G4A
10.99
11/19

THIS

SPLINTERED

SILENCE

Also by Kayla Olson
The Sandcastle Empire

THIS SPLINTERED SILENCE

KAYLA OLSON

HARPER TEEN
An Imprint of HarperCollinsPublishers

In memory of my sweet Nana,
one of the most brilliant stars to ever grace a sky

1

FIREFLIES

I FIND MY mother in the shadows—like the shell of a hollow moon, on the verge of crumbling to dust. Like I might not make it in time even though she's a mere twenty feet away.

"Hello?" My voice bounces from the steel-gray walls, from the shale-slab tile, from the panorama of glass that separates the inside of our station from the glittering ocean of stars. "Mom?"

If she hears me, she doesn't show it.

She's curled on her side on the floor, her back to me, her small frame barely moving. Still breathing—technically. I rush to kneel beside her and am relieved to see her eyes wide open, taking in the view. It is less of a relief to see the spattering of blood nearby, fresh ruby droplets smaller than strawberry seeds.

"Mom?" I sweep a thick wave of hair away from her face, tuck it behind her ear. "It's me, Lindley. Mom, can you hear me?"

Her eyelashes flutter, not quite a blink, but it's *something*. My heart climbs into my throat—I wish she'd *look* at me. "LeeLee," she says, her voice hoarse from all the coughing she's done today. "Fireflies, so many . . . pass me the jar?"

I blink until my eyes clear. She's speaking total nonsense, which is more frightening than I'm ready to admit. I've never seen her anything but composed—her mind is sharp, and it's fast. She was an easy pick for commander of our station, according to the rest of the team. My entire life, forever, everyone has always made a point to tell me exactly how much they adore her. How brilliant she is, how incredible. How she makes it look easy to lead with such calm confidence. Not that anyone needs to tell me—I know her better than anyone. But I've never seen her like this, out of her mind, not even this morning. Not even an *hour* ago.

At least she still knows who I am.

I type out a fast text to Dr. Safran, **emergency** and **observation deck 12 starboard** and **my mother**.

There are no fireflies here on the station, of course, let alone an entire jar full of them; she must be digging far back into her past, to all the years she spent on Earth. I can't even begin to count the number of times she's told me the story of that hot summer night when she was just six years old: how she and her father had set off for one of their evening walks, through the thick forest behind her childhood home. How they'd stumbled upon hundreds of swarming fireflies—thousands, maybe—and she caught enough in her jar to light their path. The sky outside our station window reminded her of that night, she loved to tell me. Stars like fireflies: they reminded her of him.

My buzz screen vibrates, and I glance at the message—Dr. Safran is on his way.

When I look up again, time tilts on its axis. I suck in a breath so sharp I'm surprised I'm not bleeding.

Her eyes are closed.

She is still, too still in every way.

My hands shake, badly, so much so that my buzz screen nearly shatters on the tile.

I squeeze my eyes shut—I can't bear to look, but I can't bear to leave. *LeeLee*, her voice echoes in my head. Her voice that I'll never hear again, ever. *LeeLee, LeeLee.* What I wouldn't give to hear, one last time, about trees taller than giants and the smell of fresh rain and the way her father's eyes crinkled when he smiled and the thousand thousand fireflies bright enough to light up the night.

I could use a jar of my own right now.

But there are no fireflies here, and no one left but me who remembers the story.

No him. No her.

Just me.

2

STARLESS

MY MOTHER ONCE told me—before she died, before her colleagues died, before everyone who wasn't born here on the station died—that each soul is tied to a star, a trail of stardust the tether. As long as the sky is full of stars, and as long as there are people alive to see it, there is hope.

She was the first to flicker, fade, blink to utter blackness.

She never saw the sky after the disease left its mark on us.

One hundred stars have gone out in the past six weeks, extinguished and smothered and choked and simply—*whoosh*—blown out—by the CRW-0001 pathogen. One hundred out of the one hundred who were sent here eighteen years ago. One hundred percent.

We are parentless. Mentorless. Medicless. Chefless. Commanderless. Less and less and less. It's been five days since the last of them passed: five days of embers and ashes and choking down the stench of death, and our grief, so we don't fall apart. Five days spent picking up the pieces of all the broken everything. All the broken everyone.

Before he passed—three weeks, two days, two hours, and fifty-six minutes ago—Dr. Safran, head medic and my mentor for the last three years, concluded definitively that only those who'd spent significant time on Earth were susceptible to CRW-0001. They're the only ones who coughed up blood. The only ones whose lungs shriveled, whose breaths became forced and far between. Their words sounded like whispers pricked with a thousand splinters as they fought, hard, just to be heard.

Until the silence took over and, one by one, the stars went out.

In my not-so-expert opinion, I believe in Dr. Safran's theory. I don't know what dirt feels like, not on Earth, not on any planet. None of us do, none of us who are left. All the air we've ever breathed has been recycled for nearly two decades inside these thick walls, steel and Plexiglas—we are a tiny dot stationed amid an extraordinary universe. Not one of us, the second generation, has coughed up a single drop of blood. We are louder than ever, now that no one tells us not to be.

We are also quieter than ever. One hundred percent of us have lost someone who meant the entire universe.

And in the midst of the losing, there are six of us who've stepped up. We've never led before, don't really know *how* to lead, but there is a need. So here we are, the six of us fumbling our way through a world that just became one hundred stars darker.

At least there are five billion trillion stars left.

Five billion trillion stars, though, are not enough light to show me this: Why is Mila Harper, age sixteen, lying dead on the cold, cold floor of the observation deck?

3

BLOODBUBBLES

I KNOW A lot of things about a lot of things.

I know about supernovas, black holes.

I know there are stars that radiate green light but appear white, true colors hidden until untangled by a prism.

I know people are the same way.

I've only ever known Mila Harper from a distance. She's the sort of girl who's had the same haircut all her life, shiny brown and sleek angles, the long parts in the front constantly falling down over her eyes. I've watched her tuck her hair behind her ears every day since she learned to read, more than a decade ago. She reads all the time, curled up in the corner of the sky lounge, one floor below this very starboard-side observation deck, always with a steaming tumbler of tea.

Correction. She *read* all the time.

Now Mila's reader sits, dead, on the floor, a crack spiderwebbing across its face. It's dotted with bloodbubbles.

Of all the things I know, bloodbubbles are only a recently developed area of my expertise. In the past six—almost seven—weeks since I found my mother, I've seen bloodbubbles on everything from butcher knives to medic-ward gowns to control panels on the commander's deck. Every day, every death.

But never from any second generation–born. Never, until now.

"Lindley?"

I look up, find Leo staring at me with those intense, unreadable eyes of his. I know for a fact he finds me equally unreadable.

"The body? What did you want to do with it?"

He looks so much like his parents in this moment it's unnerving. Deep bronze skin, and his *eyes*—his mother's eyes, keen and bright—and his father's steady, stoic demeanor. They were my mother's closest friends.

Of the six of us who've stepped up to lead, Leo and I are the roots. Tangled roots, seeds sown in the same hole by so-close parents who wanted their kids to be every bit as close. Pluck either of us up, the other would die. Leave us as we are and we might die anyway, each choking the other out. Not always on purpose.

"Don't move her yet," I say. I feel Leo's eyes on me, wanting more—as if I have more to *give*. Everyone wants so much from me now. I don't blame them, honestly. I only wish my anatomy came pre-equipped with an organ to sift through all the conflicting signals sent from my head, my heart, my gut. One that was never wrong. One that never needed sleep.

Now is the time where Dr. Safran would step in. It's hard

to believe I'd never seen an autopsy performed before six weeks ago. I'd seen surgery before—I've *done* surgery before—delicate blades and steady hands and precision, precision, precision. Autopsies aren't so delicate. I've seen eight now. Eight, before the need to identify the virus was eclipsed by the need to contain it. If only it had been containable.

Something feels off, I'm not sure what. Mila came up to the observation deck on occasion, but I didn't think it was an everyday habit of hers. Maybe it's that she's in sleeping clothes, that it's three in the morning. Of course, all of us mourn in different ways.

"Do you have your imager?" I ask, and it's out of Leo's hip pocket almost as soon as I've asked. "Snap as many photos as you can."

My brain is running on fumes. When I look at the scene after a solid stretch of sleep, I'll see things more clearly. My filters—emotional, rational—are maxed out right now: CRW-0001 wiped out one hundred out of one hundred in just under two months.

Eighty-five of us were left. Now there are eighty-four.

Maybe Dr. Safran was wrong; maybe the virus latched on to *all* of us—maybe it is simply smothering the second generation more slowly.

Or maybe it's mutated.

4

WOBBLE, SQUEAK

OUR GURNEY LOOKS nothing like it did at the start of all this.

We did away with the sheets weeks ago, when stubborn stains settled in for the long haul. A deep dent mars one end of the bed, a scar left over from those first days when we still believed the virus could be stopped by an urgent, slam-into-whatever-necessary trip to Medical. Also, one of the wheels squeaks. Another wobbles.

Leo and Heath spread Mila's body onto the bare metal bed, cold against cold. Wobble, squeak, wobble, squeak. It never gets any easier to walk with the dead.

I hope the wheels don't wake anyone. No one needs to see Mila like this, for one. Mostly, I want to keep this quiet as long as I can—people are going to panic.

There's no one I trust more than Leo and Heath, except maybe Heath's sister, Haven. What Leo and I are to each other, seeds in a hole, we are as a group. Living here, there's nowhere to hide when you don't want to see someone. We know—we've tried. We've torn at each other, torn *from* each other, more times than I can count. We've said things we don't mean, and worse, things we do. In the end, we always settle back together. It's made us strong.

Zesi, Natalin, and Haven wait for us in Medical. It doesn't look right, seeing them here, especially in sleeping clothes. I called an emergency meeting, all six of us. I didn't say why.

I don't have to.

Natalin springs to her feet. "Is that—*no*." Tears well up in her eyes, spill out.

She and Mila were close.

"You said we were immune, Lindley." Haven turns her face away, wavy blonde hair falling over her eyes like a curtain. The sight of blood spins her stomach. "You said we were safe!"

I did say those things. I said them loud and clear, at a station-wide assembly we called last week. People believe me when I speak, they always have. *You have one of those faces people implicitly trust,* Leo told me, when the six of us were settling into our roles. *You're the one to lead us.* I didn't argue, and neither did anyone else, because it's true.

"She's doing her best," Heath says, always the first to my defense, unfailingly, for better or worse, often at the expense of his own sister. "Let's not start blaming—"

"I'm not blaming," Haven snaps. "I'm *worried*."

"Well, get it together." Leo now. He, more than all of us, has a way with Haven. "Worrying doesn't change the fact that we have a situation on our hands. Linds"—he's the only one allowed to call me that, and everyone knows it—"are there any hazmat suits that aren't contaminated? And if the answer is no, how screwed does that leave us?"

Even if there were, there aren't enough for all eighty-four of us who are left. We may have already contracted the pathogen, anyway. It lies low, lingers, then explodes.

Or it did. Who knows what it does now.

"We burned them all, and spaced the contaminated air tanks," Zesi answers for me, shaking his dark, thick dreadlocks out of his eyes. "Back when we thought that would help." Before he took over as systems tech, he spent his free time in the crematory. Brilliant mind, strong heart: he does the jobs no one else can, and the ones no one else wants.

"Right," I say. "So this is where we are." All eyes are on me, as they so often are these days. I'm finally past the point of my mouth turning dry, finally past nerves that shake my voice— finally mustering a fraction of the composure my mother had when addressing her crew. "It doesn't matter if it mutated, or if we made the wrong assumptions about the original strand. Mila is dead—*any* of us could also already be carriers. We aren't necessarily screwed without hazmats, Leo. The scrubbers used them at first, but if you remember, Dr. Safran suspected the suits actually made their symptoms worse."

Five scrubbers in five pristine suits. All dead within the first two days. This is where our theory of *lie low, linger, explode* originated—Dr. Safran believed the pathogen invaded days, even weeks, earlier than symptoms began to manifest. Turns out our most recent supply delivery pilot, based down in the States, was infected when he came aboard. Nothing happened for a while, but when it did, it was too late. The hazmats were supposed to keep contaminated air out and clean air in. Instead, the scrubbers ended up dying inside their own personal gas chamber suits, more and more pathogens concentrated in the air as it recycled itself. The insides of the face pieces were worse than anything, Zesi told me. Bloodbubbles everywhere.

"You thinking we should put her on ice or fire?" Heath asks. His piercing gray eyes are still so bright, so alive in the face of death after death. It's easier to turn a blind eye, some days, pretend away the pain so it won't feel so raw. For me, anyway. For Leo, too. Heath's not like us, though. Heath stares at the sun, eyes wide open, daring it to burn him.

"Fire," I say, mostly because I'm pretty sure it's what Dr. Safran would do if he were here. I *wish* he were here. "I'm almost positive the mutation's already started spreading, but if I'm wrong, we should wipe it out in the crematory, destroy all traces of it. Just in case." I pause, think. "I could do a full autopsy—"

Haven scoffs. "Right, because you've had so much experience with those?"

I shoot her a look, although she makes a good point. I could make the cuts, sure, but I'm not experienced enough to *really* know my way around. My skills are serviceable, if that. "I could do a full autopsy—*but*—in the interest of limiting my exposure and everyone else's, I think the best way to go is to stick to blood analysis. Natalin, I'm going to get on that first thing, so our meeting needs to wait until midafternoon at the earliest."

"Sorry, but can we do it at noon?" she asks. "It's not looking good, food-wise, and I'm worried—"

"If it's so bad it can't wait until three, we should have had that meeting yesterday."

Ask for cooperation, I'm learning, and forgiveness. Not permission.

Haven and Natalin share a look. They whisper sometimes—about everyone, not just me. I do my best to let it roll off my skin. It's not always easy.

"What do you want me to tell everyone?" Haven asks. While I'm our designated leader, and the face of our assemblies, Haven is a natural at station-board communications. She makes twice-daily announcements, at nine-morning and early evening, that echo through every inch of our station's twelve sprawling decks.

"About the food?"

"About Mila," she says. "About the mutation."

I hesitate. My opinion isn't going to be a popular one—not with Haven or Natalin, anyway. "Don't tell them anything yet."

Natalin's perfectly arched eyebrows go through the roof. "It's their right—"

"Before you rail me," I say, "I said *not yet.* I didn't say *not ever.* What good is it to tell them now? We don't have answers, and you know they'll have questions. We may not be able to stop this thing, but we need to at least look like we're trying. Telling them immediately isn't going to do anything but make people panic."

"You don't know that." Natalin won't meet my eyes.

"I really, really do."

We all do. Paranoia and panic, that's what happened the first time around. I hid out in Medical with Dr. Safran, preoccupied myself with *fixing* our situation instead of agonizing over it, but still, I heard all the stories. Some people wouldn't touch the food. Some wouldn't leave their cabins. Some hoarded supplies, soap and antibac and breathing masks.

None of this mattered, in the end.

"What happens when they ask about Mila?" Haven asks. "Why they haven't seen her around?"

I'm not a fan of slippery lies. It's too hard to keep your footing with one, and lies tend to multiply. "She's helping out in the lab," I say. "That's the official word."

5

FIRE AND THE SEA

WHEN WE BREAK, Leo walks me to the lab. I hear the gurney wheels long after Heath and Zesi roll Mila out of sight. Zesi is intimately familiar with the layout of the entire station, thanks to his time at systems. He'll know how to get to the base deck, where the crematory is, without drawing attention. No one's finding out about this tonight—if anyone knows how to keep a secret here, it's him.

"You should sleep, Linds."

The other girls went back to bed. Their work centers mostly around a daytime schedule, when everyone else is awake. Mine doesn't.

"It's important to check this out," I say.

"It's important to check it out *when your mind is fresh.*" He mimics my tone. It sounds too haughty.

"Listen, don't start with me tonight, okay?" He's almost never wrong, and he knows it, and he knows *I* know it—but his exceptional clarity can be really inconvenient.

I reach for the lab door; he catches my hand, turns me around to face him. His eyes are wide, deep brown with flecks of gold. If his are fire, mine are the sea. "When is the last time you slept? No, don't look away, I'm serious."

"What do you mean by 'slept,' exactly? An hour here, an hour there? All night? Every night? Or—"

"Lindley."

It isn't a matter of wanting to sleep. No more sleep, no more dreams—not for me, at least. Now my nights are full of *what if, what next, what now?*

We've lost so much more than just our parents.

His hand is soft in mine, but I pull away. If I'm going to give him something real, I'm taking something back in return. "I don't know how anyone sleeps anymore."

He doesn't press me after that.

The lab is just as I left it last night, steady and bright and predictable and certain, crisp and clean, my own personal oasis. Unlike Medical, the lab spans an entire wing: station after station of equipment, ready and waiting to unlock the entire universe.

Except all our experts are dead.

Dr. Safran was an expert in everything. Most of the one hundred were experts in two or three fields—only the best of the best made it onto the station, this *beacon of hope for humanity*, as it was deemed nearly two decades ago at its christening. A few limited themselves to a single area of concentration, but that was rare. Our station is the main hub in our fleet's trio, home-base support for the two teams stationed much farther out in the galaxy. Each and every member—on our station and both of the others—was recruited for a lifetime of service from an extraordinarily capable pool of candidates.

Let's hope we who are left inherited enough of their intellect and instinct to keep ourselves alive.

I settle onto the tall stool near the nanoscope. It's more comfortable than my own bed lately.

"Can I help with anything?" Leo asks, taking the stool across from me, on the other side of the station. For all his *you know I'm right* superiority, he's really good about not pushing back when I've drawn my lines.

But this—stopping, sitting—changes everything. I'm tired, more so than I care to admit. I squeeze my eyes shut. Open them. Still exhausted.

"I . . . should go to bed." I slide a sample I drew from Mila's blood, just after we found her, across the table. "File this for me, please?"

He gives me a sleepy smile and doesn't dare say *I told you so.*

6

ETERNAL LIGHT,
ETERNAL NIGHT

IF ANYONE IS to blame for all that has happened, it's the moon.

Those who found the loophole in the international lunar treaty, anyway, those who staked their claim without ever actually *owning* anything: I blame them for this present misery.

If they hadn't found the loophole,

if they hadn't discovered a way to channel endless, renewable solar power from the moon's pale face—a sea of panels bathed in eternal sunlight—

if they had worked together,

if they hadn't raced to be first,

if they hadn't spurned those who came next,

if they hadn't threatened nuclear measures to control what was never truly theirs to begin with . . .

We would not be in danger of suffering the consequences.

We would not be in danger of an obliterated moon, of Earth

quite literally spinning out of control, of instability and chaos and seasonal extremes, of hailstorms with a side of asteroid showers. We would never have begun the search for an off-planet home, *just in case*. No one has blown the moon to pieces yet, to be clear, likely because the solar power payoff continues to be worth the escalating territorial tension.

But things can only be stretched so thin before they snap.

So they made their long-game contingency plan. If not for all of this, the *Lusca* would never have been created, and my mother would never have been its commander. They would never have filled our station with experts who could support the terraforming efforts on Planet RDX-4, more commonly known simply as Radix—and would never have had such a strong reason to begin terraforming efforts at all. They would never have planted the *Nautilus* at the edge of everything, a station one-tenth the size of ours, home to a smaller team of specialists who explore the far-off places we don't even know we don't know about. *Lusca*'s experts would not have been sent here to support that team, either.

And if the *Lusca* were never created, and my mother never its commander, and if I'd been born on Earth like every other generation that came before me, I would not be *here*.

I would not be grieving the effects of this particular virus, in this particular place.

I would not be stranded in eternal night, fumbling my way through darkness, wishing for starlight or fireflies or the dimmest rays of hope.

*

When I step back to think about it, how my life is what it is because of a string of choices made by people on Earth I've never met, it makes me feel terrifyingly small.

How can I get things back under control if control was never truly mine to begin with?

7

TOMORROW AND TOMORROW AND TOMORROW

THREE TONES RING over my cabin speakers. *It's a new day,* Haven's chipper voice announces. *Time to embrace it!* This is her stage voice—we all have one. Hers is more exaggerated than mine, though. More exaggerated than everyone's.

People complain, say she isn't being sensitive enough. I even agree, some days, but I think Haven's mostly in the right. We have to give the station what they need, not necessarily what they want. We *can't* give them what they want. We can't give back their yesterdays, can't take away their fear or their regret. We want those things, too, as much as anybody.

If only.

So Haven puts a smile in her voice. If they don't want it today, she likes to say, maybe they'll take it tomorrow. We'll see.

I slept, not well, for almost four hours. That's a record this week. I have a feeling I'll crash soon, and crash hard, but there's no time for that now. Now is for the lab. Now is for finishing what I couldn't even start last night.

I pin my hair into a low bun, throw my cleanest cardigan on

over last night's clothes. This is as good as it gets today. Haven will have a fit when she sees me. When it comes to securing people's trust, she says, presentation is half the battle. I never argue, and I don't disagree—I simply prefer to focus on the other half of that battle, the part that could actually keep us alive.

It takes ten minutes to get to the lab from my cabin. That's on a good day, when it's seven-morning and the station is still and quiet. Today is not a good day. Despite the pleasant-but-focused face I put on, despite keeping my eyes fixed at a neutral point ahead of me, I barely make it out of my own residential wing before someone stops me. Siena Lawson, this time.

"Hi, um . . . Commander?" She's fourteen, a rule-follower to a fault, and I've told her three times to call me Lindley. Haven referred to me as Commander Hamilton one time in an announcement, and it was the most uncomfortable thing I've ever experienced. The gift keeps on giving.

"Commander was my mother. You know you don't have to call me that, right?" I loved my mother. I don't love talking about her. "Need something?"

Siena shrinks back, just a little. She won't meet my eyes. "Sorry, Com—Lindley. I'm sorry."

"What's going on?" I attempt to soften my tone so I'm not so intimidating, try to pretend my mind isn't running full speed toward the lab. I'm not very good at pretending.

"It's Yuki and Grace," she says. "I . . . can't find them." The three of them are inseparable. I've learned more about station life these past few weeks than I ever cared to know. This recent shift—paying close attention like I never have before, learning everything I can about everyone—all of it makes me feel a bit like someone looking in. Like I'm not quite one of them anymore, now that I've stepped into the role of commander.

"You've checked their cabins?" I ask. "You're sure they aren't sleeping?" I take a deep breath to quell my simmering annoyance.

Her cheeks flame. "We were all together last night," she says. "At Mikko's."

Siena Lawson is not a stupid girl. "Walk with me," I say. This could take all morning—I don't have all morning. I put a call through to Heath. He picks up immediately, like always, unfailingly reliable.

"Meet me in the lab," I tell him. "I've got a project for you."

Heath agrees, even offers to bring me some tea. I need it.

"We weren't doing anything, I swear," Siena says when I'm off the call. "Just a few drinks, and then we passed out."

"Just a few drinks," I repeat. *A few drinks* isn't like her. *One* drink isn't like her.

"I *swear.*"

She shouldn't be drinking at all, but I don't say that. I'm not her mother—she doesn't have one anymore, none of them do. That's the problem. "You need to be careful with Mikko, Siena. Turn here," I say. "He's not himself these days. He didn't try to take advantage, did he?"

She's quiet, too quiet. "He didn't have to," she finally says. "Grace started it."

Right. Excellent. "And now you can't find her? Was anyone else there?"

"Just a couple of other guys, with Yuki and me," she says. "Dash and Reed."

Dash and Reed are good guys. Mikko's always been a quality kid, too, but he's made some terrible decisions lately.

All of us grieve a little differently, I guess.

Heath meets us at the lab, as promised. He smells fresh, just-out-of-the-shower fresh, and his not-quite-dry hair looks darker than its usual sandy blond. Did he cut his shower short just to answer my call?

"Wait here," I tell Siena. "He'll be right back for you, okay?" The old rules restricted under-eighteens from entering the lab without adult supervision, but I make the rules now. And right now, I want two minutes alone with Heath.

I enter the code, and the door slides open. Heath and I slip inside quickly, before it closes. Dr. Safran helped me memorize every code he had access to in the days before he passed. It's good he did—only a couple of others thought to share their intel, to Zesi and Natalin. Their knowledge keeps us alive.

"Thanks for this," I say, taking the tea. It's too hot to drink, so I set it on the first island I see.

When I turn around, Heath is *right* there. His eyes—his lips—soft on mine—

I push him off. "Heath—what?!" I brush the kiss away with the back of my hand, catch my breath. "What was that?"

We haven't, we've never . . . this is not what I meant by *two minutes alone with Heath.*

A curse falls out of him. "I'm sorry, Lindley, I thought—"

He's breathing hard. So am I. I pulled back before, but not far. Only a couple of inches separate me from a face I've known forever. We've always been close—*friend* close, like I am with Leo or Haven. We've never been close like this.

"I didn't think," he says, catching his breath. "I'm so sorry, Lindley." He rubs his hands over his face, kneads his temples. "With Mila—and the mutation—I was up all night thinking I might never, um. Never get the chance."

I bury my face in my teacup. Burn my lips on purpose.

"I won't do it again, I promise." He stays where he is, lets me have my space.

I've never thought of Heath like this before—I don't know *what* I want, but it's too soon to say I want him to promise that.

"Listen," I say. "It's fine, we're good. I'm just . . . not in that headspace right now. So much going on, you know?"

"Sure. Yeah." Even the smallest grin gives him dimples on both sides. "I know what you mean." Heath's every bit as busy as I am. He's taken up a swing role amid our six—peacemaker, peacekeeper, the one who deals with social issues as they come up all over the station. And, oh, have they come up. "So, you've got a project for me?"

His subject change is a little too abrupt, a little too sunny. I know him well enough to see past his dimples.

"Right, yes." I avert my eyes, look anywhere but at his lips. "Siena Lawson can't find her friends." I fill him in on Yuki and Grace, and the Mikko situation as I see it. "Talk to those guys, check their cabins. See if Siena did anything to make the girls want to keep her out of the loop."

I hate drama. It's so unnecessary, such a black hole.

"Got it," Heath says. "What if"—he glances behind him, at the door—lowers his voice—"what if I find them, and they're like Mila? What if Siena sees?"

"Make sure she doesn't," I say. "You're good at this. It'll be fine."

His eyes are so deep I could drown. I blink, look away. Focus.

"I really am sorry, Lindley."

I take another sip of tea. Carefully, this time. "If you say that one more time, I'm never speaking to you again." He smiles, and so do I.

"Don't work too hard," he says.

And then he's out.

8

AGAIN WITH THE LOSING

MILA'S BLOOD SAMPLE isn't in the file.

"Leo," I say as soon as he picks up my call, "what did you do with the blood?"

"I filed it, like you asked," he says. "Why, did I do it wrong?" His words have jagged edges: it's rare that Leo makes a mistake, rarer still for him to *admit* it.

I rummage around in the refrigerator, dig in places that aren't so obvious. "Looks like you didn't do it at all." Not in the drawer, not in the door. "You put it in the fridge?"

He's silent on the other end. "I mean . . . I *know* I did. You're positive it isn't there? On the first shelf, right in front?"

"Definitely not." The first shelf, right in front, is jammed full of weeks-old cultures I should've discarded by now.

Leo exhales loudly. "I'm sorry, Linds. I don't know what to tell you."

I clench my teeth, count to five. I know he's only frustrated with himself, not with me, but still. This is what I get for going to bed last night. I knew I should've looked over her sample.

This is why I do things myself, why I've *done* them myself since the day I started studying under Dr. Safran. I don't make these sorts of mistakes—I can't afford to, not if I want to lead as well as my mother did. Details matter, not just to me but to the entire space program.

Think, think. How do I get more blood from a body burned to ashes?

"I'll head over right now," he says. "Maybe I screwed up. Zesi, you good on your own?" There's a pause. "He's good. I'll be right there."

"Wait," I say as an idea hits me. "What did you do with Mila's reader? Last night, when we cleaned up?" I remember him sealing it in an airtight bag, bloodbubbles and all.

"Brilliant," he says. "It should still be back at Medical. I only grabbed her blood sample out of the cooler before we left for the lab."

I'll believe it when I see it. The official sample should be here, but it isn't. Samples don't just walk away.

"Good, good." I'm not thrilled, but this will work. If it's there.

"You're worried."

"Do you blame me?"

I hear Zesi in the background, then Leo's muffled voice. "No, I can't blame you," he says when he comes back. "I'm coming down there."

For as long as I can remember, it's been my dream to follow in my mother's footsteps. Medical training first, station duties next—and, eventually, assuming her role completely when the time came for her to pass down the torch.

Eventually was never supposed to happen this soon.

None of this was official yet, of course. *Try medicine for a while*, my mother said. *You might find you don't enjoy it—you might want something different.*

But I've always known. I've never been like Heath, constantly taking in the possibilities, equally tempted to pursue them all. I've never been like Haven, or the handful of others on the station who dream of living life on Earth—as if lakes and sky and forests and mountains could ever hold a candle to the glorious field of stars outside our every window. I would never trade the station, and not just because of the view—in all the universe, the station is the only place my mother and I ever coexisted, where every memory I ever made was born. It's *home*.

Now tomorrow is darkness.

Tomorrow is me starting a fire with my bare hands, not the passing of a torch.

Tomorrow is slippery for us all now—and today is for staying alive.

Mila's reader is in Medical's cooler, exactly as it should be. I tuck it inside my satchel—my mother's old satchel, with an insulated pocket—and head back to the lab. Already, it's past noon. I've let too much time slip away.

Leo should be waiting for me by now. He has codes to everything; all six of us do. We keep them to ourselves.

Which is why, I think as I walk back, it's so very odd that the blood went missing. Leo's sharp and he's trustworthy. Haven and Natalin went to bed, Heath and Zesi were at the crematory. The doors lock automatically, so no one could have broken in. And even if they could have broken in . . . why would anyone want to?

When I enter the lab, Leo's seated on one of the tall stools, at the never-used island right beside the scope station that's started to feel like home. His back is toward me, and he doesn't budge. It isn't like him.

"You didn't mean this fridge, did you."

The station where he sits is meant to support exoplanet research missions, but ever since the *Nautilus* got an equipment upgrade a few years ago, they haven't needed our lab except to run extremely specialized sample diagnoses. We always have advance notice to prep on our end, so at the moment, none of those appliances are even operational—we unplug them at stations that aren't used often in order to conserve energy. The mini-fridge is right next to the one I checked so thoroughly.

Oh, no.

Now that I'm closer, and not behind him, I see why he's staring: Mila's blood sample sits, lonely, on the island. I don't even have to ask to know it's ruined.

"The other refrigerator was just so full . . ."

He meant well, he meant well. Still, it's frustrating. "It's full for a reason." Leo is usually so on top of things. He runs systems and tech with Zesi, and works with Heath to keep the peace. "Did it not tip you off that there wasn't anything else in that fridge? Did you not think it felt a little warm?" I close my eyes, breathe. Bite back my disappointment before it slams him in the face.

"It did, but—you know how last night was, Linds." His voice is low, crackling. Too little sleep, too much stress. "It was late, and everything with Mila was just too much. And I was worried about you."

"I get it." I do.

Our mistakes might be understandable, but it doesn't mean they don't matter.

"It's too much," I say, settling onto the stool opposite him. We lean on our elbows, head in hands. Mirror images. "We shouldn't have to deal with this."

"I feel like I'm losing it." He stares, unblinking, straight through Mila's blood and into something only he can see. "Losing my footing, you know? Trying to do everything, all at once. Failing miserably."

This is why we go so well together, why we're closer with each other than we are with Heath, or Haven, or even our own parents before they . . . well, before. We feel the same things in the same way, fracture under pressure the same way, crack and break and try to hold ourselves together in the same way. We're both reluctant to accept the reality that we're capable of breaking at all.

I train my eyes on him, wait quietly until he meets them. "You really worried about me?"

"Every hour, Linds. Every hour."

This room is so white, so clean, so vast, so empty. No place for his words to hide.

"How about this?" I say. "If you ever lose yourself, I'll come find you. Bring you back."

I wouldn't have a choice. If I lose him, I lose parts of myself. Then again, we're too tangled together for either of us to go far.

"You're in luck," he says with a small grin. "Deal works both ways."

9

SOLAR FLARE

ONE DAY WHEN we were young, maybe seven or eight years old, the entire station flipped from chill and predictable, from rhythm and routine, to a blazing-hot panic. It took less than a minute for the station to turn to chaos.

Lieutenant Black, stationed in Control, had detected a powerful solar flare on the radar—the last one of similar severity had given astronauts a mere fifteen-minute window to take shelter before the burst of radiation passed through. It could have been worse: the engineers could have left the magnetized flare shield off *Lusca*'s exterior entirely, could have failed to consider it at all. But it also could have been better: the flare shield takes a full eleven minutes to settle into place, like a shell around the station. We were not rich in time.

Leo, Heath, Haven, and I were sent directly to the safe room at the station's core, along with everyone else who wasn't critical to handling or monitoring the situation. We were to wait it out there, in that dull gray box of a room right at *Lusca*'s center; it had been primarily designed to shield us from rogue asteroids, not solar flares, but it must have made our parents feel better to do *something*. When I asked my mother why she couldn't stay with me, she only replied, *I'm the heart.*

Haven chattered away nervously the entire time we spent huddled together. Heath picked at her words—as Heath still does, to this day—calling out her exaggerations, her half-truths, her flat-out lies. Leo and I sat back-to-back, silent. I hugged my knees and thought about my mother's words. What did it mean to be the heart? It was obvious why the hands had to stay on duty, because the hands do the work. I would have understood why the head had to be there, too, all strategy and solution—honestly, I was surprised my mother hadn't chosen that one for herself.

But the heart? The more I thought about it, the more I understood. The heart works all the time. The heart keeps pumping because that's what a heart *does*, because that's how it keeps everything from grinding to a halt. And the heart is more than just a muscle: it's a mystery, too. It has its own electrical supply, Leo told me once, and will continue to beat even when separated from the body. Like my mother: she was never truly able to leave her mind at work when she came home. And in reverse, she was never truly able to leave me out of her mind when we were apart.

Leo, Heath, Haven, and I—along with everyone else—stayed in the safe room for much longer than the eleven minutes it took to activate the flare shield. We stayed for at least two hours, until they were sure it had passed, sure we were well out of radiation danger. Sitting together that long, just the four of us in our dark little corner, was the first time I noticed how different Leo and I were from Heath and Haven, how different Heath and Haven were from each other. And how, much like my mother was part of a body, I was, too. Despite our differences, though, I had a harder time labeling our little group.

We all felt like the heart.

10

CRACKING OPEN
THE UNIVERSE

I SCRAPE MILA'S blood from her reader, careful not to waste a single drop. Half goes onto a plate for the electron microscope; the other half will go under the microsphere nanoscope. I'm going to crack this virus open inside and out.

I prepare a concentrated stain so I won't have to wait as long, immerse the plate in it. It'll have to sit for ten minutes at least before I can take a look. Growing up on a station full of scientists has certainly come with its advantages—I could run tests like these with my eyes closed. Which is good, since it's been so hard to keep them open lately.

Leo left a while ago—River, who's eight, locked himself out of his cabin. Again. There are only a few under-tens, and they have their good days and their very bad days. The girls, Evi and Elise, moved in with Natalin; River stays with Leo now. Evi cries a lot at night, Natalin says, only when she thinks no one can hear. Elise is the opposite. She talks nonstop and hasn't shed a single tear. Neither will discuss anything real.

And River forgets everything, always.

I put in a call to Heath. Take a deep breath, hope the awkwardness I feel over what happened between us doesn't find its way into my voice. "Find the girls yet?" I ask when he picks up.

"Negative," he says. He sounds totally normal, like he always has—like he never kissed me at all—and it's a colossal relief. "Talked to Mikko and the guys, but they say they haven't seen them since around three-morning."

About half an hour before we found Mila.

"At Mikko's, or where?"

"Yeah," he says. "Dash said they all crashed out around then in Mikko's main room, except for Grace and Mikko, who were . . ."

"Right."

"When Siena and the boys woke up, Grace and Yuki were gone. Mikko slept on the couch, alone."

I glance at the clock, at my stained sample—not done yet. In just under two hours, I'm supposed to meet Natalin, and she'll kill me if I'm late. Multitasking has never been my thing, but lately, I've had to embrace it.

I let out a long breath. "Okay, here's what I think," I say. "Tell Haven to put out a station-wide call for a mandatory check-in on the mezzanine, and tell her not to say why. I can be there in twenty minutes." We've done too many of these lately. I've been trying to avoid them as much as possible, for my sake and everyone else's. If I call too many meetings, people will stop taking them seriously. The check-ins eat time on top of that. And people ask too many questions.

"You got it." He pauses, and the silence starts to gape. It's not like him to be at a loss for words, especially around me. Right as I start to fear the worst—the conversation I'd really rather avoid until we absolutely have to deal with it—he adds: "If we find them before then, I'll have Haven cancel the check-in."

"Sounds good." My timer is about to go off, a conveniently true excuse for me to cut this call short. "Got to rush the labs if I want to make it on time—I'll see you in a bit."

"Want Haven to tell them thirty or forty-five minutes instead?"

I do, but that would push my meeting with Natalin. "No," I say. "I'll be there. Don't start without me."

Haven's announcement echoes over the speakers just as my timer beeps. *Mezzanine in fifteen, everyone! Anyone who doesn't show will be put under curfew for the next two days.*

Even though my timer's gone off, the plate isn't quite ready. I have to wait another minute before sliding it under the electron microscope. When I do, vivid purples and pinks light my sample into something otherworldly, beautiful and bright. I focus with the knobs, try to get a better look.

I'm positive my process is correct; it's my analysis I'm less sure about. Things don't look like I remember. Almost like the sample is too old to give clear results, but that can't be right— we pulled it just this morning, and it was definitely in the cooler that whole time. Maybe I messed up the concentration of the stain somehow, tried too hard to rush it. Maybe I should have asked more questions when Dr. Safran was alive to answer them.

Before the virus hit, he mostly spent our time teaching me how to heal the living, not how to study the dead.

After a few more minutes of fumbling with the microscope, I give up. If the mutation kills as quickly as the original strain did, it won't be long before we have more blood to test. And if it doesn't, it's possible we have a different virus on our hands entirely. One that isn't so contagious, maybe.

I clean the station, get it ready for next time.

I'm fairly certain next time will come soon.

11

HEARTBEATEN

IT'S GOOD THE balcony has a railing.

Meetings in the mezzanine were never this empty when my mother stood over them, in this very spot. It feels ridiculous to continue with the formalities from before, to put ourselves in this high place like we know everything about everything. As a population, we're less than half what we once were, in number and in age, in nerve and in hopes. We're all in this together.

But Haven was persuasive. *Formalities will help*, she said, when our six first joined forces. *If we want them to listen to us, we need to act like we're worth listening to.*

So, here we stand, behind our railing.

From below, seventy-eight sets of eyes stare up at us, a full spectrum: patient to compliant to desperately irritated. Seventy-eight, assuming Yuki and Grace are among them. I scan the room, don't see either girl, but that doesn't mean too much. I'm commander now, but I'm not infallible. Quite the opposite.

"Thank you for your patience," I begin. I was late. "We won't keep you long."

My amplified voice echoes over the clean, curved walls of the mezzanine. Silver and steel, backlit in varying shades of blue, this deck has always been one of my favorites. The station's architects added sleek touches, designed it to feel light despite its hard heaviness. This room was never meant for mandatory check-ins—it was a place where we assembled to hear of the latest victories in the terraforming efforts on Radix, and of the samples *Nautilus* brought back from the fringes of the universe for the team here to examine. It was a place to celebrate being alive, and the hope of future life. Now we simply number our people who are not yet dead.

"In just a few minutes," I continue, "Leo and Zesi will come around with tab-screens—you know the drill." Line up, thumbprint, leave. "Please arrange yourselves by residential wing and wait quietly until you've checked in. After that, you're free to go."

I bow my head deeply, hold it for two seconds—my mother's closing gesture. The commotion begins, everyone shifting into their check-in groups. I turn, eager to leave the balcony. Eager to escape.

"Where's Mila Harper?" a voice rings out.

Akello Regulus. Extremely tall, extremely dark, extremely kind.

He loved Mila like a sister. She loved him, too.

I knew we wouldn't be able to keep her absence quiet for long, but I'd hoped it wouldn't be quite this public when the news broke. Our excuse that she's helping out in the lab won't work, not at a mandatory check-in like this—she'd be obligated to show up, just like everyone else. Lesson learned: be more proactive next time. Tell the people who will notice so they won't make a scene.

I hate that I have to think about a next time.

Haven steps up to the microphone. She knows how sick I'm getting of all the questions. "Mila Harper isn't feeling well at the moment," she says. "We were in contact with her in the early hours of this morning, and she's been excused from this mandatory meeting."

I sigh, brace myself. This is why I hate lies. Haven worded it carefully, but saying Mila isn't feeling well—in the wake of a viral crisis? No.

Silence turns to whispers, whispers turn to a low hum, and then, all at once, the questions erupt. "What do you mean, she isn't feeling well?" and "Is she going to die?" and "Is her sickness airborne?" and "You told us we were immune; why did you tell us we were immune?" It's lava, and I can't run. I can never run.

Haven's cool voice cuts through the noise. "No," she says. "I should have worded that more thoughtfully, my apologies. Mila came down with a migraine last night, a bad one—I'll spare you the messy details of her nausea, but in short, we feel it's in her best interest to rest in her room, where it's quiet."

"So we shouldn't worry?" asks Kerr Barstow, a girl who lives a few doors down from where Mila lived. I'd see them together sometimes, at the rec center track, several years ago before Kerr shifted cliques and left Mila to her books. "It isn't contagious?"

"The only thing contagious here is paranoia," Haven says. "So take care of yourselves, and try not to worry."

They seem to accept this, mostly. No one else questions Mila's absence, or anything else we've told them—not loudly enough for us to hear, anyway. They line up by residential wing, leave their thumbprints on Leo's and Zesi's screens.

But I feel a pit forming in my stomach. Yes, it was my call to keep the truth from them, and Haven's doing a pitch-perfect job of stopping the fear spiral before it gains traction—it's just not a thing I *enjoy*.

"Crisis narrowly averted," Haven says under her breath, just to me.

"For now," I say. I scan the lines, try to find Yuki or Grace in the crowd. No sign of either girl in Leo's line, and I don't see them in Zesi's—

My sight catches on Akello Regulus, whose eyes are locked on me. I blink, look away, pretend I haven't seen him staring, that it hasn't unnerved me.

He knows. We aren't being truthful, and he knows.

He steps forward in line, nods at Zesi, presses his thumb to the tablet. When he's completed the check-in, he once again turns toward the balcony, our balcony, and fixes his eyes on mine. I don't look away this time, and neither does he. He holds my stare for a second too long before slipping out of the room.

I don't know why he's chosen to keep quiet.

All that matters is that he stays that way.

12

SHADOWS AND SUN

"THIS ISN'T GOING to work for long," Haven says as soon as it's just us. We're alone in the corridor now, behind closed balcony doors. "Did you see Akello? Did you see how he was looking at us?"

He was looking at me, not us, but I'm not in the mood to split hairs. "I saw it."

"What if he starts talking? Asking questions? What if he knocks on Mila's door, goes to check on her?" She glances over her shoulder, makes sure no one's there to overhear us. "I'm going to look like a liar, Lindley. We all are. They're going to hate us."

I pinch the bridge of my nose, will the headache away. "They won't *all* hate us," I say. "Some of them will get it. Some will understand."

"Keep telling yourself that," Haven says.

We're long past the days of tiptoeing around each other's feelings. It isn't often we agree, and I think she sometimes pushes back just for the sake of being contrary. I know I do that, anyway, to her. Occasionally. She can be a thorn in my side, the shadow to my sun, but I wouldn't have it any other way. We're better for it.

"Hey," she says when I don't answer. "Hey—you doing okay?"

I'm not, but it isn't like anyone's going to benefit from knowing I'm depleted. "It's just a lot, you know?" A station to run. All the death, all the grief. Stepping into this role ten years too early under all the wrong circumstances.

"I'll help however I can, you know that, right?"

I cut my eyes at her—my eyes are too sharp, and I know it, but I don't let them soften. "It's not like I can't handle it, Haven."

"Did I say you couldn't handle it? No. No, I did not." She makes a show of rolling her eyes. "It's just a lot to handle, that's all. And I'm here if you need me."

"You're doing a good job," I say, *thank you* in disguise. "Now I should probably go do mine."

Natalin is pacing around inside the refrigerator room when I arrive for our meeting, as if I'm late. I'm early, for the record. For once.

"We're low on pro-packs," she says before I can even say hello. "Not critically low, not yet, but if we don't get another shipment within the next seven or eight days, it isn't going to be pretty. We have to have protein, Lindley, we need—"

"I know." I raise a hand, cut her off. "I know. Let me think."

The hum of the refrigerator room is loud in our silence. I scan the shelves; they don't look as bad as I expected, actually.

"We have a lot of VPs, it looks like?" I make my voice bright, as if VPs aren't the absolute worst. The vege-packs are no one's favorites—we prefer our celery and spinach in the context of meat stew or chicken soup, not plain. Green things must taste better on Earth. "And we have loads of rice and pasta, right? And potatoes?"

"Good luck getting everyone to actually *eat* the VPs," she says. "The rice and pasta are good options, you're right, but they could cause more problems—we're on our last backup water filter, and there's only so much water to begin with. We can't cook as much rice or pasta as we'd need, because we'd be maxing out our filters *and* draining our drinking supply."

She's obviously put a lot of thought into this—and she's the expert, not me. "You're basing the math on our current number, right? Not the original population?"

Natalin's jaw twitches. "Do I look like an idiot to you? You honestly think I wouldn't have considered that?"

I shrug. "Had to ask."

"You *didn't* have to ask. I don't make mistakes like that."

"None of us are above making mistakes," I say. "I was just hoping for an easy solution."

"If there were an easy solution, we wouldn't be having this meeting." She picks up pacing where she left off, from the VP shelf to the dry grains shelf and back again.

"Listen, Nat, we're on the same side here." I try to meet her eyes, but she deftly avoids me. "I'm here to help, okay? Don't treat me like this is my fault—"

She turns to face me, and her glare is a force. "So whose is it? Mine?"

"I didn't say that. And that isn't what I think, either." I grit my teeth, try to summon my mother's patience so I don't make things worse. Because *seriously*?

"They're going to *say* it's my fault," she says. "When they're starving and thirsty, they're going to blame me, right? We have to *fix* this."

"So let's fix it. Let's focus on what we can do about it, okay?" I'm talking to myself as much as I am to her—there's a fine line between handling things and spiraling into panic, and I'm doing all I can to stay on the calm side of that line. "We have plenty of VPs to last us. If they starve because they won't eat them, that's on *them*, not you."

Reluctantly, she joins me at the shelf. We stare at the pouches, their slick SpaceLove logos and glossed-out vegetable artwork. "What if they won't send another shipment? They've already skipped one, and look where we are."

There it is, the real problem. I'd be lying if I said the same thought hadn't crossed my mind—right before I shoved it into a drawer and locked it inside. "They know we need food, Nat, and I'll put in a call for extra measure. They're not just going to leave us up here to starve."

"But what if they do?"

I try not to let it show that I'm every bit as unnerved by this as she is—one of us needs to act calm, right? Even if it's the furthest thing from what we feel? We usually get a shipment every fourth week, but we're closing in on seven weeks since the last one—our rations have stretched this long only because we're smaller now by half.

"They didn't cancel the last delivery forever," I say. "They just postponed it until we were all in the clear." It's my best effort at encouragement, and it falls admittedly flat.

"But we're *not* in the clear," she says. "You really think they're going to risk a delivery when they find out the virus has mutated? That it killed Mila? We could send a new strain straight back to Earth."

I squeeze my eyes shut, try not to let her fear get under my skin, where it will only stir up my own. "Let's just focus on what we can control, okay? We have enough food to last seven or eight days, longer if they'll eat the VPs, even longer if we ration those." I think, do a couple of quick calculations in my head. "Sit with the numbers this afternoon and figure out a way to make them stretch—take body weight and muscle mass into consideration. Age, too. We'll give new guidelines first thing tomorrow." I have no idea how much these will actually help, but Natalin seems to be turning things over in her head, so I guess I at least *sound* like I know what I'm talking about.

"They're not going to like this."

"Pretty sure they'd like starving even less." I crack open the door, feel the warm air rush in. "All we can do is our best."

13

ORIGAMI

I SLIP UP to Control, find it deserted and dead silent. It isn't unusual to find Zesi tinkering up here with our systems—it's become his safe place, where he can lose himself in tech and forget about flesh and blood for a bit. Many of our people do the same, I'm noticing, only it takes different forms: they read, they run, they party more than they used to, they do flight sims until it makes them dizzy or sick. I hear rumors of hookups. Rumors of theft. Rumors of words that cut like knives, rumors of nightmares. Everyone wants an escape from reality, but there's nowhere to go, so people end up folding in on themselves like origami, flightless paper cranes.

It's my job to smooth over the resulting paper cuts—never mind that I'm still healing, too.

I settle onto the rolling stool, its unforgiving metal cool even through the thick fabric of my pants. I'm not nearly as familiar with the control board as Zesi is, but the message-system panel is pretty easy to pick out amid the various knobs and dials. No one ever got the chance to train me on this, but how hard can it be? Two seconds of poking around pulls up a directory—I tap *Nashville*, where our Earth-based team is planted, then *connect*.

And then I wait.

And wait.

Having never put a call through to anyplace other than inside our own walls—let alone all the way to Earth—it's entirely possible I simply need to be patient. We're far out, *very* far out, and perhaps fifty unanswered rings is only half as many as it takes?

By the hundredth ring, I cut the call short.

This doesn't feel right. This is unsettling.

A chill spreads over me as I realize: not only is there no answer, but there are no missed calls in our log, either. According to the history of my entire life—the faithfully recurring calls my mother took every first day of the month, for *every* month in the station's entire existence—they should've attempted to get in touch a few days ago, at the very least.

Not that anyone would've been around to answer. Zesi spent that day down in the crematory. Just in case, I tap out a text: **You haven't picked up any calls from Nashville recently, have you?** The log is likely confirmation enough—it would be listed here if Zesi had picked up a call—but maybe I'm missing something. Maybe it's possible for things to slip through the cracks.

He replies almost immediately, a simple **no**, ellipsis, that somehow makes me feel even worse than before.

The virus was swift; the virus was deadly.

The virus came from Earth, Dr. Safran theorized. From our supply delivery pilot.

If it caught Nashville off guard like it did with us—

If it spread like wildfire—

If we are more alone out here than any of us realized—

If, if, if.

I'll try again in the morning, I resolve. Perhaps their comm lines are simply unmanned, like ours have been while we've dealt with all the death. Perhaps tomorrow will be better.

Perhaps.

14

LIKE FOREVER, ONLY NEVER AGAIN

ALL I WANT is a single day where I can walk to my cabin in peace. One day where I don't feel pressured to stand up straight, keep my shoulders back. A day where I can slow down. Smile. Answer their questions instead of doing that thing I do, the eyes-trained-straight-ahead, on-a-mission, don't-have-time-to-hear-you thing I've developed as of late.

Today is not that day.

I feel their eyes on me. Hear their questions bubble up, then evaporate, as I walk past without so much as a glance.

If there's anything I'm learning, it's this: when there is no peace, when there is no silence, you simply have to carve some out. You have to, or you'll crumble.

As soon as I'm inside my cabin, doors closed, alone, it's like the weight of the universe falls off my shoulders. It's like I'm myself again, the Lindley I used to be before I started trying to be everything to everyone. I'd spend whole hours near the fireplace, the blaze swiped up to the perfect heat, sketching while curled up in my mother's soft leather chair. The chair was one of her two luxury items from Earth, inherited from her great-grandfather. I've taken to sleeping in it every night. Makes me feel like I still have family.

It isn't the same. Even when I swipe the blaze up as high as it will go, I'm always cold. Now when I sit, I spend my time untangling the station's problems until I'm so exhausted I succumb to an hour or two of restless sleep.

I don't sit there now. I stay right where I am, back pressed up against the inside of my front door, and sit down on the cold concrete floor. Lean my head against the smooth steel, close my eyes. Breathe.

My head pounds. I do my best to turn off my worry—about Mila, about Yuki and Grace, about the look Akello gave me, about Natalin and the food, about the unanswered call I just attempted to put through and what it might mean, about all the questions I probably should have answered on my walk home. I try to tune it all out, just for a few minutes, focus on my own thoughts. But where a swarm of inspiration and hope used to be, now all I hear is the swish of rushing blood.

None of this was ever in the plan. Life has flipped so drastically as of late that it's hard to even remember what it was like before—it's as if the past and the present have been equally eclipsed by the blinding need to . . . not die. Does everyone feel this way? Or do I simply feel consumed by it because it's on me to keep *everyone* alive and not just myself?

The six of us asked for this by stepping up, I realize this. We were the obvious choice to do it—we are the oldest and the most experienced, the ones who took apprenticeships and inherited all the codes—but still. None of that makes anything easier.

Beyond the life and death at stake in our present situation, I feel a subtle pressure to be *flawless* in how I handle things. If I ever want a real shot at my dreams—for the space program to take me seriously as a contender for commander, especially since the need for a replacement came years sooner than it should have—I absolutely cannot screw this up.

Assuming the space program hasn't been completely obliterated by the virus, that is.

Assuming the virus has left anyone alive to care.

I'm getting a call on my buzz screen—it's Natalin. The part of myself I'll never be able to turn off, the curiosity, it nags at me to answer. I don't, though. I'm sort of dreading our next conversation, am not exactly eager to tell her how no one picked up when I attempted to reach out. She's verging on panic as it is. And besides: rest is important, my mother always used to say, and as our former commander she knew that better than anyone. She made it a priority to tune out, to spend time with me no matter how busy she was with station demands. Whatever Natalin needs, it can wait ten minutes.

I hope.

So I sit. Rest. Try to summon the calm my mother was known for.

I still think of this cabin suite as *ours*. Mom's and mine. It's the largest residential space on the station by far, and every inch of it was full of *us*. Now, though, it's just me living alone with the larger-than-life memory of her, a lingering presence that feels thicker by the day. Her earrings, still in the silver dish beside her bed. Her favorite blanket, still sprawled out and waiting for her to return to it. Her stash of dark chocolate and exquisite coffee, the secret privilege of her position: in her monthly updates to Shapiro, based down in Nashville, she'd occasionally mention she missed certain things, only to find them hidden in the next SpaceLove delivery, tucked discreetly between pro-packs. I haven't touched her secret stash, not yet, though I am desperately tempted.

Another call buzzes in, Heath this time. This one is even harder to resist—what if he found Yuki and Grace? What if he found them the same way we found Mila? That thought alone is enough to help me ignore the call. I don't want to know, not yet. Not ever, really. I don't want to know if he's found them dead.

What would my mother do? For all her training, for all her years of experience, she never had to deal with anything even close to this. She was always prepared, never surprised. I feel like the opposite: constantly surprised, not nearly prepared enough.

One thing I know for sure, though, is that she had the strongest mind on the station, maybe even the strongest mind out of everyone stationed on Earth and at the Radix terraforming site. Not only in terms of intelligence, either—strong in terms of never bending once she'd set her mind to something.

That's how I'm trying to be now. I may not be prepared, and I may not have her brilliance, and the challenges I face may end up eating me alive—if the mutated virus doesn't devour me first—but one thing I'm trying out is her resolve: believing I can do this, as strongly as she would have.

Believing the station won't die out under my command.

Believing I won't be crushed under the pressure of it.

A third call comes in, the third in ten minutes. This can't be good. Either they're all calling about the same huge thing, or they're calling about three separate problems. Not ideal either way. It's Leo—I never ignore Leo, and I'm not about to start now.

Break over.

"What's happening?" I say, rising to my feet.

"Heath and Zesi did another scan on Grace and Yuki, to see if they'd used their prints to access any of the common rooms—Grace's prints came up at the rec center. Natatorium, specifically."

What a relief. Assuming they went to the pool together, Grace could have opened the door for both herself and Yuki. "Timestamp?" I ask.

"Four minutes before Haven announced the mandatory check-in," he says.

"They wouldn't have heard it in the pool," we both say at the same time.

"Great work," I say. "You going down there now?"

I hear him exhale, low and slow. "Heath already went—didn't find them," he says. "But what he did find is concerning:

tiny drops of blood on the tile near the pool's ladder."

My hope plummets. "You're sure it isn't old? Did we clean down there after Katri's mother . . . when she . . ."

"It's fresh," he says. "And yeah, Fitch and Pava volunteered to help Zesi and me scrub it a couple of weeks ago."

Right. I remember now. Fitch and Pava and Katri are close like I am with Leo and Haven and Heath, the two-years-younger version of our tight-knit group. Katri loved the pool like her mother did, and they wanted it spotless for her. As if she'd ever go down there again, with the memory of her mother fresh on her mind.

Then again, I've made a bed of my mother's chair. Perhaps Katri swims laps every day to *remember*.

"Okay," I say. "Okay, let me think." Leo's quiet on the other end—this is why I never ignore him. He gives me the space I need when I ask for it, and even when I don't.

I make my way over to the floor-to-ceiling window, look out into the infinite star-studded blackness. My mother always stood in this exact spot when she wasn't sure what to do, said it gave her inspiration to see how far we've come—how much humanity has learned, how much there still is that we *don't* know. It always made her feel better to remember she didn't have to know every answer to every problem.

"Tell Heath to search their rooms again, and all the places that don't require a print-scan for access. They could've slipped out of the natatorium while everyone else was at the check-in," I say, trying not to jump to conclusions. "If the blood you found was from the virus, if they were far enough along to cough up bloodbubbles, there would've been more of it, I think, even if only one of the girls is sick." The image of my mother's blood on the cold, dark observatory-deck floor slips into my memory, broken free from the cage where I put it.

"Got it," he says, at the same time that there's a knock at my door.

No one ever knocks at my door. Mostly because I'm only ever home in the middle of the night, but that's beside the point. "Someone's here," I say. "Check back in soon, okay?"

He agrees, and then he's out. The knocking starts up again, a little louder this time—

It's Heath.

"Sorry to bother you," he says, in lieu of a greeting. "You didn't answer when I called earlier, and this, it's kind of urgent, I—"

"I just talked to Leo," I cut in. Heath's definition of urgent doesn't always line up with mine. "He told me about Grace, and the natatorium, and the blood—that's probably him calling you right now."

He checks his buzz screen, and I can see I'm right. He ignores the call.

"You probably shouldn't ignore that," I say.

"Like you ignored my call, but took Leo's?" His words are playful, but not without a bit of sting.

Our kiss, his lips on mine—suddenly they're all I see when I look at him. Yet another stretch of uncharted territory I haven't learned to navigate. "Look," I tell him, "I just needed a break, I didn't mean anything by it, okay? It's been a long day."

"Sure, I get that," he says, sheepish. "You deserve a break—I was just giving you a hard time. Sorry."

"So, Grace and Yuki?"

"Oh, no," he says. "That's actually not what I was trying to get in touch about. I mean, that was a big part of it, yeah, but the most pressing thing is that Zesi's having a separate issue in Control and wants to get your input—told him I'd relay the message while he works on it."

This definitely qualifies as urgent, and I feel a twinge of guilt over cutting him off earlier. I close my eyes, take a deep breath. If things keep spiraling at this rate, the station is basically doomed. Heath grasps my shoulders, his hands soft but firm. I open my eyes again, only to meet his. They're the color of shining steel, a burst of gray that turns dark at the edges. Haven kept all the colors for herself, apparently, all the green and gold and blue; the precise shade of her hazel irises shifts with the light.

"One thing at a time, Lindley, okay?" Heath's smile is small but steady. "You're not alone in this. You're *not*."

He sounds so sure. I nod, let his words sink in. Try to feel them.

He's right, in a way. The six of us are in this together. They're not going to let me break.

So why do I feel like everything is on me, when it comes down to it?

Maybe because I'm the most visibly in charge. Commander, like my mother was, no matter how hard I try to separate myself from the title. Maybe because I get all the questions, and tend to have the most answers.

That's the problem. I only have *most* of the answers.

Heath squeezes my shoulders. "I'm here for you however you need me to be, all right? If that means you need to ignore my next hundred calls, I get it. Okay?" He searches for my eyes until I meet them. "Just call me back within a quarter hour, though, if you do that. Might be urgent."

I grin, and his smile cracks into a laugh. "I think I can manage that," I say. "Speaking of urgent, I think you should go find Leo instead of coming with me to Control."

"Yeah," he says. "You're probably right."

"And Heath?"

He looks up from his buzz screen. "Yeah, Linds?"

He's never called me that, and it throws me off for a split second. I decide to let it slide—I'm not sure I like him using Leo's name for me, but I'm also not sure I don't.

"Thanks," I say. "I needed this."

His mouth turns up at one corner. "See you in a bit."

15

BLINK TO BLACK

HAVEN AND LEO are already in Control, waiting with Zesi, when I arrive.

"Is Natalin coming?" I ask, noting her absence.

"Oh," Zesi says, messing with a section of the control panel, not taking his eyes off it. "No, she said you told her to work on some sort of food plan—should I have told her to ditch that for this?"

"No, no," I say. "That's exactly what I would've told her, just wanted to make sure she wasn't on her way. What's going on? Heath said it was urgent?"

Zesi, on his rolling stool, spins around to face us. "Okay," he says. "Don't kill me."

"*Not* the most promising way to begin," I say, crossing my arms. "What?"

"So—okay—okay." He's nervous, fidgety. I've never seen Zesi like this before, and it's unsettling. "This whole time, I've been looking in the wrong place for incoming messages, right?

I thought I'd get an alert here, where it says *message alerts*. I mean, seems logical enough."

I look where he's pointing, at the same dark stretch of unlit panels I used for my failed attempt at contact with Earth earlier.

"I thought it was weird we hadn't heard from anyone in a while, from down below, but at the same time, I never really paid attention to how much of our communication before . . . before everyone, um . . . before I was alone up here . . . was initiated by us, not them. Looking back, I think we initiated most of the calls. Also, I've been busy lately, distracted—"

"Is there a point to this?" Haven asks.

Zesi sighs. "I tried to use this message system, tested it to make sure it's working, and you know what I found? It's our *internal* messaging channel, not the one we use between the station and Earth. *This*"—he rolls to the far end of the board, where a smallish red light blinks angrily—"is the channel we need. I only noticed it because it used to be steady and green. I didn't think much of it when it turned yellow, but the red was sort of hard to overlook."

"So we have a message," Leo says. "What's the problem with that? What'd they say?"

"Well," Zesi says with a nervous laugh, "that *is* the problem. I can't get into that particular system just yet. And red could mean anything from *this message is ten days old* to *ALERT, ALERT, TAKE ASTEROID PRECAUTIONS*, right?"

Asteroid.

As if we don't have enough problems.

I stare at the angry red light, as if it's showing me our bleak future: I imagine an unwieldy space rock, hurtling toward us—ripping through us—ending us.

"Find a way to break in to the system, find a way to unlock the message," I order. "Stay up all night if you have to. If there's an asteroid headed for us, we won't have much time to shift position." Not that we're equipped to make a *significant* shift—our sheer size renders us mostly inert. We weren't designed for travel, only self-defense in emergencies. "Are we even equipped to do a scan for that sort of thing? We'd have to be, right?" I've been so consumed with dealing with disasters inside the ship, I hadn't yet considered the potential disasters from out-side. Excellent.

"We are, but I can't keep a close eye on the radar *and* try to break in to the message system at the same time," he says. "I can tell you what to do for the scan, though; I can walk you through it—any of you up for taking lead on that?"

Our eyes collectively land on Leo. He's the best with tech, other than Zesi himself. Nice to not be the expert for once.

"Yeah," Leo says. "I'll help."

"I can help, too," Haven says. "I mean, if that would actually *be* helpful? Not too many hands on deck? And that way, we can rotate out if any of us needs to focus on something else for a bit?"

"The more minds, the better," Zesi says, and it almost makes me feel bad for being the only one to not volunteer. Almost.

"Let me know when you break through," I say. "I want to

be with you when you listen to the message, even if it's in the middle of the night."

It's very possible I'll regret these words, but what I'd regret even more? An asteroid slamming through our station. Blinking out to blackness. If that's even a remote possibility, we need to take immediate precautions.

"Get some rest, Linds, okay?" Leo says. "You deserve it."

I smile, nod. Keep my mouth shut, because he means well.

We all deserve rest, and I should tell them to make sure they get some, too. More than deserve, we all *need* it. But we can't afford to rest, not really. So I stay quiet.

It isn't like I'll be stealing any more time for myself, though, not tonight. It isn't like I'm a hypocrite.

I leave them all in Control and head for the lab. I've got work to do.

16

TO SHATTER, TO SPLATTER

OF ALL THE long days I've had lately, today takes the prize. It's only five-evening, according to the lab's analog clock, but a week's worth of problems have crept in and wedged themselves between minute marks. The hours are bursting at the seams.

I take a seat on my old, familiar stool. Lean my elbows on the crisp white Formica countertop. Think. It helps to have this empty surface in front of me—it's calming, like an alternate universe where nothing is wrong or out of place or broken, where nothing is shattered, or splattered with blood. Like I have endless possibility in front of me, the good sort.

It isn't easy to clear my head. I came down here to focus on Mila, to see if there's anything else I can learn from the hazy results of the lab work I did this afternoon, but my mind is slippery. Every few minutes, I find myself steeped in thought over the problems I've assigned everyone else. And not only those—unofficial ones, too. Like the thing Haven said today after the mandatory check-in: *they're going to hate us.* Or Natalin's fear that a station-wide food crisis will fall on her shoulders. And then there's this new Heath situation, whatever's changing between us—it definitely rubbed him the wrong way that I picked up Leo's call and ignored his, but it isn't like I did it to hurt him.

I feel like I'm walking on glass, carrying armfuls of glass, in a glass world that's tipped off its axis.

At twenty after, I hear the lab door slide open. It's Heath.

"Linds?" Again with the nickname. "I don't mean to interrupt . . . whatever it is you're doing?" He eyes my still-clean table. "Thought you might want to take a look at this."

He slides a petite plastic bag to me, zip-sealed to contain the tiniest bit of blood inside. I look up and find him staring at me, not the bag.

"From the tile near the pool?" I ask.

He nods. "Scraped as much as I could. Still looking for the girls themselves—thought I'd stop by here before I head to the far wings so you could get to work."

It isn't what I came down here to do, but then again, it's not like I'm actually *doing* what I came down here to do. And if Yuki or Grace coughed up this blood, it could certainly be another route to answers about the mutation.

"Thanks, Heath," I say. "That was really thoughtful, thank you."

He looks like he wants to say more, but no words actually

make it out of his mouth. Things are definitely shifting between us—he's never measured his words with me.

"Look," I say, then pause. How do I call attention to the awkwardness without making it even *more* awkward? "I just want to make sure everything's okay. With us, I mean. I'm sorry about this afternoon, about not answering your call—"

"And I'm sorry about this morning," he says.

"I told you not to apologize, remember?" I smile, trying for playful.

His smile is small and heavy, barely a smile at all. "No, seriously, Lindley," he says, "I should have thought more about the timing. I don't want you to have to worry about me on top of all the other things you have going on right now. I just thought"— he looks away, runs a hand through his hair—"I don't know what I thought. I think you're amazing, and I'm crazy impressed at how well you're holding up under all the pressure."

I half laugh, ready to protest, but his words keep coming. "It's true," he says, brightening. "Things would be falling apart here if you hadn't stepped up and pulled us all together, is what I'm trying to say." He glances down at his hands. "Last thing I want to do is stand in the way of that. Be a distraction, you know?"

Things *are* falling apart, despite my best efforts, but I don't say that. He'd just pile on more praise I don't deserve. "I don't want you to disappear on me, either, though," I say. "Like, because you're afraid of distracting me? I want you . . . I want things to be like they always have been."

I *think* I want that? I don't know. Until he kissed me this morning, I'd never considered that things with Heath could *be* any different than they've always been.

But it looks like I've said something wrong. His lips are a tight line now, and his eyes aren't as bright. "Yeah," he says. "Yeah, sure." He glances at the clock, backs toward the door. "Should probably keep looking for the girls now. I'll let you know if I find anything, okay? Good luck with the blood sample, hope it's helpful—I'll buzz you if there's any more to test, or maybe have Haven buzz you, whatever."

The door slides closed behind him, cutting off the end of his sentence.

"Um, goodbye?" I say to the door.

Add any more glass to the pile in my arms, I'll be a bloody mess within days.

I adjust the pins in my hair, make sure everything is smooth and tight. It's a lucky ritual of sorts, one I picked up from my mother years ago. Whereas hers was an unconscious habit, mine was born out of fascination, admiration. I loved her hairpins, for one. More than that, I wanted to be exactly like her.

Ironic, that it took losing her for me to follow in her steps.

I can almost hear her: *LeeLee,* she would say, if she were here, *you've got a job to do.* She was always going on about jobs, how they weren't going to take care of themselves. *Nothing holds the power to crush you unless you hand over that power.*

So I take a deep breath. It's just me and the microscopes, alone together in this pristine, empty room. I prepare another slide, the Grace/Yuki blood barely sufficient. And then I get to work.

17

HAZE AND FUZZ

WHEN THE RESULTS are in, the first thing I notice is the sample's crisp clarity: this slide bears no resemblance to the haze and fuzz of Mila's sample from this morning. I must have sleepwalked through that procedure, screwed something up along the way. This one is perfection.

Speaking of perfection, the second thing I notice: there's no trace of an active virus at all. It's reassuring, for sure, but not conclusive—just because Grace or Yuki haven't contracted the mutation yet, it doesn't mean they won't.

My buzz screen lights up, not with a call this time, only a message from Leo: **Heath found them.** A second later, another message edges out the first: **Alive.**

It's the first thing to go well all day, and the relief is physical. My eyes flutter closed, trapping tears that've sprung up out of nowhere. Heath found the girls. I want to know everything.

My finger hovers over the screen. I could call Heath directly for the details, *would*, on any other day. We've never had a day like today, though, so I find myself buzzing Leo instead.

"He found them?" I say. "Tell me everything."

It isn't lost on me that Heath didn't call me, either.

"Yeah, hang on a sec," Leo says, but then there's a long pause, Haven's voice in the background. "Sorry," he says. "I'm in the middle of something"—a series of beeps tramples over his voice—"can I call you back in a few? Or just buzz Heath, it might be a while before I finish."

"Sure, yeah." I want to ask about their progress in Control, too, but now is obviously not a good time for that. "Talk to you in a bit."

I busy myself with cleaning the lab station, calm myself with the familiar rhythm of clearing the table of scopes and trays, wiping it down with disinfectant until it sparkles. The whole process takes less than two minutes, but it's two minutes well spent. My head feels clear again, too.

I buzz Heath before I have time to talk myself out of it.

"Hey," he says, picking up immediately. "Find something?" He's so different from his sister in that way, and I'm grateful for it—when Haven and I have our tense stretches, she freezes me out.

"Where are you?" I say, nudging my stool into its hiding spot under the table. "Leo says you found the girls?"

"Yeah, I'm with them now. Starboard-side lab."

"What? What were they doing in there?" There's hardly ever a good reason for *me* to go into SSL, let alone two fourteen-year-olds who have nothing to do with cold storage. "Never mind, don't answer that, I'm going to ask them myself. Stay where you are and don't let them leave."

He doesn't protest, but then, he never does. Heath genuinely loves being on the receiving end of orders like this—he's said so on a couple of occasions. He takes a lot of joy in following well, on following *through*. I guess he's had a lot of practice, having Haven for a twin. She's just the opposite.

The lab door slides shut behind me. Portside, we call this one—even when our station was new and running smoothly, full of brilliant, vibrant minds, Portside was the more heavily trafficked of the two. It was where active experimentation happened, where 90 percent of the equipment was installed, since we often ran tests for *Nautilus* before they received their equipment upgrade. SSL, on the other hand, occupies twice the space for a tenth of the science. Which isn't to say it's small—Portside itself is quite expansive, taking up half of this deck. It's just that SSL takes up the *entire* starboard side of its deck.

For the life of me, I can't imagine why Yuki and Grace would go to SSL. Not for anything useful, not that I can think of. Maybe for its beauty? Its mystery? SSL houses rows and rows of glowing pillars, so ethereal and white like starlight. It takes two people to wrap arms around each pillar, that's how thick they are—but for their expanse, they're mostly just filled with chilled, transparent gel. Tiny sprigs of plant life dot each pillar with green, floating embryos put on pause, waiting for the day when Radix is ready to be fully terraformed.

As I enter my universal access code to get into SSL, that brings up another question: How did Yuki and Grace get in here in the first place?

I weave in and out between pillars, find Heath and the girls in the dimly lit lab station in the middle of the room. The station is a wide white oval rimmed with thick countertop ledges, all storing a limited range of equipment—Yuki and Grace sit cross-legged on top of the counter, quietly staring at their hands. Nothing seems out of place, so at least there's that.

"What exactly is happening here?" I let my question dangle, resist the urge to fill the silence when it goes unanswered.

Heath stands, his back against the oval's curved inner wall, his arms crossed. I join him, mimic his pose. We're like a set of twin statues.

It's so quiet, so still, we might as well be caught up in the cold storage pillars with the countless sprigs of plants. Life, put on hold.

Do I break them with questions? Pile on the guilt until they splinter beneath it? Either of those would be effective, I think, for this single moment. But what about tomorrow? What about pulling this problem up at its roots rather than simply tearing off dead leaves?

I uncross my arms, hope it makes me look approachable rather than like some sort of commanderly force. "You're not in trouble, okay?" It takes effort to soften the edges in my voice, especially after this day. Yuki glances up at me—progress. "We were just worried when we couldn't find you. And we didn't think to look . . . here."

"How did you—" Heath starts, but I hold up a hand to cut

him off. His tone is too sharp.

"Heath and I know you were at the pool earlier—"

"We didn't know about the check-in until we were already at the pool!" Grace cuts me off, finally emerging from the silent pose she's maintained since we arrived. "We would've come, but we were dripping wet."

So they *did* hear the announcement? And they still didn't come? I could absolutely give them an earful for this. Could, possibly should. I'm torn—but they obviously already know it was wrong to skip it, otherwise they wouldn't be acting so weird. Is that the *only* reason they're acting weird, though?

"Forget about the check-in for now," I say. "Heath found blood near the steps. Did one of you fall or something?"

I found no trace of the virus when I studied the blood sample, so I definitely don't want to ask any leading questions to give away that I studied it in the first place—we'd only end up on a slippery slope ending in questions about *why* I studied it. I'm not about to discuss Mila with anyone who can't even be bothered with mandatory check-ins. I'm not about to discuss Mila, period.

"I got a nosebleed," Yuki says shyly.

"She gets them a lot," Grace adds. "Always has."

Yuki nods, the more soft-spoken of the two. "My dad was— did you know my dad?"

"Her dad was a nurse," Grace says, making Yuki blush. "He let her do this all the time."

"Let her do *what* all the time?" Heath asks, adopting my purposefully patient tone. "This isn't Medical, so what does your father have to do with it?"

Yuki's cheeks are cherry-blossom pink now. "Pillar Ninety-Seven," she says. "It's full of witch hazel. Well, half full now. He'd extract a sample here and there, whenever supplies were low, and mix it with some other things to help my nose stop bleeding."

I try to stifle the surprise on my face—all of this is news to me, and wow, so many rules broken all at once. Like, so many *major* rules broken, and not just by these girls. "He taught you how to do it, too? And gave you the access code?"

"I'm sorry!" Yuki says, burying her face in her hands. "I know it's wrong, I just—they don't stop, sometimes, the nosebleeds, and he was worried I might bleed too much, or that I'd have an emergency while he was working, and—I just—I didn't know what else to do. I'm sorry, Commander, I won't do it again, I promise I won't—"

"It's fine," I say, even though it really, really isn't. "It stopped bleeding this time, though?"

Grace is notably quiet now. Trying to absorb as little attention as possible, I'm sure. As little *blame* as possible.

Yuki nods. "On its own, this time. We only stayed because it's so peaceful in here." Her face twists, and she stares at her hands. "It reminds me of him." Her voice is so quiet, I barely make out the words. "My dad."

I'm overcome with the sudden urge to hug her, because I know that feeling. I know it so, so well. But I keep my distance: if there's one thing I've learned in these weeks, it's that grief doesn't always want a hug.

"Don't disappear on us again," I say, making sure to meet Grace's eyes, not just Yuki's. "It's imperative that you attend every check-in, dripping wet or not, and in the future, please buzz me if you need more witch hazel." We've had enough blood on this ship—if it takes breaking the rules to stop more from spilling, so be it. Better to know what's happening on the station, better to not have people scurrying around in the dark trying to hide things. "And a word of advice—be careful at Mikko's parties? Things have been hard lately for everyone, I know. Make your choices with a clear head, not with a broken heart, okay?" I overheard my mother say that to someone once, and it's stuck with me ever since. Only recently did those words take on true power—I'd never known brokenness before she died, not really.

Now it's Grace whose cheeks are pink. "Yes, Commander," she mumbles.

That's twice now with the *Commander*—both times dig, like hairpins to the heart. I resist the urge to correct them. I downplay my authority, usually, but in this case it's more reinforcement than burden.

"Now go find Siena," I say. "She's been worried sick."

The girls slide down from the lab ledge without a word,

leaving Heath alone with me in the wide white oval.

"Well," Heath says. "This is not good."

"Not good at all," I agree.

Because, really, when it comes down to it, we should be celebrating. That we found them—that they're alive.

In truth, it's unnerving. I thought I had a pretty good handle on station-wide activity, on the secret things people think they're so good at hiding. Between the six of us, I thought we knew everything.

Today proves me wrong. In so many ways, I'm starting to feel like I'm in over my head.

"Good work today," I say, meeting Heath's eyes.

He doesn't look away, not for a long time. "You, too, Linds."

His *Linds* hits both of us at once, brings back in vivid color how quickly things are shifting between us. We stay still for a minute, steadied by the hum of the pillars, their ethereal glow. Yuki was right, it really is peaceful in here.

"I, um," I say, my store of eloquence depleted for the day. "We should go. Rest while we can, right?"

He clears his throat. "Right. Yes, you're right."

We leave the room as empty as it should be, no trace we were ever there.

18

TURN UP THE BLAZE

I WAKE FROM another short stretch of uncomfortable sleep just after midnight. My legs are sweaty, stuck to the arm of my mother's leather chair, fire still blazing at an eleven. I should know by now that eleven's much too high—it's just so beautiful, the rhythm of the flames. Mesmerizing. I've come to rely on them lately, when my mind is too full and I can't sleep. I turn up the blaze, then let myself get lost. Sleep, sweat, wake, repeat.

My buzz screen lights up, though, and now I see it isn't just the heat that's pulled me from sleep. It's Zesi: **Meet in Control ASAP.**

I straighten, throw off the blanket I love but can't quit. The blur of sleep falls instantly away.

Be there in ten, I reply. I slip into a clean pair of pants, zip my favorite hoodie on over my camisole. Zesi wouldn't wake me unless he's had a breakthrough—ten minutes is generous in light of how fast I plan to move.

There are a surprising number of people still awake, clustered inside one of the enclaves I pass. They're very into themselves, listening to Sailor Salvato sing as he plays his acoustic guitar. Good for me: no one asks a single question. I'm pretty sure no one even sees me slip by.

Control looks almost exactly the same as it did when I left earlier, except like an older, more haggard version of itself. Coffee mugs outnumber people two to one, varying degrees of full, varying degrees of fresh. One look at Haven, Leo, and Zesi explains it: they've been busy, more than a bit distracted. They're running on fumes.

"Someone want to start talking?" I ask. I can't shake commander mode, not even in the middle of the night. When I doubt myself, this sort of thing always affirms that I'm not the worst person they could've chosen. As much as the pressure gets to me, the role comes more naturally than I like to admit.

Leo glances at Haven, then back at me. "Good news is, there's no asteroid," Leo says. "We've been running scans for hours now—each vector scan takes a while, since it's calling out so far into the galaxy, and each one pinged a number of potential problems. I ran the scans, and Haven zeroed in on the pings, trying to track velocity, direction, all that. Long story short, we haven't found anything to be concerned about, nothing on a collision path."

It's a lot to take in—no wonder they look exhausted. "Good," I say. "That *is* good news. So what's the bad news?" Surely Zesi wouldn't have called me all the way here in the middle of the night if there were only good news. He could've just messaged

no asteroid instead of sending out an ASAP summons.

My eyes drift to where Zesi sits, near the message-system light. It's no longer blinking and angry, no longer bright at all. I feel my heartbeat in my throat—a wave of anxiety rushes into the void left by my asteroid panic.

"You did it?" I ask. "You broke into the message system? What did it say?"

Zesi glances at Haven and Leo, bites absently at his lip.

"*What?*" It comes out more demanding than I mean it to, but I'm not exactly sorry. "What's going on?"

Zesi takes a deep breath, meets my eyes. Barely. "Not *it*. Not what did *it* say," he says. "A more accurate question would be what did *they* say. *They*, as in the *seventeen* messages we missed."

Seventeen.

I can only imagine what this means—what they're *thinking* down in Nashville. Seventeen messages with no answer: it's a problem, and not just because there could be critical, time-sensitive information there.

Seventeen messages with no answer could mean they think we're all dead. It could mean we won't see another shipment for a good long while, since those things take time to prepare, time to launch.

"Let's hear them," I say.

Zesi nods, wordless. I brace myself, rest my elbows against the silver ledge with all the coffee mugs, stare out the window into the endless sea of stars.

Shapiro here, for Hamilton, the message begins. Hamilton

meaning my mother, I'm sure, definitely not her seventeen-year-old daughter. In all the years I've heard my mother speak of her monthly check-in calls with Shapiro, this is the first time I've ever heard his voice. It's deeper than I expected.

Please report back with your status ASAP, the message goes on. *I'm sorry to leave this information on a recording, but it's urgent, so better here than not at all. Just got word of the report you sent down about two isolated instances of contagion—I hope that's all it's come to, two isolated instances. I trust you've put the patients under quarantine already, but if not, you are under strict orders to do so immediately. We've taken a hard hit down here, to say the least— Roberts is dead, and similar symptoms have begun to manifest in another delivery pilot from the same division. I need to know your status—head count, supply levels. We're locking down the base, putting ourselves under quarantine so this thing doesn't spread. We can't promise any future deliveries until we're sure our pilots are in the clear, until we know more about the incubation time. It'd be bad for you to ration food, but it'd be worse for a dead pilot to crash his bird into your station. Okay. Report back immediately, Hamilton. Stars and sun—Shapiro out.*

"How old was that message?" I stare at my reflection in the window, half here and half not. It's as faded as I feel.

"February twentieth," Zesi says. "Looks like the commander put in a call less than a minute later, so my best guess is that she never actually listened to his message."

February 20: the day after the first symptoms began to manifest, nearly seven weeks ago. I remember it clearly, because my mother died the very next day. I can hardly believe it was *only* seven weeks ago—so much has happened since then—and yet the sting of loss is as raw as ever, like we lost her just yesterday and have been living in one long nightmare ever since.

"Ready for the next?" Zesi asks, pulling me out of my head. "This one's only five days old." He presses a button and another message begins to roll.

Hamilton, this is Shapiro—things have been hell down here, and I regret that I haven't reached out in a while. Quarantine knocked out Mission Control for weeks, along with both sectors where our backup systems are located. Lesson learned for the future, right? He laughs, but it is tight and strained with stress. *Anyway, I was expecting to find a full inbox waiting for me, and the board's pressing me for updates—you know how they get—but there's nothing there. I know you've got everything under control, but it isn't like you to just go dark, so I'm worried. Report back at once.*

The messages pile on top of themselves: *We're concerned about your utter silence!* and *Is anyone left alive?* and *Please, Linsey, let me know you're okay.*

Only my mother's closest friends called her Linsey. Shapiro's voice is more strained with every message, like he's been up all night, every night, for days. He sounds exhausted. He sounds like me.

Sixteen messages roll from over three straight days of panic, according to the timestamps—but then there's a gap afterward, two days of silence. The final message is a long one, dated yesterday morning at nine sharp, and it's the only one where

Shapiro doesn't start with some form of my mother's name:

If you're hearing this message, he begins, *it means I'm wrong and you're not all dead. Hell, I hope I'm wrong. If you're hearing this, you're alive, and your systems have been down, or something else is preventing you from getting in touch.*

The board has spent the last forty-eight hours in strategy; we've lost a lot of sleep over you, and for the sake of closure, we need to know your status. Since our attempts at contact have been met with silence, and our pilot division is still under quarantine, we've made contact with Sergeant Vonn at the exca site on Radix. He's making preparations to send a supply crew over, but we've told him to hold off until we're sure the station hasn't been occupied, that this isn't some hostage situation or an act of war. I've flagged this message as urgent—if I don't hear back from you within the next twenty-four hours, Vonn will launch his crew in preparation to attack, rather than aid.

He pauses, clears his throat.

If you're all dead, he says finally, *this won't be an issue. Shapiro out.*

I run some fast math in my head: it's one in the morning now, so we have just under eight hours to deal with this. Just under eight hours to figure out how to tell Shapiro about all of our dead—that if anything's holding us hostage or declaring war, it's grief.

It would be a simple call, if not for the Vonn piece of it— or if Shapiro were able to make decisions on his own without first getting board approval. Vonn's system of ethics is abysmal at best, and the board's willingness to turn a blind eye in the name of advancing the mission is equally odious. Well, the board minus Shapiro—Shapiro and my mother were consistently like-minded, always the minority no matter the vote. Shapiro, I trust.

It's everyone else who makes me wary.

Several years back, Vonn tried to steal some of my mother's team when he got into a bind, but she ultimately won that fight because of her team's invaluable expertise. She needed them here, she told him. Her people were not expendable.

I have no doubt Vonn would help us only so long as it helps him: feed us, harvest us, use us for slave labor on Radix until we have nothing left to give. It's how he's always operated, pushing workers to their limits for the sake of getting the job done quickly—and the board spins it so the workers believe they're sacrificing to save humanity. How desperate are they, now that Vonn doesn't have ready access to a refresher crew from Earth? Even if a new crew was willing to give everything for the mission—new crews always are, what with the incentives they offer for families left behind—how would those crews *get* to Radix, if they can't even manage to launch a simple supply delivery?

Honestly, I'd almost rather starve than accept interference of any kind from Vonn. *Surely* there's some other way to stretch or replenish our supplies that doesn't include our being indebted to him down the line? More than just our short-term relief, we have to consider the potential for long-term misery: if Vonn and the board eventually put their heads together and realize they can solve two problems at once by sending us out to Radix to replenish Vonn's team, that's it—that's our entire miserable future, right there, and not even Shapiro will be able to stop it from happening.

We are not experts like our parents were. Aside from Shapiro, we have no one left to defend our worth but ourselves.

The infinite sea of stars curls in on itself, and for one silent, dangling second, I think I'm going to lose it. I steady myself, cradle my head in my hands. It's too much, this. I can't do it. I can't do everything I need to do to keep everyone alive. Today has been too much, too much in every way.

There are six of us, yes, six of us in this together. But they're waiting for *me*. Leo, Zesi, Haven, silent and waiting for my word.

If I can't handle this, who will?

I shift four mugs of old, cold coffee to the side. "Let's get a fresh pot going," I say. "Meet at my place in twenty, make sure Nat and Heath are there, too."

We never meet at my place, but with so much spinning out of control, I need to be somewhere I feel safe, steady. We're going to handle this, handle *everything*, and we're going to handle it on my terms.

19

LIKE A FALLING STAR

LEO'S THE FIRST to arrive. He takes a long look at me, then breaks into a wide smile. "Look at us," he says. "We look like we've been left to fend for ourselves on Mars or something."

His smile is contagious. Just when I forget how much I need him, he's there, bright and beaming and warm. "Not that far off, really," I say.

"Not that far off except for *everything*." He smiles again. Mars exploration never did take off, especially once they learned more about the conditions on Radix, how perfect it'd be for terraforming. Mars has been reduced to a primitive reminder of all we thought we knew—and how very little anyone actually knows, compared to the vastness of the universe.

"How are you always this fresh, Leo? How do you do it? How do you not need sleep?"

"How do you know you're not sleeping now?" he says. "How do you know this isn't a dream?"

"I always wake up at the worst parts," I say, purposefully

taking him seriously. "I would've woken up a long time ago if this were a dream."

His smile fades, and he looks at me, really *looks* at me. "C'mere, Linds." He pulls me in close, wraps his arms around me. They're strong, and he's strong, and it turns out I need this right now in a major way. I bury my cheek in his chest, he rests his chin on my head: perfect fit, as always. We've done this for years, ever since his height drastically outpaced mine. "We're going to get through this, all right?" His chest rises, falls. "We *are.*"

We.

"Yeah," I say. "It's just—little things, you know?" Her chocolate. How everything in this place is always exactly as I leave it, because I'm the only one who lives here now. The stars outside our every window, a constant reminder of all I've loved and lost.

"I get it," he says. And I know he does. He was incredibly close with his father, and loved his mother to pieces. They were good people, the best. "I think it's okay to think about them, you know? I think they'd want us to remember."

I don't know how to think about those things without falling apart, is the problem. And if I fall apart, the station does, too. But I don't say so—I can't. I try, but the words won't come out.

Someone pounds at my door, startling us apart.

"Helloooo?" Haven calls, her voice ever clear from the far side of the door. "A little help here? Hands are full of coffee!"

I rush over to let her in, find everyone else close behind her.

Haven and Natalin and Heath carry two mugs each, full to their brims. Zesi has a French press in both hands, each wrapped in a little neoprene sweater to hold in the heat.

I shift things around on our—my—coffee table, make room for the French presses and mugs. Haven and Natalin curl into the love seat, a functional purple built-in that's too big and too small all at once. The guys spread out around the table, each claiming a piece of the woven, rust-colored rug that makes our cork-on-concrete floor slightly more bearable. They leave my mother's chair for me.

The mood settles like a falling star, bright and brighter until it burns out to blackness. I take a sip of coffee, set the mug carefully onto the table. "It's been a long day, and it's late, so let's jump right in," I say. "I'll follow up with each of you on an individual basis tomorrow—especially you, Natalin, I know the food situation's looking pretty grim—but for now, we need to talk about Shapiro and the messages."

Natalin starts to protest, but I cut her off before she can derail me. "The messages present a number of issues," I say. "For one, we've been silent so long they think we're dead. We're already low on supplies, and it sounds like they're not planning to send us more anytime soon—even when they find out we're alive, they won't be able to, due to their pilot quarantine. I know this complicates the food crisis in a major way, Nat, so please be assured that isn't lost on me."

I glance at her face, try to get a read on how irritated she is that I'm steamrolling her like this. She nods, lips tight, but doesn't interrupt.

"Making contact with Shapiro isn't the hard part, thanks to Zesi's breakthrough with our external comm system—our system seems to be working just fine, we simply didn't know how to get into it until today," I continue. "Problem is, we need to come to a consensus on what to tell him."

"How is that a problem?" This from Natalin. I knew she wouldn't keep her thoughts to herself for long. "He thinks we're dead, and we can easily tell him we aren't. Zesi mentioned, on the way over, about some sort of shipment from Radix?"

Leo catches my eye. Clearly, he gets my hesitation even before I spell it out. "It's not just a matter of supplies," he says. "I think what Lindley is concerned about, rightly, is supplies *with strings attached.*" He glances at me, and I give a small nod in thanks.

Leo gets it, always. He's well acquainted with my flashes of intuition, with how nine times out of ten they're spot on. I only hope this isn't the one time I'm wrong.

"Sergeant Vonn and Lindley's mom didn't get along," he goes on—understatement of the galaxy. How many times did we stay up until three-morning, just the two of us, Leo listening patiently as I spilled over with worry for my mother? Vonn and my mother were fundamentally different in every way imaginable—he, with his condescension and his insults that sliced like knives—she, with her wisdom and unwavering commitment to treating humans like humans.

"That's putting it rather mildly," I say. "The only thing worse than Vonn attacking us? Accepting his help and finding ourselves indebted to him." I take a deep breath, taste the words on my tongue before letting them out. "We're up here on our own—Vonn will need a replacement team sooner or later. How long do you think it'll be before they decide to ship us out to Radix in the name of 'what's best for everyone'?" I sharpen my tone so the words cut through any lingering notions of invincibility the others might have. "You know the board will side with Vonn if it comes down to it—they always do."

How many times have we heard *what's best for everyone* to justify what they do? Only then, we were the everyone benefitting at others' expense. *The board thinks they own the entire universe*, my mother always said. *They think they can grind people into dust and suffer no consequences.* For a long time, I thought she was speaking metaphorically, but then I overheard her one night, talking about how an entire shift of exca workers had died under the sergeant's command. No virus responsible, only Vonn—not enough water, not enough sleep, nothing but *do more and do it yesterday.*

No one says anything for a good long minute. The fire dances in place. Zesi pours more coffee from the French press.

"Do I need to remind you?" I say finally. "Vonn tried to poach my mother's crew when he got in a bind, and she only barely won that fight—do I need to spell out how much worse it would be for *us*?"

"It isn't like Shapiro said we were going to go, like, *work* for him, though." Natalin bites at her fingernail, something she does only when she's the perfect combination of irritated and anxious. "He didn't even say Vonn would come anywhere close to the station. Just his delivery people, right?"

"That's true, but—"

"But what, Lindley? You really think his delivery people are going to drop supplies off and then, like, take us all hostage to become drudges out at the exca site?"

My cheeks burn. "Not immediately," I say. "But, yes, I think it's a slippery slope. Accepting his help sets a bad precedent for the future."

"Refusing his help means we might never *see* our future," she shoots back.

"Look, I'm not disagreeing with you." I straighten in my chair, try to keep my voice from rising. "I agree with you, in fact. Hence the problem."

"I am not going to stand by and watch the station starve just because you're too prideful, and too afraid, to accept their supplies. That's a *lot of life* on my hands, Lindley. A lot of *death*."

"Our hands," I say. "Not just yours."

"*Your* hands." Her eyes are steely blue-gray, never too tired to fight for what she feels is right. We have that in common. "I'll go on record if it comes to it, tell the entire station whose decision it was to deny us access to food."

"We can make it work if we ration properly, right? If every-one could just get over themselves and eat what they need, not only what they like—"

"We have to live in reality, Lindley. We can't put our hope in what would *ideally* work—"

"You're expecting the worst out of our people," I say.

"And you're proving me right." She glares at me, eyes fierce through narrowed slits.

"Wow, Nat, nothing like your bleak outlook on reality to make us feel better," Haven says.

Natalin sets her jaw. "It's hard *not* to have a bleak outlook with a reality like this."

"Rather than dwelling on how terribly this could all turn out," I say, doing everything I can to keep calm, "I think it would be most useful—*for now*—to focus on a plan B. You're absolutely certain we don't have enough food to last us?"

"To last us how *long*? Not indefinitely, that's for sure," she says. "Probably not longer than late next week—*maybe* a day or two after that. Depending on how many more, um, die. Assuming Mila wasn't a fluke."

My head pounds with the other crisis I've tucked away, the one I've thoroughly attempted to compartmentalize so it doesn't tear my mind in two. Even if we manage to keep everyone from starving, who's to say the mutation won't take us out anyway?

I close my eyes. Take a breath.

"We have to think long-term, Nat," Heath cuts in. "I agree with you that we need supplies, for sure. I think it's dangerous to completely write off what Lindley's saying, though. Can we come up with a third option? Maybe we can get supplies from *Nautilus* instead of Radix?"

"That's not a bad idea at all," I say. *Nautilus* is tiny compared to our station—fifteen people, total—but since they're so far out of the way, their shipments are infrequent and comparable to ours in size.

"What if we're carriers?" Haven says. "For the virus, I mean. Everyone on *Nautilus* came from Earth, right? Could we spread the virus, even though we're immune to it?"

"We don't even know if we *are* immune to it now," Zesi says. "Who knows what we might pass to them."

The thought of spreading the virus in a supply handoff hadn't even occurred to me. If Vonn and everyone on Radix are still alive, business-as-usual, that means they never came in contact with CRW-0001 at all. We could infect everyone at the entire exca site if we spread it to one of their delivery people, kill a multitrillion-dollar endeavor just because we can't stretch our food supply for another few weeks. As much as I dislike Vonn and his twisted way of getting the job done, there's no denying his wealth of knowledge and experience. I may think him despicable, but it doesn't mean I want him dead—to lose him could be disastrous for the future of humanity as a whole.

A wave of nausea slams into me as I realize: these convictions I've drawn all on my own are deeply rooted in the very same *what's best for everyone* ideology I so despise—there's no way we can jeopardize the space program en masse just because we're having a crisis. And I don't know which is worse: the fact that what's best for *us* falls on the wrong side of what's best for everyone else . . . or the fact that it feels almost wrong to prioritize our own survival.

What would my mother have done? Surely she would have protected me, along with her team and their families, if it came down to it. She would've found some miraculous way to save everything and everyone all at once.

"What?" Leo says, nudging my knee. "What's this look on your face?"

"We're just going to have to work with what we have," I say. "We could infect everyone on Radix, not just *Nautilus.*" There has to be some way to save ourselves without jeopardizing the rest of the space team—without jeopardizing the future of *humanity.* There *has* to be.

"They could wear hazmats, though, right?" Leo says. "We could scrub the air in the delivery chamber, make sure it's clean? It might be clean enough already—no one's been in there since the last shipment."

"I've never tried to scrub an entire chamber before," Zesi says. "I'm not sure I'd be able to eliminate all traces of the virus, or if there's any way to be sure our air-qual measuring systems are as precise as they'd need to be."

"Like I said, though, it might be clean enough already. It could work."

"But what if it doesn't?" I counter. "Our entire station was compromised by a single delivery guy whose only contact was with that chamber. We make the tiniest mistake, and they're done. That's a lot more life at stake than just our station, Nat."

For once, she doesn't argue. I feel no satisfaction at having the final word, though. This is a problem.

"So what do we tell Shapiro?" Haven asks.

The exhaustion is heavy in this room, sunken eyes on tired faces. I don't know how we're going to survive all of this, but I have to believe we *can*. Under different circumstances, I would have no issue with telling Shapiro the truth in its entirety—but it's only a matter of time before the board finds out we're running the station on our own, and that's where I get nervous. They've only ever acted in their own interests. Why would they act in ours now?

"We tell him only what's necessary," I say. "And it doesn't all have to be true."

20

ALONELY

I WAKE TO an empty room at nearly eight-morning, disoriented from the coffee and the stress and the late, late night. The fire isn't on anymore—Leo must have turned it off after I fell asleep. He and Heath stayed with me after the others went home, played a game of cards near the window so I wouldn't be alone. I insisted I wanted to be alone, of course, but they know me too well. What I say and what I mean don't always align. They can almost always tell the difference.

I have a dull headache, the sort that comes from tucking too many thoughts away, and too many feelings. Water will help, I think. I hope. I fill my glass at our refrigerated dispenser, watch the water sparkle under the purple-white spotlight that turns on whenever it's in use. It's such a simple thing, that spotlight, but I've come to love it. It's steady. It's always been there, my whole life. If the light goes dark, I'll just replace it with one of the hundred backup disks in our supply drawer, and how easy is that? *So* easy. Easy is nice right now.

The water helps, at least with clarity. Yesterday comes back in screaming color: if only all the problems, all the pressure, had evaporated overnight. I really should get going—I'll need to get in touch with Shapiro before the next sixty-two minutes are up, and beyond that, I should probably deal with Natalin before her frustration spirals out of control. I've also been neglecting the lab for too long now already, and should really spend some time later poking and prodding at the failed test results Mila's sample yielded. If I can approach the mutation from a different angle, somehow, maybe I can find a way to stop it before it claims its next victims. If we had a cure—or a vaccine—we could get supplies from *Nautilus* without fear of spreading incurable sickness.

Should, should, should.

I miss the freedom I had two months ago, when no one's life depended on my ability to keep it together, or to keep up with all our rapidly multiplying issues and magically produce all the right answers at all the right times.

The pressure . . . is . . . a lot.

Despite feeling torn by the urgent need to fix everything, I force myself to slow down. Take deliberate sips of the water. Breathe deeply. I slip over to the window, where Heath and Leo left the playing cards stacked neatly on the floor. It's been a while since I've actually played. Years, maybe. I pick up the deck, muscle memory working them into a bridge shuffle. The slap of card against card, the rush of air—it's soothing, mindless. Something to break up the silence. I never deal them into a solitaire, never pause to see the mocking face of the joker staring back at me, or the royals, smug and smirking.

Three minutes of shuffling and I can't take it anymore, can't bear to sit still for a second longer. I set the deck down, faceup, and see the queen of clubs staring back at me. Her eyes are sad, almost, but sort of serene. I tuck her into my back pocket, a reminder that it's okay to be still, even if I can't be alone.

Alone: funny how you can feel that way while surrounded, constantly, by other people. How that sometimes makes the feeling even more pronounced.

Enough, I tell myself. Enough of this.

Time to do whatever I can to sort our issues out.

21

IT'S ONLY THE WEIGHT OF THE WORLD

I COME TO a sharp halt just outside Control, close my eyes, breathe, breathe. *Shapiro will be happy to hear we're alive,* I tell myself. *No need for nerves.*

So why do I feel so anxious?

Why do I feel like my six-year-old self, playing dress-up in my mother's uniform?

I open my eyes to find Haven staring at me, dead-on, six inches from my nose. The look on her face reminds me of one of the royals from the card deck.

"What?" I say, scowling, and she cracks up.

"It's just—you—you looked so *terrified*!"

"I don't see what's funny about that." I *am* terrified. I usually hide it better, I guess.

"I can make the call, if you want?" she offers, remnants of laughter still on her face.

It's tempting—there's a reason she's the one who does our station-wide announcements, the face of all our communications. I sound too severe under pressure, I've been told. Really,

I'm just measuring my words so they don't come out wrong. The irony.

"No, no, I've got it," I say. No part of me is looking *forward* to the call, but as our designated leader, I feel like it's my official responsibility to take care of communication with Nashville. This isn't just a morning announcement we're talking about. Besides, the way she assumes I may need her to do it for me rubs me the wrong way.

"Okayyy," she singsongs. "If you're sure."

I grin, tight-lipped, so what I'm actually thinking won't slip out.

This lack of sleep is becoming problematic for my patience.

Zesi, Leo, and Heath are already inside when Haven and I enter the room. Zesi and Heath are on the rolling stools, both looking a little fidgety. Leo paces the room, runs a hand through his hair every few seconds. Leo rarely shows his nerves like this—most days, you'd have to look close to know he felt nervous at all.

Good to know I'm not alone in my uneasiness.

There's a gleam to the countertop's steel this morning, no trace of last night's dirty mugs or coffee splatters. Zesi must have been the one to clean up, I'd bet my mother's chair on it. He's always been a bit of a clutterphobe. Also, I recognize a stress-clean when I see it—I do the same thing when I need to calm down.

Leo stops pacing when he sees me, and Heath rises from

his stool. Both look like they're about to go in for a hug, to hug *me*, but are each caught off guard by the other. We all end up rooted in place, the world's most awkward quadrangle, Haven its fourth corner.

"So," Leo says, eyes on me. "You're good to go with what you'll tell Shapiro?"

"Good on my end." I avoid everyone's eyes, Haven's especially—I'm still technically working the words out in my head. "Zesi? What about communications? You're all up and ready, too?"

"They couldn't have made it easier," he says, gesturing to the display screen. I peer down over his shoulder and see options for *quick reply, voice,* and *video* beside the log entry labeled *Shapiro—Nashville.*

"Great," I say. "This is great."

Suddenly, heat floods my cheeks like I'm standing in a spotlight made of pure sunbeams. It's only a call, I tell myself, swallowing my panic. It's only a call to the head of Earth-based station relations, only a call full of slippery not-quite-lies, of half-truths—unless I decide to tell him the *full* truth, which could be significantly more helpful, but still feels risky. Either option feels like a playing-card fortress that could collapse under the force of a single breath.

"Do you want us to leave so you can be alone?" Heath asks. "Would that help?"

The idea alone is pure relief. "Yes," I say. "Yeah, I think that would help a ton, if you don't mind." I'm worried enough about how the call will sound to Shapiro—taking out the worry about how I'll sound to everyone else is a weight off. "Thank you. I'll catch you up right after."

Heath, Leo, and Zesi file out, but Haven lingers. "You sure you've got this?"

She's overdoing it today, and I feel more insulted than supported, but maybe that's just me and my lack of sleep; maybe it's just me projecting my fears that I'm not doing well enough quickly enough for everyone on board. Either way, it's more motivation than ever to make it through this call.

"I'm *fine*, okay?" My words bite, sharp-toothed and snapping, and I only minimally regret them. Maybe they'll save us in the future, make her think twice next time before she says something that makes me want to cut even deeper.

Haven backs away, hands up. To her credit, she doesn't say anything more, but I know from experience that that's worse, sometimes. I also know from experience that we'll recover, that we just need some time to cool off. Her sleep was interrupted last night just like mine was—there's a reason I don't wake her up unless it's absolutely necessary, and it's that she doesn't handle it well. She gets prickly.

Finally, it's just me and the display screen, alone in Control. It's time.

My finger hovers over *voice*. No way I'm choosing *video*, where Shapiro will see the fear on my face, and the cracks in my truth, too. I tap the audio-only option before I can take it all back, before I take Haven up on her offer. The timer starts counting, and the call connects before even two seconds tick past.

"*Shapiro,*" says a breathless, sleepless voice. "Shapiro here— *Lusca,* we thought you were dead." *Lusca* is the official name of our station, but I've only ever seen it in written form, on supply order forms and carved into the wall just outside Control.

My voice catches at first, but I collect myself and force out the words. "We're—we're alive. This is Lindley Hamilton—"

"Linsey, *Linsey,*" he breathes. "I thought—I was sure—sure you were—"

His voice breaks, and now I'm extra relieved I can't see his face, because I'm pretty sure what I'd see is the head of the space program completely breaking down. I almost wish he could see *my* face, though; I am not Linsey, and I really should correct him—should clear up the confusion, that I only *sound* like my mother—but—

But—

How? I can't seem to get the words out, and even if I could, would they even be helpful? Would he crumble under the weight of knowing that someone he cares deeply about didn't make it? Would Nashville crumble along with him, and maybe even the entire space program, already tenuous in its recovery after the virus hit so hard?

I can still be honest about the most important things— get his advice on the virus, request a supply delivery ASAP. It might actually work out better for us, now that I think about it, because my mother was a voting member of the board. I, obviously, am not. If any major decisions come down to a board vote, perhaps I can have a real say in our future, vote like she would have wanted to.

Still. Pretending to be my mother was not part of the plan.

My window is closing. I could tell the truth. I could tell him right now.

"I'm so sorry I couldn't call before this morning," I say, and with that, it is done.

At least the words I've actually said are true.

He's speechless on the other end, but I know he's still there. I can almost hear his tears. Do I really sound that much like my mother? I never realized it before, but I must.

And grief hears what it wants to hear, I guess.

Fortunately, he doesn't linger on the personal. He has his moment, and then it's on to the urgent. "Good, good," he says, more to himself than me. "This means the quarantine worked up there and you caught it in time—virus spread like wildfire down here, Lins, it's unbelievable. We've taken a pretty bad hit. I thought for sure you were—"

He cuts off, choked up on his own fear, or relief, or both.

"But you're not, you're *not*."

The silence stretches between us, and again, I'm tempted to fill it with all the things he really should know—but there's no way the board would let us have a say in our own future if they knew all our parents, all our experts, were dead. There's no *way*, not if their majority vote was finally all but unopposed.

They'd trample Shapiro without a single look back.

"My apologies for letting your messages go so long unattended," I say, putting on my best Mom/commander voice. I never heard her on these calls, only in station-wide assemblies and the like, but she had the tendency to be . . . overly multisyllabic. Not with me, of course. I'm not sure how casual she would have been with Shapiro. "We've been caught up with the quarantine, and unfortunately, one of the hardest-hit areas on board the station was Control—Lieutenants Black and Brady—hence our silence."

My mind spins with strategy, trying to stay two steps ahead of my words at all times. This lie should be safe: it gives, at once, a reason for our silence *and* a reason for Zesi to pick up communications in the absence of our lieutenants, should he ever have to answer a call.

He mutters a curse. "I'm sorry to hear it," he says, not a single trace of suspicion in his voice. "Very sorry indeed. What a loss." I can almost hear him bowing his head.

He believes me. I'm doing this, I'm actually pulling this off. Not that I enjoy having to.

"Have any other areas been so drastically affected?" he asks.

All of them, I want to say. But I dodge the question instead, saying, "We could use a shipment whenever your team has fully recovered, but otherwise, we're managing." Not too much, not entirely untrue.

"Good, good. Are you able to give me a current head count,

just so we know what sort of damage we're dealing with?"

I freeze, panic. I've just let him believe I'm my own mother—the *commander*—and that our quarantine has been successful. How can I give him a current head count without immediately backtracking? How can I ask his advice on how to deal with a mutation?

I may have made an enormous mistake.

"Just let me know as soon as you can," he goes on, mistaking my panic for the confident silence of someone who's neck deep in tracking down the requested data. "If you've lost any other critical team members, we need to know ASAP so we can make arrangements to get their replacements and their families up to the station, too—as well as the arrangements for relocating any members of *Lusca's* youth community who find themselves unattached, now that the virus has had its way."

My head snaps up.

That—

That sounds like—

That sounds like I've been right to fear the worst, like every single one of us is in danger of being relocated from the only home we've known for our entire lives. With the whole universe at our fingertips, it isn't unthinkable that we'd want to explore it—but when we've lost so much already, and have so little left to cling to, I can't see a forced relocation going over well with *anyone.*

Especially not those of us whose dream it is to stay.

And where would we even go? It's only a small leap of logic

before the board has the same idea I did, that they could send us to Radix to work with Vonn. That would be every nightmare come true—for us. For the board, it would be a brilliant, expedient solution. What's best for everyone in the long run.

"Yes," I say, just to say *something*. I'm starting to fray, will unravel if the silence stretches any longer. "Yes, I'll get you a head count as soon as I can, but"—I squeeze my eyes shut, force the lie—"rest assured things are running smoothly up here."

"Anything else I should be aware of?"

I clear my throat, dry my nervous palms on the crisp fabric of my pants. I'm not exactly sure how to approach the subject of Vonn without sounding one thousand percent panicked. I'm not sure how to say *anything* without sounding panicked. I need to ask about the shipment, and should probably put feelers out about mutation strategy—but the way this conversation has gone down so far has me hedging.

"In your most recent message, you mentioned sending intervention from Radix," I begin. My voice is as even as I can make it; hopefully it sounds smooth and confident on Shapiro's end of the call.

"Oh, yes—about that," he says. "We've taken another look at the logistics of it all, and at our situation down here. Jack thinks it would be comparable in both time and expense to launch your supplies from here instead of from Radix." Jack is on the board, according to hundreds of my mother's venting sessions I wasn't supposed to overhear. "Trajectory from Radix puts a shipment there at seven to eight days; ours would be less costly and we could get it to you in just under ten."

Relief washes over me—this is good news, *very* good. Mostly. As long as we can, in fact, stretch our supplies that long.

"Don't get me wrong, Vonn's ready to go if you're down to critical levels," he continues. "But if you're confident you can stretch what you've got, we've got you covered. Tell me honestly, Lins—do you have enough to last? Only you know how well you've rationed since the last delivery, but I'm worried you won't have enough."

It's not even a full two weeks. I think back to my conversation with Natalin—about how we'll be fine if we can just get people to eat what they *need* instead of only what they *like*.

We can do this. Eating vege-packs for a few days seems like a small sacrifice compared to being indebted to Vonn and potentially forfeiting our future freedom. Worst-case scenario, we find a way to get what we need from *Nautilus* instead.

"We . . . we should be good until your shipment arrives," I say. I shut my eyes tight, hope for the best.

"Great, *great*," he says. "I'll let everyone know. We'll shoot to get a shipment to you from here as soon as we can—I'll confirm liftoff within the next day or two." He sounds almost relieved. If I had said we were critically low, would he even have been able to convince the board to go forward with the faster delivery?

"Excellent," I say, suddenly anxious to start wrapping this up before more surprises spool out of my control. "Thank you . . ." Would she call him by his first name, Julian, or some sort of nickname? He began all his messages with Shapiro, so I'm not sure. Too late for me to add a name now, though, so I just close with, "We've got everything under control."

"Here if you need anything, as always," he says. "And Linsey?"

He says her name with such kindness it puts a lump in my throat. "Yes?" I force out.

"Don't forget to take care of yourself, okay?"

"You, too."

And then it's over.

Don't forget to take care of yourself.

I'm not my mother, but we shared more than the sound of our voice: I needed to hear this every bit as much as she would have.

I sit, staring at the communications screen, the call log's *07:08:43* still blinking up at me. If only I could stretch time, make each minute feel as eternally long as those seven did.

22

THERE IS NO AWAY

PRIORITY NUMBER ONE: I need to keep my people alive, and I need to give them a future worth living for. No one will ever love this station more than I do. I refuse to lose a single person more—I refuse to lose our *home*. Even if it means I'll only ever be commander for this brief, terrible moment in time, before they replace me with someone far more experienced.

Everything in me wants to prove—to myself *and* to the space program—that I'm capable of stepping up and taking care of my people. If I were to tell Shapiro exactly how alone we are up here, and how desperate, the board would most definitely relocate us, possibly to the most horrendous place in the entire galaxy. We'd lose the only home we've ever known—our only tie to the past and, for many of us, our dream for the future.

That's not how it will happen, though, not if I can help it.

So here I sit in my lab, digging for answers that could not only stop the mutation from spreading to *our* people, but also to those on *Nautilus*, since it's our best option at replenishing our supplies, if things come down to that. I'm curled over my lab station, studying the Mila sample from earlier. Nothing about it makes any sense. I've stared at it for an hour now, breaking my brain over what could have possibly gone wrong in my test process, and what I could possibly do about it with nothing left of her to test.

The most sobering thing is, no amount of testing will bring her back to life.

It's heartbreaking, when I take a step back from trying to *study* her death and remember the actual life lost—when I remove myself from the feeling that death after death is just our reality now, when I think of the individual people who are no longer with us.

Mila was nearly my age. We never spent much time together, but she knew Natalin well. She was friendly enough with Haven. Otherwise she kept mostly to herself, was never really *involved*. Still, our station feels incomplete without her. Even the absence of one quiet person can be devastating, it turns out. Added to the hundred who died before her—

I resist the urge to throw the petri dish against the wall, and only because I don't need any more messes to clean.

I bury my face in my hands, try to ride out this useless surge of grief. After some time—a few minutes? half an hour?—there's a knock at my glass.

Leo.

Instead of inviting him in, I join him in the corridor. We walk together, our footsteps and the hum of electricity the only sounds. I don't ask why he's come to find me, and he doesn't ask anything I don't feel like answering.

How does he do it? How does he feel so much like *home*, like the past I long for but will never reclaim?

And then a thought slips in so suddenly it stops me dead in my tracks: the mutation could take out any one of us. Leo could be next. Any *one* of us could be next.

"So?" Leo says after a while. "How did the call go? Are we good?"

A half laugh falls out of me before I can stop it. "Define *good*."

"Were you successful in convincing him not to flood our station with Vonn's team?" Leo says, a mix of playful and pointed he's somehow mastered over the years.

"Good on that front," I say. *For now,* I want to add. I don't feel successful so much as that I simply postponed an inevitable disaster. I only hope my lies have bought us enough time to prove ourselves, if it comes down to defending our worth and right to have a say in our own futures: that we are as capable as any of our parents were at running the station, at keeping ourselves alive. That this may have started as a station full of science experts, but life ran its course and it's become so much more than that—it's become our *home*.

I want, desperately, for our home to stay a home. Our home to stay *ours*.

"What's this look?" Leo asks when I don't offer anything else. "What's wrong?"

We're stopped now, in the middle of a corridor that overlooks one of the common areas. Leo deserves to know the details of that call, probably *needs* to know, in order for us to pull off the fact that I just led Shapiro to believe my mother is alive and well and it's business-as-usual up here, save for some extended quarantine and a hard hit to the lieutenants who used to run Control.

Once I try to put it into words, though, it doesn't sound like I've done us any favors.

It sounds shameful. Slippery and shameful. Would my mother have done what I did? Would she find it dishonorable that I lied about her death—my own mother's death!—to her faithful colleague, who knew her well enough to call her by her first name? Who cared enough to sneak luxuries into the shipments for her?

"Just relieved that part is over," I tell him, forcing a tight-lipped smile. "Everything's fine."

Because I had to say *something*. Because I can't handle a lecture from Leo right now.

I'll tell him later, when I'm not fresh off the call and another failed round of lab work and have figured out how to say it in a way that sounds like I've helped us—which, despite everything, I still believe I have—instead of backing us into a corner. It's a matter of how I choose to frame it, is all.

Leo glances back at me, clearly concerned. "Are you sure you're o—"

He's cut off by a commotion down on the mezzanine. I peer over the railing and see Akello Regulus step between Mikko

Sørensen and a girl, a girl who is fierce and flailing, practically eclipsed by Akello's intimidating frame. He towers over Mikko, too, but that doesn't stop Mikko from trying to get around him at the girl—Cameron Cade, I see, when she darts away from his furious hands, grasping at her shirt like he wants to rip it right off.

"Hey!" Leo calls over the balcony. "*Hey.*"

His voice is loud in my ear but is swallowed up by the noise. Leo runs to the nearest staircase, takes the steps two at a time, and plants himself in the middle of the fray. I follow, fast as I can.

Two guys drag Mikko backward by his elbows into the small crowd that's gathered, stunned, because how are they supposed to *not* watch? Akello relaxes, just a little, but it's a mistake— Cameron slips out from behind him, beelines toward Mikko, and drives her fist dead center into his face. Blood rushes out, even onto her hand, and she shakes it off.

"Everybody *stop*," Leo bellows, and this time, now that we are right in the thick of things, a sudden and forceful silence falls all around us. It is a still, silent freeze.

I take the first step, purposefully meeting eyes with Cameron, then Mikko, and back again. Cameron's always been passionate to a fault, for better or worse: she feels everything and she feels it deeply. If you get in her way—watch out. As for Mikko, he's an explosion waiting to happen, more agitated and volatile by the day. This collision won't end well, not on its own. I make myself like a lion, starved and stalking its prey. Teeth are necessary in this case. This isn't a Yuki and Grace situation—this is claws out, blood spilled. This is something I need to put a stop to *now*.

Mikko glares at Cameron, then shifts his heavy stare to me. I glare right back. At least he's not struggling against the guys who hold him in place anymore.

"What did you *do* to her, Mikko? What's going on?"

"What did *I* do?" His eyebrows shoot so high up they practically jump off his face. "She nearly gives me a *brain injury* by breaking my nose, and it's what did *I* do? Why don't you ask Cameron what she's hiding underneath her shirt? Why don't you ask what she broke into my place and *stole* from me?"

"Please," Cameron hisses. "I didn't break in and you know it."

"You went into my dad's room, even though I *clearly said* that was *off-limits*—"

"You shouldn't invite half the station over to parties if you don't want people all up in your place."

"I wasn't the one who invited you, and you know it."

"It isn't like you kicked me out when I showed up, though, is it?"

"Are you saying this is *my* fault? You steal my dad's razor blades and—"

"Just be happy I didn't use them on your face," Cameron spits.

"*Enough!* Enough with this." Blood crashes through my veins, and it's a struggle to not be ruled by it, caught up in the same wild fury. "Hand them over *now*," I order Cameron.

She glares at me, unflinching.

I step closer. Cameron has a few inches on me and is clearly relishing the fact that it makes her look like the dominant one between us. Eye to eye, voice low and even, I start again. "Hand. Them. Over."

"Yeah," she says with a half laugh. "And *you're* going to make me . . . how?"

It's a good question, one I hope she can't tell I don't know the answer to just yet.

"Don't push me, Cameron." I hold firm, stay steady, try not to let the panic I'm starting to feel show. I honestly *don't* know how I'll make her cooperate. Even if it works out this time, what will I do next time, for a future incident? What if it were Akello towering over me? What then? He could crush me. This could all spiral, and quickly.

Her glare finally falters, just for a second. She reaches inside her shirt and pulls out two thin silver blades, their sharp edges tucked into thin, protective sleeves.

"*Thank* you," Mikko says, shooting a pointed glare at Cameron. He reaches for the blades, but I push his hand away.

"Don't thank me," I say. "These aren't going back to you, either."

"But they were my father's—they were one of his personal items—"

That explains why they were in his cabin in the first place, I guess, but it doesn't change the fact that it's against policy to keep blades outside of Medical and the labs. "I'm sorry," I say. And I am. I wouldn't want anyone else confiscating my mother's things. I get it. "I wish I could turn them back over to you, but even under normal circumstances, these really shouldn't have been in your cabin in the first place."

Like when Heath and I discovered Yuki and Grace inside SSL—that they had access to top-secret entry codes—a wave of unsettledness washes over me. If these blades were in Mikko's cabin, what else is hiding out where it shouldn't be?

No one's ever used a blade against anyone else in the history of our station, as far as I know.

Then again, we're living in a season of firsts these days.

"So that's it?" Mikko says, pressing his forearm against his still-bleeding nose. "She steals my father's things, rams her fist into my face, and on top of that, you're not going to give the blades back? Real fair, Lindley."

Leo steps in, grabs the neck of Mikko's shirt. "It's *Commander*, Mikko, and don't forget it. You're on probation, both of you." Cameron rolls her eyes, but Leo doesn't let it faze him. "Any more incidents like this—from *anyone*—there will be privileges lost for everyone on board. Got it?"

"*Fine*, whatever." Mikko shakes Leo off.

"Yeah," Cameron says, no longer meeting any of our eyes. "Whatever."

No one moves after that, and no one says a word. The silence is so thick it could explode at any second. Leo and I wind through the crowd, make our exit. One foot after the other after the other after the other.

As soon as we're out of the lions' den, I split off from Leo, turning down an empty corridor.

"Lindley!" Leo calls after me. It's just us now. "Lindley, slow down!"

But I can't, I can't, the blood is crashing around inside me again, carrying me faster than I want to go. I'm not sure where I'm headed, I just want to get *away*. Even from Leo.

He picks up his pace, catches up with me. I walk faster.

Eventually, when I don't slow down and don't say a word, he gives up.

"Never seen you run away from something before, Linds," he calls from where I left him behind. It's almost enough to make me stop. "You're not alone in this, okay? We'll get through it."

"Not running away," I reply, eyes trained straight ahead. "Just running."

Because here, on the station, there is no away.

23

STARDUST

WHEN I WAS younger, and my mother still told me bedtime stories, I always imagined stardust like this: sparkles made of glittering gold, the tail of a shooting star, never fading, full of bright-burning magic. She'd tell stories of being back on Earth, of sitting in the backyard with her father, cold nights spent wrapped up in warm blankets, eyes wide and locked on the sky. The meteor showers were incredible, she said. Like fireworks, only even more wondrous, because no human had set them in motion.

I don't remember how old I was when I first learned that shooting stars are not, in fact, actual stars. Rather, they are stone and mineral, catching fire once they enter Earth's atmosphere, not inherently bright or blazing. They're glorified rocks.

It never bothered my mother that what she'd seen from Earth was, in fact, only an illusion. *The change in perspective makes things* more *beautiful,* she insisted. *Even a glorified rock can be beautiful given the right circumstances.*

In all the ways we were similar, this was not one of them.

I saw her point, sure. But for me, the change in perspective worked the other way. Shooting stars were not magical, or made of gold, or glitter, or embers, or sparks. They were rocks in the wrong place at the wrong time. Dust, and only dust.

I inherited so much from her, a thousand things that make me feel the smallest bit capable of filling up the void she left when she died. But this thing with Cameron and Mikko—how quickly things could have spiraled out of my control, and what then?—I feel shaken by it. Unnerved.

What if I've inherited a thousand things from my mother, who was gold and glitter in her own way, but I'm missing the one crucial thing that will determine whether I can pull this off?

What then?

24

A GASH IN THE GALAXY

NATALIN'S WAITING OUTSIDE my door when I get home a while later, arms crossed. Angry.

No surprise there. I blew off our meeting and didn't bother to let her know.

"You were supposed to meet me half an hour ago," she says, blocking me when I try to slip past her. "What, you've got nothing to say?"

"Can we *not* talk about this in the corridor?"

"At this point, I'm about to tell the entire blasted *station* about this food crisis, Lindley. I hope someone overhears! They deserve to know the truth, and they deserve to know who's doing everything they can to keep us alive."

And everyone who's not, her narrowed eyes say.

"You have no idea what you're talking about, Nat. I accepted a slightly delayed shipment that will be better for us in the long run—"

"*How* slightly delayed are we talking about here?"

"A couple of days," I say. "It's not like I declined their help altogether."

"Well, you may as well have," she shoots back.

"That isn't fair and you know it." I meet her glare, hold it. "Now *step. Aside.* I'm not talking about this unless we're behind closed doors."

For a fraction of a second, I fear I will have to physically remove her if I want to access my entry panel. Finally, though, she shifts. I open the door, gesture inside. "After you."

I walk straight over to the window, stand with my toes right up to the edge of it. Incredible, how we've come this far: that humanity has made incomprehensible advancements in space exploration, yet humanity itself never seems to change. For better or worse, we remain passionate, and disagreeable, and prone to making innumerable mistakes. Has anyone in history ever wanted blame placed upon her head like a crown of fire?

"Look, Lindley, I know you're probably only suffering a major guilt complex about opting to deprive our station of a quicker shipment, but I never expected you to no-show our meeting. That isn't like you. It isn't something I expect—"

"We will work. Something. Out." My breath fogs the glass. "And you can stop being so melodramatic. While you're at it, you can also stop with the accusations."

"It would help if you weren't so worthy of them."

I turn, look her dead in the eye. "It would help if you weren't so quick to panic. If you could have just a *tiny* bit of faith that I'm doing what I think is best for us. You think I want to starve? You really think I want to walk around this ship and see our people wasting away? You really think I would *choose to look them in the eye while that happens* if I didn't think the direction we're headed in is the best one?" I should stop, I really should. I can't. "We don't have to eat things we like. We just have to *eat*. We can do that, mostly, for a little while longer. So in the meantime, I need you to do your job—and quit telling me how to do mine."

"'Mostly,'" she says. "'For a little while longer.' Do you hear yourself? What does it matter if we have enough to eat for ninety percent of the time we *need* it, if it's not going to be enough to last?"

I knew those words were a mistake the second they slipped out. I knew she'd latch on to them, throw them back at me.

"We can make it work—"

"I ran the numbers again, twice, and we'd barely have enough to last until the first date they offered us. We need another delivery or we're basically dead."

Her words hang in the air, linger just long enough before crashing to the ground. Different perspectives aside, in this moment we are coming from the exact same place: terror.

"I'll figure it out," I say, too sharply. *Alone*, I want to add. She doesn't move, just stands there like she's grown deep roots through my floor. "I need some space, Nat."

Finally she turns, heads for the door. "Unless you can get

back on a call and *fix* this," she says before she leaves, no fight left in her voice, "you should start with the water. Find a way to get more of it, and we *might* have a chance."

I spend the entire next hour at my window, alone except for the queen of clubs. She is the best sort of company, the silent sort who can't judge the ideas I toss around: she doesn't expect too much, and she doesn't expect too little. That's the problem with people—all their expectations, all their expectations *for good reason.* Queens on cards have no stake in staying alive. Queens on cards cannot die. If someone were to burn or shred or otherwise destroy them, they wouldn't care because they cannot think or see or feel.

But our station is not occupied by cards. Our station is full of living, breathing people, who I care desperately about despite— because of!—all the messy complications that come along with blood and soul and heart.

Unless you can get back on a call and fix this plays on a loop in my head. *Fix this, fix this, fix this.* It would be so easy—in theory. So easy to head up to Control, press my finger to a button, and tell him I was wrong.

I hate being wrong.

I could spin it with the truth, though—that after taking a closer look at our supplies, we can't make the delayed option work after all. But what then? What about Vonn, what his intervention could mean for us down the line? If I was too optimistic before on the food front, maybe I'm being too paranoid about what could happen to us later. My gut twists at the thought of asking for his help—but is that worry worth people's lives? Is my pride worth people starving?

I have to admit it isn't.

I close my eyes, count to ten. Steady my nerves. This is the right decision, I tell myself. This is the *only* decision, now that I know what I know. I only wish we had better choices.

Control is deserted when I arrive, which is a relief. It's hard enough to face the mistake I've made on my own—it would be worse to have to do it in front of everyone else. I take a seat on the stool, roll over to the message-system section of the control board. Before I can think twice, I put in a call, press *video* this time. Better not to leave myself any openings—with a video call, there's no chance I'll sabotage my own good intentions with more lies. Once Shapiro sees my face, he'll see I'm not my mother. With that lie unraveled, the rest will fall out easily.

They will, anyway, if Shapiro ever actually picks up. Five rings go unanswered, then ten. At eleven, the message on screen blinks from *INITIATING VIDEO CALL* to *THANK YOU FOR YOUR PATIENCE*. At twenty, it says *FAILURE TO CONNECT, TRY AGAIN LATER.*

Well. This is . . . not ideal.

I try again with audio-only—perhaps there's just a satellite issue of some sort making the video option unavailable? Twenty rings pass, with the same basic messages. No luck—and no missed calls, no voice mails on the log. Nothing at all to assure me this outage is due to regularly scheduled maintenance, or any other reason that implies it will be up and running again soon. I'm definitely using the right system—last time I put in a call, Shapiro picked up on the very first ring. I'm fairly certain it's not a problem on our end, since we were able to initiate this new call, too, and it only failed when it couldn't get through to Nashville. I could be wrong, of course. I'm not a systems expert—and it's not like Zesi has experience with this, either.

It could be *anything*, I realize, with a wave of dread. Hopefully it's just a simple system failure, something that will be functional within the day, and not something much more severe. They're far enough inland from most natural disasters—one of the primary reasons they relocated space headquarters from Texas and Florida decades ago—but they're not immune to strong floods, or tornadoes. If not a natural disaster, perhaps the virus wasn't quite as contained as they believed it to be— perhaps they let down their guard too early in the name of getting a shipment up to us; perhaps it flared up and hit them hard.

I hope that's not it. I hope they're coasting on sugar and caffeine and adrenaline in an all-out effort to address their technical issues and nothing more. I hope they're okay.

I hope they're *alive*.

It is an incredibly helpless feeling to be this far away and have no idea what's going on.

And what of our shipment now? Unless the system issue is resolved soon, we'll have no way of knowing for sure that

Shapiro even managed to get it off the ground. If it's more than just a simple technical failure, their team could be sidelined for *weeks* dealing with . . . whatever it is that has happened.

Breathe, Lindley. *Breathe.* Just because everything else has spiraled to catastrophe, it doesn't necessarily mean things are worst-case scenario down in Nashville. And it doesn't have to mean things are worst-case scenario here, either, even though it feels that way.

I shut off Control's overhead spotlight as I head out, back to my place. Natalin seemed to think we could stretch our supplies if we addressed our water shortage—if only water filters were as easy to come by as our light replacement disks, I think. We've got *drawers* full of those, so tiny and flat. Water filters are bulkier, and oddly shaped; we definitely wouldn't have any spares hidden away somewhere. There has to be a way to get a fresh one, though. As I walk, I keep coming back to the idea of possibly getting what we need from *Nautilus* instead of from Radix.

The more I think about it, the more it seems like a viable option. It's risky, yes, for so many reasons—but compared to leaving all of our people to go hungry, it might be a risk worth taking. At *most*, our mutation could infect fifteen people. Better fifteen than starving our entire station, right?

Not that it *feels* right. What a terrible choice to have to make, when the best thing doesn't feel like a *good* thing.

My buzz screen has been blessedly quiet for a good long

while now. I put in a call to Heath once I'm back inside the private walls of my own suite. It can feel like before between us, if I just do my best to forget. I *need* it to feel like before.

He answers immediately. "Are you okay? Leo said you were upset, that we needed to give you some space—it's been so hard not to call, Linds. What's going on?"

Well, that explains the silence. "I'm . . . better than before," I tell him, though I can't quite bring myself to add that better doesn't exactly mean good. "Can you meet me right now? I want to run something by you. If Leo or Zesi are free, bring them along, too."

"Yeah, of course," he says. "At . . . at your place? Or where?"

The way he stumbles over it is like a neon arrow pointing to the truth I am reluctant to admit: it will never feel like before. There is no forgetting that kiss, no forgetting all the awkward fumbling that has come after it. It isn't that Heath and I are wrong for each other. I just never saw it coming.

If I'm honest, I don't exactly *want* to forget. But I just can't do this right now. I can't be someone to him—to anyone. Not when I have to be someone to *everyone*. It's too much pressure.

"Linds?" he says when I'm quiet. "Lindley, you still there?"

I'm making too much out of this. He can come over like he always has. We can be alone together without anything happening to make things even more awkward. Probably.

"Bring Leo and Zesi, okay? If they're not free, tell them it's urgent." Leo and Zesi will make a good buffer, for everyone's sake. "My place is fine. Just come over as soon as you can."

My reflection stares back at me as I end the call, but I can't look her in the eye. The choice I'm about to make—one that risks life to save life—feels like the furthest thing from a victory.

25

THRONE OF CHAINS

NOT TEN MINUTES later, Heath is at my door.

Alone.

"Zesi and Leo didn't pick up," he says. "I tried them each twice." He glances past me, over my shoulder. I'm blocking the door more than I realized.

"Sorry," I say, shifting out of the way. "Come in."

I follow him inside. As soon as I've stepped out from the jamb, the door slides shut behind me. "Weird that they wouldn't answer," I say. Especially with Heath trying them each twice.

Heath sits on the purple love seat, which gives me pause—does he expect me to sit beside him on it? My mother's chair feels slightly too far away, but it's the only other chair in this room. The love seat isn't a terrible option, just *cozy*, close. I'm worried about encouraging the wrong impression.

I choose my mother's chair.

"They're probably just busy," he says. "You said it was urgent, so I didn't think I should wait. What's going on?" He picks up my deck of cards from where it sits on the end table, shuffles twice before putting it back in a neat stack. Maybe it's just the way the light's falling on him as he shifts under it, shine and shadow in all the right places, but I've never noticed how attractive he is. How have we been so close for this long and I'm only just now seeing it?

"I—" Now that I'm sitting in the chair, Heath really does feel too far away, awkwardly so. I don't want to have an entire conversation with ten feet between us. "Sorry," I say, "I feel like I should move closer."

I move over near the love seat, sit on the cork floor and lean back. I turn, resting my elbow on the purple cushion, so I can see his face.

"Better?" he says, amused.

My cheeks flush. "I just tried calling Shapiro about our shipment," I start. Better to get right to business. "It . . . didn't work. The system wouldn't connect." I take a deep breath. If there's anyone I can confess my mistakes to, it's Heath—he's never given me a hard time for making a mistake, ever. "I'd told Shapiro earlier we'd be okay waiting a few extra days for a shipment, but after talking to Natalin . . . I . . . needed to tell him ASAP that the delay wasn't going to work after all."

I watch as it sinks in, wonder if he's leaped to the same fears as I have. "So," he says, "on top of the obviously unsettling system issues—you're worried he might send the shipment as planned, and it'll get to us too late?"

"I'm worried about what the system failure itself implies," I say. "That they might not be able to send a shipment at all."

He's quiet for a long moment. I can feel the empathy radiating off him—like he's *with* me in this, trying to figure out how to fix it, and not just thinking about how I shouldn't have made the mistake in the first place.

"I've been thinking about the idea you mentioned earlier," I finally say. "How *Nautilus* could be an option—the more I think about it, the more I'm convinced they'd be able to spare a water filter. Surely they have a backup, right? I've been looking through my mother's records, and Nashville sent a comprehensive delivery itinerary for this year's shipments to *Nautilus*, Radix, and our station—looks like *Nautilus* received a heavy cargo load just two months ago. With their tiny crew, their current filter should still be going strong. Heavy cargo loads tend to come with backup supplies, right? I'd bet all the stars they received replacement filters."

Heath is quiet, not nearly as enthusiastic as I expect for someone who came up with the idea. Not nearly as enthusiastic as I'd expect from Heath, period. "So . . . you're not worried anymore about infecting them?"

"No, I still totally am, but I've been weighing the risks." I take a deep breath, look up into his eyes. "I think we should go to them. I think *you* should go to them."

This, *this*: this wakes him up.

"Lindley—no—I haven't flown in a year!"

"We'll tell them to leave supplies in one of their small-craft hangars," I say, as if he's just wholeheartedly agreed. "And they can block that one off indefinitely, since they have another hangar, so we could make this work, we could really—"

"Linds. I haven't flown a bee *in a year.* And even then, Jaqí was in my ear the whole time telling me all the things I was doing wrong."

"Flying a bee is like riding a bike, right? You never forget how?"

My argument would be much more convincing if either of us had ever actually ridden a bike.

"I *crashed* last time, okay? I crash-landed, smashed a wing off on my way back into our dock."

His words hang between us as last year clicks into place.

The scar on his eyebrow, once a thin slice of blood, but nearly undetectable now. He'd opened his medicine cabinet too carelessly, caught a sharp edge to the face. That was the story I knew.

The bruises on his head that he'd said were from a fight—a fight I'd never been able to imagine, because Heath? Fighting? And over *what*? Yet it still put distance between us, because it seemed like such a primitive way to handle a disagreement.

"Why didn't you tell me the truth?"

He looks down at his hands. "We weren't supposed to be out. Jaqí was . . . he and your mom didn't see eye to eye on the necessity of flight training."

"What? She never told me she didn't want you training."

"Probably because it was *me*, Linds. Come on, what would

you have said if she'd brought it up?"

"Seriously?"

"Yeah, seriously. You would have told her I loved it, right? And that I was pretty good at it—how Jaqí always said I was the fastest learner he'd ever trained?"

I think back to those months Heath went out with Jaqí, just the two of them, tiny specks flinging themselves out into the infinite universe. Heath had just turned sixteen, three weeks to the day before my own sixteenth birthday. *Jaqí taught me corkscrews today,* Heath would report. *We did speed runs and death dives and twelve loops in a row!* And, and, and.

"Honestly?" I say. "I would have told her you were more flash than substance, that I thought you took too many risks." I pause, dare to meet his eyes. "And that Jaqí encouraged too many risky things."

Maybe sending Heath to *Nautilus* isn't such a great idea after all. I knew he loved the rush of it, the thrill—I assumed those things came along with basic knowledge of technique and precision. Hearing he crash-landed is *not* reassuring. Hearing that my mother discouraged his training isn't reassuring, either.

It does make sense, though. She never talked about flight school, but I know that's where she and my father first met. She talked about my father almost as little as she talked about flight school.

When I meet Heath's eyes again, they aren't full of wounded pride, like I expect—they're happy, almost. "This right here," he says. Slowly, thoughtfully. "*This* is why I like you."

I can't help it. I laugh. "I'll make a mental note to make disparaging remarks about you more often."

He grins. "I mean, I could do without the disparaging remarks," he says. "But I like that you're honest." He looks me straight in the eye, and I blush.

"Honesty doesn't always feel like a good thing," I reply, cheeks on fire. "If people knew how I honestly felt, I don't know that they'd like me so much."

I'd rather curl up in bed with a good read than try to figure out how to keep us all from starving or socially imploding, for example. I'd rather be the kind of person who could easily trust other people to untangle all our problems.

I'd rather put up walls between Heath and me, pretend I feel nothing for him, keep telling myself that—keep telling *him* that—than deal with the very real possibility of letting this, whatever *this* is, distract me from all the things I have to do. When the truth of it is, if he had kissed me before the virus hit, I can't say for sure there wouldn't have been a spark between us. I can't say for sure there isn't one now.

Does it make me a horrible person if I don't admit there could be something between us? If I don't admit this *right* after he's praised me for my honesty?

He slides down from the love seat, sits beside me on the cork floor. "We're not talking about other people here, right? We're talking about you and me." He smooths a hand over my hair.

My breath catches, but when I loosen up and let myself *feel*, it feels . . . rather nice. "You can tell me anything, Lindley. You know that, don't you?"

For the first time since my mother died, it's as if I have the freedom to just be in a moment, rather than trying to keep everything from collapsing. As if the entire weight of the universe is off my shoulders, as if someone is taking care of *me* for a change.

I didn't realize how badly I needed this. How badly I needed a break from being strong, for however long this moment lasts.

Everyone deserves a break, right?

I shift closer, try to put the station and all our problems out of my mind. Maybe Heath could help me deal with my stress, rather than just being something else to worry about. Maybe he is exactly what I need.

I burrow into him, rest my cheek on his chest. He leans his head against mine, warm and comforting. "You're sure you want to do this? I'm sorry, Linds, I know you said—"

Before he can finish, I sit up again—lean in—cut his words off with a kiss. He is all softness, all kindness, gentle and easy and careful; I press a little harder, kiss a little deeper, showing him *yes, I'm sure* without so many words. It's new and familiar all at once, not as far a leap as I first thought from friendship to . . . this. Not as strange, not as awkward. Not strange or awkward at all.

We lose a long stretch of time, linger in this brand-new thing that is just between us. For once, I'm not counting the minutes.

Until there is a knock at my door, and we break away, his face as flushed as mine feels. I jump up to answer it, smooth my hair and straighten my shirt.

I open it and find Leo on the other side.

"Am . . . I . . . interrupting?" he says, eyeing Heath, eyeing me.

Is it really that obvious?

"Sorry I missed your calls, man," Leo says mercifully, not forcing us to answer his own question. He turns back to me, and, oh—something isn't right. Something is very, very wrong. "We've . . . got a situation."

We've got a situation.

The words paralyze me, make me feel sick.

Leo has no way of knowing how eerily similar his words are to the ones Dr. Safran spoke, back when the virus claimed its first handful of victims. And yet I have this feeling, I just *know* even before he says it, it's happening again.

"Who?" I ask. "How many?"

Heath is at my side now. Both of us look to Leo for answers. I don't know about Heath, but I'm hoping, hard, that Leo will tell me what I want to hear, not what I fear.

"Two dead," he says. "Jaako Solano and Kerr Barstow."

Kerr was one of the most beautiful girls on the station, and also one of the brightest. She and Jaako were like movie stars from back on Earth—how I imagined movie stars to be, anyway: everyone watching their every move, secretly wanting to befriend them, to *be* them. They were untouchable, especially after they finally started dating a few months ago.

They were untouchable.

"We won't be able to keep this quiet for long," Heath says, and it's like he's plucked the thought directly from my head.

"We won't be able to keep it quiet at all." Leo grimaces. "Zesi and I weren't the first to find them."

26

ROCK TO A STORM TO AN OCEAN

"NO, NO, NO—THIS is *not* good." I pace the room, borderline panicked. "I should have spent more time in the lab, I should have—"

"You've had a lot on your plate," Leo says. "You've done all you could."

Leo is the rock to my storm, steady and unmoved. Heath is somewhere in between: Heath is the ocean, steady and wild all at once.

And I was *kissing Heath* while Jaako and Kerr lay dead. While someone discovered them.

"I could have done more," I say. "I should have run more tests—why didn't I run more tests?" More death should not come as a surprise, given Mila, given what happened to our parents. And yet. Perhaps I've been deluding myself, holding tight to a small bit of hope—that Mila was a fluke. That there was no mutation. That if I could just make sure we're well-fed, make sure we're not the target of some asteroid's collision course, make sure we're not positioning ourselves to be overtaken by a ruthless slave driver, I could keep us alive.

My best is not enough. My best is not enough, and now I can't even call Shapiro for help.

"Linds. *Lindley.*" Leo is face-to-face with me now, his hands on my shoulders. "You could not have stopped this no matter how many tests you ran."

Look at what happened to our parents, he doesn't have to say. "So, what, I'm not even supposed to try? This is obviously a mutation—just because we weren't able to stop the virus the first time around, maybe there's a way to stop this one. Maybe three deaths will be the end of it."

Three deaths are already three too many.

And three deaths confirms it: Mila was no fluke. It's already begun to spread.

"Who found them? Where were they? Tell me everything."

"Noël found them, technically, but Sawyer and Bram were right there with her," Leo says. "Noël said she was supposed to go for a run with Kerr, but Kerr never showed. When she went to find her at Jaako's place, no one answered. She'd been staying there since her parents . . . well. You know." He clears the tightness from his throat. "So, yeah, Noël decided to try Kerr's place instead—but on her way, she saw Jaako and Kerr huddled together in one of the mezzanine alcoves. At first she thought they were just, uh . . . making out."

Leo's face takes on a deep red flush, and so does mine; is he thinking about Heath and me? Because I am *definitely* thinking about Heath and me.

"They were too still, though," Leo continues. "Bram and Sawyer were nearby, saw Noël freak out when she discovered them unconscious, blood all over them."

"This is—I just—*no*," I say. "Was anyone else around?"

"I mean, yeah. It's the mezzanine, you know? And it's not like I was right there when they found them—Bram had to come looking for me. A crowd had gathered by the time I got there."

"A crowd? A *crowd*? How big of a crowd are we talking about?" It doesn't make a difference, I realize, even as I say the words. If Noël had been the only one to see them, word still would have spread. If *no one* had seen them, word would have spread. Unlike Mila, the absence of Jaako and Kerr—the golden couple—would not have gone unnoticed.

Heath comes to stand beside me, brimming with pent-up energy that could explode any second now. "Okay," he says. "Okay. What are we going to do?"

We need to figure out how to handle this; he's right. But I'm stuck on a thought: Mila was not in the same circles as Jaako and Kerr, not even close. Their circles were polar opposites.

So how is it that these three people—these three, who were never in contact with one another, especially since Kerr started spending so many nights at Jaako's place—are the only ones who've died from the mutation? *Lie low, linger, explode*: there must be more at play here than with the original strain. Perhaps something in each person's DNA determines how quickly they succumb to it? Or maybe they were the first in contact with the original strain, and it has only just now turned into something deadly?

Whatever the reason, I have my work cut out for me.

My buzz screen vibrates—Haven.

"What's going on, Lindley?" she says as soon as I connect. "Why am I hearing about *two new deaths* from twelve-year-old drama queen Josie Hewitt? You have to know about this by now, right? We need to hold an assembly immediately so we don't lose everyone's trust—I mean, if we haven't already—we need—"

"Haven. Stop." I close my eyes, move into the kitchen, where I can talk without Leo and Heath watching me. "There's no way we can assemble right now—that would be a complete disaster. Can you imagine how many questions? How volatile? I'm not giving any answers until after I have some time in the lab, and that's the end of it."

"I told you we should have told them the truth right from the start," she says. "You're right, this *is* a complete disaster. And the longer you wait to address it, the less they'll trust you. Sorry, but it's true."

It is true, and I know it. But I don't see any way around it. It isn't like half answers and reassuring lies will win any trust, either. "I'll talk to them. I *will*," I say. "Just not today."

She sighs loudly on the other end of the call. For my benefit more than hers, I'm sure. "What do you want me to say, then? I assume you just want me to do some faceless announcement and tell them everything is fine, not to worry?"

Faceless announcement, yes. They'd never believe *everything is fine*, though, not after this. They wouldn't believe *not to worry*.

"Tell them we've decided against holding an assembly because we're spending time in the lab, and we're focusing our efforts on how to stop the virus before it takes any more lives." True enough. "Tell them it might not be hopeless, since it appears to be a different strain from what wiped out . . . everyone else." Borderline lie, the *it might not be hopeless* part, but also true enough. "And tell them to report to Medical immediately if they notice any signs of the contagion taking over—coughing fits, bloodbubbles, anything out of character or unusual."

For once, Haven is quiet on the other end. "Quarantine?" she finally asks. "Curfew?"

"Pointless," I say. It isn't like Mila spent a lot of time around Jaako or Kerr, but they are our only three dead. Several of us were right there after Mila died, but we're still alive—proximity to the bloodbubbles themselves doesn't seem to make much of a difference. "Pretty sure we've all already been exposed, and that it's just a matter of time."

"I think I'll leave that last part out," she says drily.

"Probably for the best." The idea that we've all already been exposed is unnerving, when I really stop to dwell on it: Is it inside *me* right now? It would have to be, right? How much longer do I have? How much longer do I have to try to save all of us?

How much longer will it even matter?

27

DROWNING IN AN HOURGLASS OF SAND

THREE TONES CHIME through the speakers as I join Leo and Heath back in the main room of my suite. Haven's voice fills the space, an undercurrent of energy despite the heavy news she delivers:

"Attention, everyone, attention, please!" She pauses for a split second. "It is with great sadness that I bring you news of more death on *Lusca*'s decks, this time from our own generation. We your leaders wanted to address these tragedies immediately and reassure you that we are doing all we can to contain the virus before it spirals out of control. Only three lives have been lost at this point—Mila Harper, Kerr Barstow, and Jaako Solano—and we hope to lose not a single person more. We have reason to believe this mutation may not be as destructive as the one that wiped out the first generation, and are already doing lab work in search of a solution."

Leo raises his eyebrows at me, as I am clearly *not* already in the lab running tests. Close enough, though.

"We your leaders ask that you please go on with your daily lives as normally as you can manage," Haven continues. "There is no quarantine or curfew in place, which should be reassuring—we don't think there is a need for such restrictions at this time."

I have to give Haven credit for spinning this in our favor so well: as if the lack of quarantine means there's nothing to worry about, when really, it's simply too late to make a difference.

"Please report to Medical if you experience any unusual or worrying symptoms. If no one is there to receive you, you may use any public comm channel to call me—Haven—at any time. Seven-three-two-nine-star."

I make a mental note to thank Haven for her quick thinking. I hadn't considered yet that no one is permanently stationed at Medical to receive patients. It's not like I can hang out there all day, especially now that I'll probably be eating and sleeping in the lab for the next long while—and I certainly don't mind that Haven's given *her* number out with an open invitation to contact her at any time. I'd rather not field those calls on top of everything else.

"Thank you, everyone," she says. "In the wake of these tragedies, I urge you all to be kind and be wise."

The speaker clicks off. I wait—wait—listening intently for the sound of silence devolving into chaos.

Of course I know better than to assume it would happen that quickly, or that loudly. I think most things begin to fracture without anyone realizing it's even happening, a sort of splintered silence that gives way all at once under too much weight, and without warning.

Leo and Heath watch me, wordless, as I gather supplies for a long stint in the lab: my favorite hoodie; my pillow; the throw from my mother's chair. I wish it were as easy to gather answers, or energy, or sanity.

"Looks like I've got work to do," I say, not meeting their eyes. "Leo, have Zesi send samples to the lab immediately. If one of you could arrange for Natalin to send food a couple times throughout the day, that might be nice, because I'll probably forget to—"

"Lindley," Heath says. "*Lindley.*"

When I finally look up at him, all I can focus on are his lips. My cheeks flame with guilt: for kissing him as Kerr and Jaako lay dead, and for wanting to kiss him again.

"We're here for you," Leo says. "We've got your back, okay?"

The night my mother died, it was Leo I sought. Leo who sat with me, back-to-back like we had all those years ago, during the solar flare. Leo whose only words that entire pitch-black night were *I'm here for you.*

For the first time in my life, I was without the one person I loved more than anything in the universe.

Leo stayed with me. He didn't have to say any more, or do any more—he was just there when I needed it. He's always been there. If I'm honest, as honest as Heath thinks I am, I'm afraid things will shift between Leo and me if I let Heath come any closer. I'm afraid things are shifting already: there's a new expression on Leo's face now, one I can't immediately place. I thought I knew all there was to know about him.

And maybe I did. Maybe something new sprouted up when I wasn't looking.

Everything is shifting too fast, too suddenly. I want things to be like before, I want things to be safe and steady and not so sharp. I want my mother's voice.

I want.

"What do you want to do about the *Nautilus*?" Heath asks as I head for the door. "You still want me to go for it?"

I don't know what I want.

"Let me get some tests started, and after they process, we'll talk more about it," I say. "Be ready in about an hour—let's meet in SSL this time." I can't think of a place more peaceful and quiet than SSL, with its rows and rows of pillars, of life on hold. Maybe I'll even start sleeping there. If I sleep for long enough, maybe I can freeze time, too.

28

FLOCKS OF FLIES

IT TAKES LESS than a minute before they start to swarm: a girl at the end of my hall, a pair of guys around the next turn. Heath and Leo flank me, dismiss the questions, push them away.

Over. And. Over.

It was never like this before, back when none of us had such a driving need for *why*. Everyone mostly kept to their cliques, or kept to themselves, hanging out in their cabins or the rec center, or studying in the various learning hubs scattered throughout our decks. Now, though, it's like they're afraid to be alone, like they crave the comfort of the herd. The learning hubs have been deserted lately; the rec center is a ghost town.

What felt so solid before—who we were, who we'd *become*— all we thought we knew—it's all been stripped away and reconfigured by the knife of tragedy.

Nothing is certain anymore.

Everyone wants answers I can't possibly give, and not only in regard to the deaths.

By the time we get to Portside, where I'll run the blood tests, Heath and Leo have to physically shield me—and the sliding door—as I slip inside, alone. It is a very good thing this lab is passcode protected. It is a very good thing the doors are stronger than they look.

If only they were soundproof.

I don't envy Heath and Leo right now, having to fight them off on their way out the door. In fact, I'm not sure they'll be able to break through that crowd anytime soon.

I buzz Zesi, and he picks up immediately. "Hey, Lindley—kind of a bad time right now—"

"Tell me about it," I mutter. "Listen, I don't care *how* you get samples to me, but I need blood from Jaako and Kerr as soon as possible, okay?"

In the background, a frantic voice peppers Zesi with questions. Just one, though, it sounds like. "Who's with you?" I ask.

"River," he says. "He's scared because he can't find Leo, and he got locked out again."

"I swear, when I get a spare second, I'm tattooing that code on the kid's arm." You'd think, at eight years old, he could remember a six-digit number. "Leo's here at Portside," I say. "Just bring River with you, okay? You're a lifesaver, Zesi, the best. I'll see you soon." I rush the words and tap out before he can protest.

The crowd is still thick outside my lab doors, still thick and *loud*. I need something to drown out the noise, something other than the blood rushing in my head. Usually the hum of the refrigerator is enough to calm me down, but now all I hear are their accusations: *You said we were safe! You said there was nothing to worry about! You lied about Mila!* I don't know for sure that those are direct quotes—it's hard to pick out entire thoughts from the chorus—but those are the words I hear.

There's an old data pod in the drawer filled with music from Earth, but its charger cable has been misplaced for a while now. I have a feeling it's tangled in the knot of spare cables over at one of the dormant scope stations. Usually I prefer silence while working—still do—so I haven't bothered to dig the cable out before now. It'll be a little bit before Zesi arrives with the samples, though, and with how spotless it is in here, I can't even clean to calm my nerves.

I get to digging. The knot of cables is easy to find, like a lone tumbleweed in an otherwise empty desert. There must be at least fifteen different strands tangled together, thick and thin and barely there. I see the one I need hopelessly woven throughout all the other cables.

It is the perfect project.

I pick and pull, worry at knots, loosen one area just to find another impossible snag. Already, I feel calmer. More capable. If I'd known how effective it would be to sort through this mess—this *meaningless* mess, for once—I'd have done it a long time ago. Perhaps I'll knot everything back up when I'm finished, for next time.

I'm plugging the charger into the data pod when Zesi arrives. The crowd has thinned outside my door, I realize, now that I'm paying attention again—and it looks like Leo isn't there anymore. The sliding door opens; Zesi breezes in, leaving River alone on the other side of it.

"Can't stay," Zesi says, "but here you go. Leo collected some of this as soon as he found them, and I picked up the rest." He places an array of samples on my island—not just blood this time, but tubes of saliva and hair samples, too. "Need anything else?" he says, already heading back to the door.

What *don't* I need?

"Can you try putting in a call to Shapiro when you get back up to Control?" I ask. "It wouldn't connect earlier."

He grimaces. "That . . . doesn't sound good," he says. "But yeah, I'll check it out."

"Buzz me ASAP if you get through," I say. "Leo and Heath tell you we're meeting at SSL in just under an hour?"

He nods. "I'll be there."

And as quickly as he arrived, he's gone.

I smooth my hair back, adjust the pins, and get to work.

Just as I did with Mila's sample, I prepare the slides, one each for Jaako and Kerr. These results should be much clearer since the blood is so fresh. It's sickening and surreal to have blood on the plates at all, but for Jaako and Kerr? Who woke up this morning, just like I did? They were golden, and beloved, and in love.

Not one of us is untouchable.

When the concentrated stain is ready, I immerse the plates and leave them to rest for the requisite ten minutes. I scan the room for something to do while the time passes, but there's nothing to clean, nothing to untangle. I check the data pod instead; it's finally holding enough of a charge to turn on. I scroll through the list of artists: Whitney Houston. Michael Jackson. Prince. I pick one at random—"Kiss," by Prince—and the music fills the room, its poppy beat echoing over all the lab's hard, sterile surfaces.

It's so sunny, so upbeat. So stark a contrast to the death on the plates before me, to the darkness I feel. The music defuses my tension in a way silence never has: it helps me focus on something light for once. Helps me *feel* something light. When it ends, I press repeat and listen to it all over again.

My timer goes off at ten minutes, and I cut Prince off mid-word. If I'm not careful, I could lose myself in an endless loop of sunny distraction. Now, though, it's time to focus. All the darkness of this bleak reality comes rushing back in when I see the results.

They're not any clearer than Mila's were.

In fact, they look exactly the same. Exactly as blurred— exactly as useless.

I don't know what the problem is, but I know it isn't with my process. My process is perfection.

I could easily explain away a single failed test, especially given our issues with proper sample storage. But three? With samples even fresher than some of the ones we took during the initial wave of CRW-0001? It's unheard of in this lab.

This is odd, this is unsettling. This isn't right.

29

FRACTAL

IT'S STILL TWENTY minutes until our meeting at SSL, but I can't take another second in Portside. The lab results have shaken me up, and I need to clear my head.

I take the most circuitous route I can think of—up three decks, aft toward the generator room, cross over to starboard, take the stairs back down, where they'll dump me out around the corner from the lab. It's quiet, as I suspected. I've never had need to go from Portside to SSL like this before—on a normal day, I would have just walked across the deck. On normal days I never have need to go to SSL at all.

I'll have to remember this route, now that *normal* is a thing of the past.

SSL is blessedly empty when I enter. After finding Yuki and Grace hiding out in here, part of me worried it would happen again. For once, though, something has gone as it should.

I make my way around the pillars, over to the far wall. Unlike Portside, which is bright and white and windowless, there are no overhead lights in SSL except for a few spotlights around the main lab area—it's lit almost entirely by the glow of the pillars. Also unlike Portside, SSL has an enormous panoramic view of the galaxy on this far wall. Given how dark it is in here, the stars seem to shine even brighter than usual.

I take a seat on the floor, draw my knees up to my chest. What is happening? How is it that, with everything shifting and our problems constantly blooming into complicated fractals, the one constant I've come to depend on—the scientific method—has degenerated right along with everything else? How are my tests suddenly useless? It just makes no sense.

I'll do tests on the saliva next, I guess. I'll do tests on the hair if I have to, not that the virus will show up there, but maybe just to prove to myself that I still know how to examine a sample—that I haven't completely lost my mind.

Soon, the sound of a door sliding open echoes from across the room. I'm too far hidden to see who it is; I really should get up, really shouldn't be late for my own meeting.

"Linds?" a voice says, deep and calm: Leo. "You here yet?"

"Back by the window," I say quietly.

A minute later, he sits down beside me, doesn't say a word. With everything that's been happening lately, I'd almost forgotten how it feels to sit, alone, with Leo: like I'm myself again. Like all of my pieces are in one place, not scattered. Safe.

It isn't like that with Heath. I feel safe with him, for sure, but it isn't the same. With Heath, it's like I'm only just discovering pieces of myself I never knew existed. With Heath, things are new and shiny and distracting. Not in a bad way—it isn't bad at all. I'd go so far as to say that things with Heath are *good*.

But Leo feels like home.

If it had been Leo who'd kissed me, Leo who'd said he'd only just realized he might never get the chance—

No. I stop myself before I go there, before I go too far down that path.

"How're you holding up?" he says, his voice quiet.

"I'm not," I say. "Not really."

From nowhere, a pair of hot tears slip out and run down my cheeks. I wipe them away with the back of my hand. This isn't me—I don't cry. If Leo sees, he'll know things are far worse than I've let on. That I'm breaking inside, one brittle piece at a time. I will my eyes dry, stare into the stars until they're blurred and unfocused.

"Did River find you?" I say, changing the subject.

"Yeah, I took him home." He studies me, long and slow. I'm not even looking at him, but I feel it. "You're doing a good job, Linds. You're doing the best job anyone could do."

"Not better than my mother," I say.

"Your mother would be impressed with how you're handling this," he says, "and that's the honest truth."

Finally, I turn my eyes from the firefly stars, look into his. We're both illuminated by the faint glow from the nearest pillar, by this small patch of light in a world of shadows. I don't have words. I can't possibly express how much I needed to hear what he's just said.

He puts his arm around me and pulls me close, a thing we've

done forever on days where things feel impossible—but today, *this* impossible day, it feels different. It feels almost wrong, given how things are shifting with Heath. It feels more intimate than usual.

And yet I don't pull away.

Maybe *this* is what I never knew I wanted, what I never knew I needed. Maybe I just wanted someone to be there for me, maybe I thought it was Heath—Heath is wonderful, Heath is my friend. Now that I'm here, though, I can't say for sure it's not Leo I need. Leo I *want*.

I blink rapidly. Stay calm, Lindley. First the tears, and now this new thing I can't unsee, where my best friends are suddenly becoming something more to me: Who *am* I? This is the worst time for this. For any of it. For leaning into Leo when I've just kissed Heath, for thinking about any of this at all when there is real, actual *life* at stake.

Across the room, the door slides open again. I stiffen at the sound of it, more than I mean to.

"You okay?" Leo says, just to me, as voices fill the room. Everyone's here now, it sounds like, even Natalin and Haven.

"I'm fine," I say, rising to my feet. I force a smile. "Thanks for . . . for everything."

We're close now, in near darkness. It might be my imagination, but the way he looks at me—it feels like there's something more behind his eyes. He looks like he might kiss me, like he'd kiss me in a heartbeat if he knew for sure I wanted him to. Has he always looked at me like this? Was I blind before, only waking up to the fact that a close friend could have feelings when Heath explicitly took that leap?

Or am I only seeing what I want to see?

Whatever he feels, he doesn't act on it, and neither do I. "We should probably go meet the others," he says.

There's no hiding the fact that Leo and I were alone together when we join the group in the main lab area. Aside from a brief flicker of—something—across Heath's face, no one bats an eye. Is he jealous? Hurt? Both, maybe. It's old news that Leo and I are close friends, but perhaps that reality is something Heath didn't fully consider before now.

Haven and Natalin sit on the lab's countertop, legs dangling over the edge. Zesi and Heath sit across from them on the opposite ledge. I look from face to face, landing at last on Leo's: we are the definition of exhausted. Frayed. Threadbare, barely holding it together. Natalin looks like she doesn't even have it in her to be angry at me right now, which worries me more than it should.

"I know we're all tired," I say, breaking the silence. "I know we all wish we could pull answers out of the sky, and rewind time, and just . . . not have to do this."

Everyone stares at their hands, or the floor, aside from Leo and Heath. They watch me.

I take a deep breath, try to get this over with so we can go back to our labs and our buzz screens and, if we're lucky, our beds. "I'm sending Heath to *Nautilus* immediately to retrieve a fresh water filter." Natalin looks up as I go over the basics of the plan, exactly like I did with Heath.

This time, Heath doesn't push back. Crash or not, I have a feeling he's wanted to fly again ever since he last sat in a cockpit.

"Won't Shapiro wonder why we're suddenly reaching out to *Nautilus*—let alone sending a bee over—when we've just assured him we're holding up fine?" Leo asks.

"Shapiro might not be around to notice it," I say, averting my eyes from everyone, Natalin especially. "We're experiencing . . . a bit of a connectivity issue."

"With our system? Or Nashville's?" Haven asks. "Would we even be able to get in touch with *Nautilus* before heading their way? Seems like we should make sure they even have what we need before flying all the way out there, right?"

"We can try, for sure," I say. "We should absolutely try that first."

"And if you can't get in touch, but go anyway, and get there only to find they don't have enough supplies to share—what's the plan then?" Natalin looks the furthest thing from convinced by this idea. "What if you burn through all your power before you get there and can't recharge?"

"As long as they have a spare water filter, we can stretch our supplies here—isn't that what you said, Linds? And you're pretty sure they'll have at least that, right?" Heath asks. Haven and Natalin exchange a glance, clearly in response to his use of my nickname.

"It's not *ideal*," Natalin says, "but at this point, what is? It's a good start, I'll say that much. Back to the bee's power, though—you've never flown that long of a distance before, have you?"

"It's not like Radix—or Earth, for that matter—is any closer," I say, suddenly defensive over Heath's flying skills. "This is our best shot, Nat."

"I haven't flown that *far*, but I have flown for that long of a time," Heath says, not missing a beat. "Jaqí trained me on power re-gen and how to spark it mid-flight—there's a way to do it so you actually *build* power the longer you fly, rather than losing it. I'm pretty confident I can get to *Nautilus* just fine."

If you can dock without crashing, my mind automatically fills in, and I immediately feel guilty for thinking it.

Still, it's the truth. If he crashes on entry, he could cause real damage to *Nautilus*—it's smaller than our station, for one, so he could tear up more than just a bee wing. If he tears up a bee wing, he'd have to convince them to let him take one of their crafts in order to return home; they might have only one, and who knows if it's up to the trip?

I look up, find all eyes on me. "There's a lot that could go wrong," I say, averting my attention away from Heath so he doesn't feel the full weight of this statement, how his crash history inspired it. "But as risky as it is, I believe we can pull it off."

A minute drags out, slow and silent; I wait for someone to challenge me, but no one does. If anything, I feel like everyone is finally on board—even Natalin. I suppose she's figured out her parting words to me, *start with water*, significantly influenced this idea.

"I'm going with him," Zesi announces.

"Wait, what?" I say. "That wasn't part of the plan. We need you here—"

"You need someone on the bee who can navigate while keeping a careful eye on satellite positioning," he replies. "You need someone who can try to radio with *Nautilus* while Heath keeps the craft flying smoothly."

He's right, and we all know it. Zesi's role on the station is important, but this mission is crucial if we want to extend our food supply. Leo and Haven have passable training in Control, thanks to their long day scanning for asteroids. And if we're able to get in touch with Shapiro again, it'll be my responsibility to fill him in on the truth, not Zesi's.

It's not easy to send Heath and Zesi out into the wild unknown, especially knowing all that could go wrong—they feel too integral to our survival. At the same time, though, it's probably best that we come up with a way to survive without our most crucial members. Our six may be five tomorrow.

Our six may be *zero* tomorrow.

"All right," I say. "Leave tonight—and get back here as fast as you can."

30

129,600 SECONDS

MY ENTIRE WORLD collapsed in a split second when it was my mother's time to pass. A split second seemed like nothing, no time at all, until the one when everything changed.

Eighteen hours to *Nautilus*, eighteen hours back: thirty-six hours is more than enough time for the station to implode. What will this world be like when Heath and Zesi return? And what will it be like if they *don't*?

We tried three times to get in touch with *Nautilus*—three times, with no answer. Zesi feels confident he could find a way to radio in once they're within short range of the station, that he could tap into their internal channels straight from the bee. Our internals still work, so the hope is that theirs do, too.

I hope he's right. Even if he isn't, we all agree that it still seems worth it to *try*.

Leo and I accompany Heath and Zesi to the hangar so we can see them off. In all my years, I've only been down here a handful of times. The runway spans the entire bottom deck, with openings on each end for easy entry and exit. On the far side of the runway, three bees are docked, two in pristine condition beside a broken-winged third. We're also equipped with two firebirds, but they're not as fast or nimble as the bees. Our side of the runway is lined with viewing windows—we're behind them, in an airlocked chamber. All the flight suits are here, eight in total, as if we were meant to have a robust team of pilots. Was it my mother's call to keep the flight team all but nonexistent? Why weren't more allowed to train?

Heath pulls me aside before he suits up. His eyes are bright, sparkling with excitement. Behind the excitement, though, is a hint of reluctance. "So, uh, Linds?" His cheeks turn pink as he runs a hand through his hair. "I just wanted to say, if anything happens . . . to us . . . out there . . . don't blame yourself, okay?"

My heart picks up; he knows me well. His admission that there is reason to worry—that if something goes wrong, he and Zesi go with it—

"You don't have to do this," I say, even though we both know I'm only saying it because he's right: I'm absolutely going to blame myself if something happens. I'd never forgive myself, either. I'm the acting commander, and this is my call. I could make them stay home. We could continue to take our chances with our current store of supplies—but what if Natalin's right? What if the rest of the station goes hungry? What if the only way to stretch our food, our water, is for more of our people to succumb to the mutation so there are fewer of us to feed?

How horrible, to hope enough die so that others can live. To hope someone not-Heath, not-Zesi, dies instead. To keep them home out of fear, out of selfishness disguised as love.

I would never be able to live with myself if I made a call like that.

"We've got this," Heath says. "Success is our only option, right?"

I grin. "Sounds about right."

Before I even know what's happening, he's wrapped an arm around me—pulled me close—pressed his lips to mine. It's a hungry kiss, part goodbye and part *I'm winning the universe for you, Lindley.* I don't know what to do, I don't—

I break it off.

Leo's watching.

Heath's expression—I can't bear to see it right now. I know this must feel like a door slammed in his face after what happened earlier at my place, and it's no way to start a mission. It's just that I'm still wrapping my mind around our last kiss, our last kiss *in private*, and whether it was Heath I should have been kissing at all.

I tuck my hair behind my ear, focus on Zesi, the one person whose eyes I'm able to meet. Clear my throat. "When will we know if you've been successful?" I ask.

"Whenever we get back," Zesi says. He presses a button near the door labeled *grav force*, and the entire runway takes on an electric-purple glow. "Turn gravity back off once we're out, okay?" he says to Leo. "Too much wasted power to leave it running out there for no reason."

They zip into their suits.

Secure their helmets.

Proceed through the airlocks, once, twice—and then they're out on the runway, silver suits shining in the purple glow like they're walking on a star.

The bee's passenger pod opens. Zesi climbs into the navigator chair and straps in, but Heath slowly turns back to face us. He looks directly through the viewing windows, directly at me, though I can't see his eyes through the reflective panel on his helmet. He holds up a hand, as if to wave.

"So," Leo says. "You and Heath?"

I hold my hand up, return the wave. "That's what he wants," I say.

Heath joins Zesi in the cockpit, lowers the pod shield. Seconds later, he maneuvers the bee to the center of the runway. Careful. Precise.

"And what do you want?" Leo asks.

The bee's floodbeams turn on, and I hear the engine spool up to a loud hum even through these thick walls. They'll be gone soon. In less than a minute, they'll fling themselves out into the stars, and we won't know they've made it until they return.

Or until they don't.

Is it too much to ask that the people I care about stay safe? Stay alive?

I blink, and they're out.

"A little bit of everything," I say. "Too many things I can't have."

31

PEACE IN PIECES

WHEN I WAS four years old, all I wanted was my mother.

I'd wake in the middle of the night, thirsty, and she'd bring me water. I'd wake up scared, and she brought herself.

Once, though, I woke up alone. I called out into the darkness, and no one answered. I pulled the covers up to my nose, too frightened to leave my own bed, too frightened to close my eyes. Eventually fear gave way to sleep, and I woke with her curled up beside me in bed, our noses touching.

When I was seven, all I wanted were hairpins. My mother sat me down in front of her mirror, smoothed my hair out so it looked exactly like hers, and tucked the pins in all the right places. She pulled bright threads out from the hems of two of her camisoles, teal and red, and wrapped them tightly around the pins so they were more than just plain metal: something special just for me.

At eight, I wanted answers: Who is my father? *Where* is my father? Why are we two instead of three?

My mother gave me a question instead. *Would we still be us if we were three instead of two?* I still wondered, for a long time—never stopped, really—but her words tamed my desperate need to know into mere curiosity. Things would be different with him in the picture. Maybe better, and maybe not. Not the same as what I had, though, and I *loved* what I had with my mother.

At twelve, all I wanted was space. Our walls felt like they were closing in, people's words felt electric, my skin felt too thin.

My mother gave me space, too.

At fourteen, I craved knowledge. Skill. To be important, and helpful, like my mother the commander—like everyone who'd traded life on Earth for this permanent mission on the station. The very day I mentioned it, my mother set up a time for me to meet with Dr. Safran. I've returned to his lab every day since.

Today, I want

and hope

and wish

and fear.

But my mother is not here.

Who would I be if we were still two instead of one?

32

THE LIGHT THAT BLINDS

I SLEEP IN the lab, on my stool, rest my head on the island. Its cool, hard surface is no comfort; my back grows stiff from being bent in an unfamiliar position all night long.

When I wake, it's to the sound of fists pounding at my door: the sound of a voice that yells and won't let up.

I don't move. I don't have to, for one, to see that it is Akello Regulus making all the noise. Akello, and no one else, at just after six-morning. It's very possible he might shatter my door with the sound of his voice alone, with his fists thrown in for good measure.

If I open the door, nothing stands between us.

I meet his eyes from where I sit, and very purposefully hold his gaze. His fists fall to his sides now that he has my attention. He stops shouting, though his words ring in my ears to fill the silence anyway: *LIARS! Liars, ALL of you!*

I buzz Leo. He picks up at once. "Linds?" His voice is full of sleep.

"Can you . . . could you come down to Portside?"

Akello's pounding starts up again, and the yelling, now that I've made no move to engage with him.

"What was that?" Leo says, flipping at once into alert mode. "Linds, what's happening? Are you okay? I'm coming down there now, hang on."

I swallow the lump that's formed in my throat. I don't know how to voice what I'm thinking—that Akello looks like he wants to strangle an apology right out of me? That I don't even blame him?

"Yeah," I say. "Yeah, thanks. Careful, though, Akello looks . . . upset." He's intimidatingly tall, but his height has never felt quite so threatening. Usually, he's calm, thoughtful. Steady. Warm.

What do we even do to keep this from escalating further? Akello has several inches on Leo, and it isn't like Leo's equipped with anything that could give him an advantage. If Akello turns on Leo, if something happens—I don't even know what I'd do. Heath and Leo together could hold their own, but Heath isn't here. Heath is more than halfway to *Nautilus* by now.

And what if more people join up with him outside my door? What if it's Leo and Haven and Natalin and me against all the rest? The only way Leo will have the upper hand here is if Akello never sees him coming.

"Bring some zip ties, just in case," I tell Leo. "There's a whole drawer full of them in Medical." Assuming he's coming from Control, where he stayed on duty all night, Medical will be an easy detour.

"Got it," he says. "Keep him distracted. I'll be there soon."

"I just want to talk!" Akello yells, still pounding the glass.

I slide off my stool, walk slowly to face him. Now that he has my attention, he's quiet again, though anger still simmers in his eyes. I'm putting a lot of faith in the thin pane that separates us, that it is stronger than it looks.

Our height difference is incredible—he towers over me. I straighten my shoulders, hold my head high. I may not have his height, but I can match him for presence.

"You want to talk?" I tilt my head, narrow my eyes. "So *talk*."

"You've made a big mistake." I can feel his intensity even from this side of the glass. "You lied about Mila, and no one trusts you."

I give a little half laugh. "You think I don't know that?"

"I'm just telling you," he says. "People are starting to talk. People are *saying* things, wondering what else you and the others are hiding."

"I don't see anyone else trying to break down my door. All I see is *you*."

"If you had nothing to hide, you wouldn't be holing up in here. You'd answer our questions instead of leaving us to come up with answers on our own." The way he says *answers* sends a chill down my spine.

"Well, if this is your answer—coming to my door and blatantly accusing me of making the wrong call, without stopping to consider that there was no good alternative? Your answer is no *solution*."

"Tell us, then," he says. "Tell us—"

But his words die out as Leo catches him by surprise. Before Akello even realizes what's happening, Leo has swiftly bound his wrists behind him with the zip ties. Tears spring up in my eyes at the sight of it. It's only for a minute, I tell myself. It's only temporary.

"She'll give answers when we have them," Leo says. "And unfortunately, we don't have them just yet."

Akello's usual gentle nature is overwhelmingly apparent in the way he doesn't fight back against Leo—his passion, his desire that things be *right*, are tempered now by an even-keeled calm. Perhaps he was only trying to get my attention; perhaps he was no threat at all. Are we justified in temporarily binding him simply because I *felt* threatened? Have I really become so ruled by my own fear?

"Come with me," Leo says. "Lindley's got work to do. You can yell at me all you want, all right?"

Akello nods, eyes sparkling under the recessed spotlights just outside my door. This one heartbreaking look: it says more than any of his words ever could.

He's lost everything, like every one of us.

He couldn't stand by and do nothing.

He had to do *some*thing.

I know the feeling.

Leo glances over his shoulder at me as he leads Akello away. *Thank you,* I mouth.

Always, he replies.

I spend a full ten minutes pacing the lab, walking off the emotion that's left me shaking and a little dizzy. Too much pressure, too little sleep, and now this—I'm doing everything I possibly can, and I get yelled at in return? It's not that I blame him for his frustration, or for demanding answers. I just wish I had answers to *give*.

I try to put it out of my mind for now. Do what I can. Dwelling on it will only lead to *your best is never enough, Lindley*. To the reality that people are starting to break—that we have been breaking for weeks.

Eventually, I manage to pull it together. Focus does not come easily, to say the least.

For the better part of the next hour, I mull over the conundrum of my hazy lab results. One failed sample was disappointing, but three failed samples—failed in identical ways, for no obvious reason?

It's suspicious. It isn't right.

Where did I go wrong? I pace circles around my island, go back over the test procedures in my head. I didn't miss anything. My measurements, my timers: all precise. The samples were fresh and handled properly, at least where Kerr and Jaako were concerned.

So *what happened*?

All I can think to do now is run the labs on the saliva and hair samples. Saliva first, I decide—I'm much more familiar with that process than I am with hair's. Zesi sealed two swabs each into small plastic bags. I prepare two vials of reagent solution, and am just about to settle the swabs into position when I notice something odd.

They're clean.

They're *too* clean, for two people whose final breaths were laced with bloodbubbles. As if they never coughed blood up at all.

Holy—the implications here, everything this could *mean*—

Suddenly I can't move fast enough.

If there is no trace of blood in the saliva, that changes everything.

*Every*thing.

33

SHADE AND SHADOW

THE WAY I see it, of the two possibilities at play here, one of them is impossible.

Either Zesi and Leo collected falsified samples—swabs taken from somewhere else, *anywhere* but from Jaako and Kerr—or these deaths were not due to a mutated virus at all.

If these strange saliva samples were the only odd things that had happened, that would be one thing, but they're not. Three tests in a row have failed, 100 percent of the tests I've run on this new wave of death. None of my tests failed in the first wave, so I'm relatively certain it's not simply that I'm doing it wrong. And then there's the erratic way the virus seems to have spread: the victims had so little in common—Mila, who never spent time with Jaako and Kerr—while the six of us who've actually handled the dead remain untouched, living and breathing like always.

The only logical explanation is that the virus is not to blame.

✳

I trust Zesi and Leo, would trust them with my life.

I trust them. They wouldn't lie to me.

Right?

The alternative is equally unnerving:

Someone on this station is lying. Someone on this station is a murderer.

34

ZOMBIE STARS

WHEN I WAS younger, maybe eight or nine, I liked to spend time in the sky lounge, sipping hot chocolate and staring out into the infinite star-spotted expanse. Leo would come and find me every now and then, sit beside me on the floor and talk my ear off for hours. He was very into space facts at the time, particularly the more terrifying ones.

I can still remember, vividly, the day I learned of zombie stars.

Of white dwarfs that have died, essentially, but end up coming back to life by creating an immense supernova that feeds off their neighboring stars.

I remember wondering if they knew, somehow, what they were doing: if they did it on purpose, taking and taking and taking just so they could *survive*, even if it meant draining the life out of the stars they'd seen every other day of their eternal star lives. Or if that was just their nature, some sort of self-preservation method that kicked in on instinct.

We've all suffered a death here, in a way. We still live, we still breathe, we still walk and talk and try to keep on going in the hope that one day we won't feel so broken. But on the inside? Parents who will never again be more than memories—the shattered illusions of safety and security, tiny shards lodged in our hearts, reminding us every day that we are *fragile*—

Someone here is trying to bring themselves back to life, trying to feel again in the midst of all that is numb.

And they are very good at hiding.

35

SECRET SECRETS

WHOEVER DID THIS is extremely clever. Whoever did this is extremely *calculating*.

Mila. Jaako. Kerr.

After all we've suffered, loss after loss after loss, I cannot fathom the level of delusion it would take to decide that this—*this*, the theft of life and breath and future—is the answer. I cannot fathom the numbness of heart required to break another heart, to take it and smash it and see if the shards are sharp enough to make its killer bleed, or feel. The bitterness required to spread bile into the world, just to avoid being alone in it.

Yet here we are.

It isn't like we live down on Earth, where there are innumerable places for a murderer to flee. There are no far-flung continents up here, no mountains or forests, no caves or islands or anywhere else someone might go to run from the past. Here, someone is hiding in plain sight. It could be *any*one. It's unnerving.

Worse, it's simply hard to imagine anyone on the station

who would do a thing like this. We all have our moments—we all clash sometimes, and things have certainly been escalating as of late—but we've lasted this long without resorting to murdering each other. It is world-shifting to realize that the reality we live in is not what I thought it was.

I thought we were better than this.

I dig my fingers into my temples, stare into the pristine white lab island until it is a blinding blur. This is an entirely new dimension of things required of me: not even my mother had to deal with a serial killer. A *serial killer*, holy . . . that's what this is, and it's possibly more frightening than a virus. That it likely won't end at three deaths. That there's no predicting who might be next.

That there's *motive* behind it.

With a mutation, it might have been hopeless—we might have all been wiped out—but at least I would have died knowing I tried my very best, that there might not have been a cure at all no matter how long I worked for one. Knowing what I now know, though—that these deaths are absolutely preventable, that I have every reason to believe they'll continue unless I find the killer and put a stop to this madness—it's a heavier sort of pressure, one that's closing in on me from all sides. Should I call for some sort of lockdown? Or would that only make for a smarter killer amid a sea of emotional instability? The killer could creep around in secret and take our people out one by one without anyone noticing, thanks to all the isolation. Still, my gut says a lockdown could minimize our losses if done well. We just need to go about it the right way.

My finger hovers over my buzz screen, and I'm ready to have Haven make the call—but I can't bring myself to actually do it. Not yet. Before I stir up panic prematurely, I should probably have more to back up my theory than just a simple *this is off, this doesn't feel right.* I should probably have something concrete.

Deep breaths. Calm, calm.

I need to do quick work, and I need it to be the best work of my life.

When I first stepped up as commander, I cracked open my mother's slim silver laptop and familiarized myself with file after file until my eyes gave out for the night. I spent a large percentage of my time in the manifest records of all who remained: I was familiar enough with most of their names, but not things like birth dates, or their parents' names and specific roles aboard the station, or other details I wouldn't have known simply by surviving seventeen years of station life together. Before it became my priority to know each and every resident, I mostly grew roots with Leo and Heath and Haven. I was friendly with the others, sure. But being friendly isn't exactly the same as being *friends.*

I slip out of the lab and head home, straight to my mother's bedside table. She always kept the laptop in its top drawer; I keep it there, too. A thought nags at me: *Don't waste time going through the manifests*, it says. *Better to run more tests in the lab.*

But the tests can wait. As far as the deaths go, I'm more

concerned with *who* did the killing than *how*. For the moment, anyway. Finding links and patterns among the victims could lead to their killer, which could put an end to this swiftly.

I pull up the manifest's master list, filter it by year of birth so I won't have to see the names of all our parents who died. A heaviness settles in my chest: they are nothing more than names on a screen now. Bits and bytes and memory.

Eighty-five names remain after the filter does its work, because of course the computer has no way of knowing what's happened since I last opened it. I click Mila's name, but it turns out I'm not prepared for her photo—how odd it is to have her bright brown eyes looking out, so very *alive*, as I switch her status to *deceased*. I do the same for Jaako. For Kerr.

Now we are eighty-two.

It doesn't look like a lot, but I know better. Just as our parents were more than just their names, so are we all. I wish it were as easy as sifting through the photos until I found one that obviously didn't belong, one that glowed red with anger, perhaps, or possibly even remorse. If only. So . . . what *am* I looking for?

Perspective, I decide.

A bird's-eye view of those of us who are left. Any connections I can draw between the victims, any telling details that might help me rule out—or take a closer look at—potential suspects.

This . . . could take a while.

36

BREAK

I'VE BEEN SAVING my mother's brick of chocolate, sealed up in its foil like some sort of shrine.

I tear into it.

Break off one small piece.

Things are not okay, not even a little bit.

37

UNSETTLE, UPROOT

IT ISN'T EASY to forget everything I know, but tonight, it is necessary. It's imperative that I use wide-open eyes to take a good, hard look at the familiar—that I dislodge my biases, approach each file as if it belongs to the killer.

The familiar has become strange.

Yuki and Grace, for example: no longer are they merely *two girls who went missing*, or *girls with porcelain bones who are more likely to be broken than to break.* Now they are *girls who had access codes to SSL, girls who broke in without permission, girls who stole witch hazel from Pillar 97.* Girls who might break other rules to preserve their own good.

And Akello—how he looked like he wanted to strangle the truth out of me, how he looked like he might have tried if not for the glass between us—his eyes on me during the mandatory check-in said he knew about Mila before we'd even announced it. I assumed it was because they were inseparable as friends, but it isn't like I knew the inner workings of their relationship; maybe it was an enemies-closer situation, how he always hung around her. Maybe he twisted and snapped. He's certainly imposing enough to overpower a victim or three.

It isn't such a stretch to connect some people to the deaths. Like Mikko, ready to attack Cameron for stealing his father's razor blades. The fact that he had razor blades at all—and the fact that Cameron stole them.

On and on, I sift through the files. I consider each one, jotting notes as I go, mapping connections between them, until I'm left with just six.

Five, if we're not counting me.

These are the most difficult biases to set aside. Sometimes, biases are there for a reason: because there are people who are implicitly trustworthy, people you've grown close to because they're worthy of closeness, people you know—*know*—would never do the unspeakable things in question. *Could* never, because you've seen straight down to their souls, shadows and all. That even their shadows aren't so dark as to hide murder, murder, murder.

Heath. Haven. Natalin. Leo. Zesi.

They've been working tirelessly alongside me, tending to the station just like I've been doing. I trust them, every single one.

Though, if I'm honest, Natalin doesn't completely seem to trust *me*.

And I'm learning new things by the day about Heath, when I thought I knew all there was to know—how he feels about me, for one. How he never told me about his crash landing last year.

We *all* know every turn of the station.

Every security camera.

Every single code for every single room.

I thought it would make me feel better to go through the manifests, but instead of ruling people out, all I'm left with is a mess of notes and the pervasive feeling that it could be *anyone*.

The only people I can absolutely trust are dead.

38

GIRL AGAINST TIME

IT'S FOUR-MORNING, AND I've now had three pieces of chocolate, a full fifth of the entire bar. Even at this early hour, I take great care in spreading my supplies out in perfect order on the laboratory island.

I'm running on three hours of broken sleep. Aside from obvious concerns—the who and how of these murders—we're coming up on the thirty-six-hour mark from when Zesi and Heath set off for *Nautilus*. I know well enough not to expect them to return at *exactly* thirty-six hours, since they will have had to dock and load up the fresh batch of supplies, but I find myself waiting on the edge of my stool regardless. In my limited, broken sleep, I kept dreaming of explosions: a perfect burst of fire from the heart of the bee, complete destruction in the span of a single second, all of it silent in the void of space.

I've been trying not to dwell on the things that make me afraid. Trying to find answers instead, fumbling around for something solid and within my control, rather than tying myself into anxious knots over things so far out of it. The mystery of the deaths has been a more than sufficient distraction thus far—but not a satisfying one.

Instead of neatly tied answers, I've dug up a tangle of questions.

Instead of feeling like I'm in control, I'm keenly aware that I'm *not*.

None of this helps with the fear.

I've been mostly unbothered since Zesi and Heath left, miraculously, except for twice-daily food deliveries from Haven or Natalin and the occasional text from Leo. **Everything under control**, he wrote once. I decided to treat it like an update, not a question, given the lack of punctuation. **Excellent, thank you**, I wrote back, an answer that would suffice either way.

Otherwise, I've kept entirely to myself. Natalin and Haven and Leo still think I'm trying to crack a cure for the virus— that's the only reason I can come up with for how thoroughly they've left me to my work. I'm not about to tell them the truth of what I've discovered, though. Not yet.

This morning, my objective is simple: If the blood at the scene wasn't coughed up by Jaako or Kerr . . . where did it come from? My lab is equipped with the most advanced DNA tech out there—crucial for a space station meant to analyze samples discovered on Radix or any other non-Earth planets we eventually explore. It's fast, it's accurate, it's very straightforward. I'll run tests on the blood and see what I find.

I place a droplet of blood on the slide, secure it in place by pressing another slide down on top. The slide sandwich fits snugly into the machine, right into a depression of the exact same shape. I power it on and wait.

Thirteen minutes, that's all it will take—a vast improvement over DNA machines of old. Thirteen minutes for *answers*.

It seems impossibly far away, especially now. I should have dragged myself out of half sleep at three-morning instead of four. Any other time, really. It's two minutes past the thirty-six-hour return-from-*Nautilus* mark, and there's nothing I can do now but wait. For test results, for their return.

Not even music from the old data pod is comforting. I turn it on, then immediately turn it off—the tone is too light for this moment, the beat too relentless. It only adds to the chaos in my head. I tap around, find a file labeled *Nature Sounds*, and click into it. A grid of images fills the screen, each matching its label: *thunderstorm, ocean breeze, jungle nights, bamboo forest*, along with a planet's worth of others.

At first, I assume this file exists simply because the first generation wanted a reminder of home. Once I select *bamboo forest*, though, it's clear that isn't the only reason. It's peaceful, steady in a way that doesn't compete with the noise in my mind—rather, it tames it. I close my eyes, rest my head on the island. For the first time, I feel like maybe I've missed out by never having been on Earth. I start to wonder: Does this soundtrack do justice to a real bamboo forest? Did my mother ever visit one? Was it full of fireflies like the one from her childhood? Did my mother miss these sorts of sounds when she traded them for the constant hum of the station?

It simply never occurred to me that Earth would sound so different than the station—that there would be so many *different* kinds of sounds, on top of that. I've always loved life on the *Lusca*, but for the first time, it makes me wonder if my mother ever questioned her decision to live out her days here. If she ever regretted it.

I wish I could ask her. The hole in my heart cracks around its edges, crumbles. It gets a little wider each day.

I close my eyes, do my best to shake off these feelings. Focus on all the things I *can* try to fix, not the things that are impossibly broken.

Six minutes and forty-two seconds have passed since I started the test. It's still a little early to expect Heath and Zesi to return, but not impossible—assuming they coordinated with *Nautilus*'s team and the supplies were already in the hangar, like they were supposed to be, that seems like a reasonable amount of time to load them up and settle back into the bee.

I take out my buzz screen, type a message to Leo. **Any sign of them yet?**

Heath and Zesi? he immediately sends back. I resist the urge to ask, well, who else?

It's ten past 36 hours, I reply. **Let me know as soon as they dock?**

For sure, he sends back. **Sry, of course you meant Heath and Zesi. Just woke up.**

Right. Not everyone gets up at four-morning. **Thanks. I'm in Portside if you need me.**

Things going okay there?

I sit so long trying to come up with the perfect response, the DNA machine startles me when it beeps.

I'll let you know, I type quickly, but delete it before hitting send. **Going like usual,** I send instead.

I abandon the buzz screen on the island, hurry over to see the results as they fill the machine's display panel. The display is a mess of information, more details on it than I could ever hope to decode. That's the thing about this machine: it may be simple to operate, but it still requires a trained eye to interpret the results. Fortunately, its creator recognized the need for a basic summation of results in addition to results that could be mined for months—that's what I'm waiting on, for the field that says *SEARCHING FOR MATCH* to replace itself with something I can use.

I wait. And wait.

Finally, *SEARCHING FOR MATCH* disappears, leaving a void behind. Two seconds pass, and then: *MATCH FOUND— Alexandra Tovar, DOB 09/15/2107.*

My heart climbs to my throat.

Alexandra Tovar was Leo's mother.

39

UNRAVEL

ALEXANDRA TOVAR WAS one of the last to pass.

The days leading up to it were excruciating: Alexandra, watching the others die off, one by one. Watching as I lost my mother, as Heath and Haven lost their parents. As Alexandra herself lost her *husband*.

Knowing with certainty that she'd be next. If not next, then soon.

Leo was remarkably strong in her final days. He felt he had to be, I think. Seeing Leo devastated would have been worse for her than the dying itself, and if there was one thing left in his power, it was to keep it from being worse.

He practiced so long at tucking himself in—all the wayward anxiety and fear and sorrow—that he's kept at it ever since. Only once have I seen him unravel, and that didn't happen until they were all dead, every single one of them. When it hit him—hit *us*—that we were really, truly, irreversibly without them. Alone.

We sat on the floor near my window, just the two of us, in

silence, all night long. Neither of us slept. I was in too much shock to cry, in too much denial. He was shaking, hard, even with the blaze turned on full force, even when I slipped my mother's favorite blanket off my shoulders and wrapped it around his.

We counted stars.

We laid out the deck of cards, piled it back up again.

We didn't talk. We didn't need to.

He might walk around like he's fine now, might even seem like he's doing *well* to anyone who doesn't know him like I do. I know better, though. I know *him* better.

And I know, because I do the very same thing.

40

EXCEPTIONS

IT'S FORTY-TWO PAST the thirty-six-hour mark, and I haven't heard another word from Leo. I've spent the entire time with my fingers hovering over the buzz screen, trying to decide what—how—*whether*—to tell him about his mother's blood.

On one hand, there's not a soul I trust more. There's not anyone I know better than Leo, and I am one thousand percent certain he would never even think to murder someone, let alone actually do it. And the crime itself is worse than just a single straightforward murder—it must have taken extreme planning and calculation to stage these deaths to look like a viral muta-tion. I don't *think* Leo is our liar. The one thing holding me back from telling him everything, though, is that these deaths required extreme resources.

Codes, first and foremost. The samples scraped from all the others who died—Alexandra's blood included—are stored in a single location: the mini-fridge two feet behind me. In order to access it, the killer would have needed all-access codes to this lab, an awareness of my time spent here, and the knowledge that we kept all those blood samples in the first place. There are only a few people who have *all* of those things: six, to be exact. Five, if we're not counting me.

Leo wouldn't have done something so coldhearted, though. And if he had, surely he wouldn't have used his own mother's blood.

Right?

Except that's exactly the sort of calculated forethought the killer must possess, if they're hiding right here in plain sight—to think of the person most likely to discover the deaths as murders, if they're discovered at all. To orchestrate the details in such a way that would rule them out as suspects.

I can't make any assumptions. I have to work based on *facts.*

And the fact is, Leo and Zesi collected these samples from Jaako and Kerr in the first place. Leo was the one who called me in the middle of the night when Mila died, too. And he is the one who put Mila's blood sample in the wrong refrigerator after we found her—could that have been on purpose, to make it unusable? Could he have planned things out to that extent, that even then he was setting himself up to have no apparent knowledge about which mini-fridge we used for sample storage?

My head is spinning; my world has inverted.

I thought I was alone before, but now, *now* I am truly alone. Because, really, what it comes down to is that someone is very much not who I thought they were. I can't even trust my own judgment—is there anything more isolating than that?

But then I come back around to the truth, that I usually

have very good judgment, that I have sharp instincts. And that I shouldn't rule out the rest of the station just because I can't understand how they would have had access to the codes, to my schedule, to the inner workings of how and where we stored the blood samples, or that we stored blood samples at all. It seems just as plausible that someone could have figured out *all* of those things—more plausible, possibly!—than if Leo had suddenly turned into someone I don't actually know. The same holds true for Heath, for Zesi, for Haven, for Natalin, differences of opinion aside.

So I sit here, finger hovering over my blank buzz screen.

I don't want to live in a world where I can't trust Leo. In that world, I can't trust anything, not even myself—and how is that going to help? It's going to take more than just me to figure out what exactly killed our three; I'll definitely need to run more tests in the lab, but it's more complicated than just that.

If I trust Leo and I'm wrong, that would be devastating. If he's kept this much from me, he's not the person I know, not even a little bit—and what would keep him from killing me? To what lengths would our murderer go to keep their secret? I could end up just another body, sprinkled with the blood of Alexandra Tovar. *She spent all that time in the lab*, Haven would say, in the obligatory station-wide announcement. *Of course she was more susceptible to the mutation.*

If I *don't* trust Leo, though—if I fumble around in secret for answers instead of asking for help where I need it—someone else might die in the time it takes for me to make all the necessary connections.

I pick up the buzz screen, type in a message. **Question: Do you know how to access the security vid-feeds?**

As soon as I hit send, I realize: I'm hoping for a *no* as much as I am a *yes*. No more than two seconds later, my screen lights up with a new message.

Yeah, Leo writes. **Need something?**

I let out a long exhale. It doesn't mean anything, doesn't have to mean anything except that he'll be able to help me. I push aside the lingering thoughts that say otherwise. Choose faith.

Meet in Control ASAP, I reply.

For once, I don't bother to clear my lab island, except for the sensitive materials that require proper storage. I pause briefly to make sure the door is locked behind me, but what good is a coded entry if the code isn't secret anymore? A broken door would almost be better—then, at least, it would obviously rule out the people I trust most.

The station is still and silent at this early hour. Even Control is empty when I arrive, and dark; I'm alone in a field of backlit panels. Still no new-message alerts on our comm system, I observe on instinct. I look through the wide window into the endless sea of stars, wish I could press pause on this moment without ever having to take a hard look at reality. In reality, the axis of my world has tilted, suddenly and drastically, and everything I thought I knew is in the process of sliding out from under me. I don't want to know who has it in them to take life. I don't want to know if my fears have played out against this very backdrop of stars, if Zesi and Heath and their bee exploded into one more ball of flaming fire amid the millions that will outlive us all.

But there is no way to stop time. I would have stopped it a long time ago if there was.

I hear the door slide open behind me, hear the rustle of Leo's pants as he enters. I don't turn around, and he doesn't say anything, and for a long moment it's like the night we sat by my window, soaking in the truth of all that had happened. He comes to stand by my side. Watches me like I watch the stars.

"We . . . have a problem," I say finally. I steal a glance at him, see his profile lit up by the glow of the control panels. Once I meet his eyes, I can't look away: he would not have done this. Not with his own mother's blood—not at all. In this moment, I choose to believe I can trust him.

What is trust if you know all of the answers?

Hopefully it is not a mistake.

"Did they—did Zesi and Heath—"

"No," I say quickly. "Not that. Well, not yet—I haven't seen anything, good or bad." We're at thirty-seven hours and counting now. "They should be back any minute."

They should've been back already.

Leo's concerned, too, and trying to hide it on his face. Not that he's trying to hide it from *me*—it's himself he's trying to

198 |

convince. He's probably not even aware he's doing it.

"So," I say, when the silence has drawn on for too long. My voice is crackling and low, barely more than a whisper. "I made a breakthrough today."

I want to say more, but the words curl up in my throat. I want to protect him, because after I tell him, there will be no going back to the not-knowing. I want to protect *myself*, in case I'm wrong and this is a huge mistake.

"About the virus? How it spreads—how to end it?"

He sounds so genuinely hopeful. It's enough to put me at ease, at least a little. *How to end it*: if only.

I take a deep breath. Whisper, because even I don't want to hear what I have to say. "It isn't the virus this time. Someone— somebody—" Tears spring up without warning, and it is such a foreign feeling I'm caught completely off guard. "Someone *killed* them, Leo. On purpose."

My words hang between us, heavy and hovering, like they could fall and crush us at any moment. Maybe they will. We are already being picked off by a threat we can't see; even if spoken word doesn't have the power to kill our bodies, what about our hope? Words hold more power than people give them credit for, I think.

"But the blood . . . ?" Leo says after a long pause. He's turning the problem over in his mind like I've been, I can tell. Trying to reconcile fear with surface-level fact.

I shake my head. "Your mother's blood," I say, staring out

into the stars, not at his face, *anywhere* but his face. "Someone pulled it out of storage and used it to stage the whole thing. They only made it *look* like the virus."

He's still, too still.

It's the sort of stillness that comes right before an explosion.

But instead of exploding like Leo does—all at once, very rarely, extremely supernova—I feel the full force of his energy surge through me as he takes my hand, as he laces his fingers in mine, as he holds on for dear life.

We've not done this before, and now that we have, how have we never?

So often, we sit back-to-back when working through our mutual discomforts. Side by side, if not that.

I turn, face him. His lips find mine, perfectly soft against his days-old stubble, and I don't pull away, definitely do *not* pull away. If anything, I pull him closer, my free hand at the back of his neck. I kiss him harder, taste a hint of sweet spearmint on his tongue. In this moment, when everything else in the world feels like it's slipping away, it is everything to me to have Leo here, now, close and closer than we've ever been. Like we can stop tomorrow, if only we commit to keeping this present moment alive.

So we stay in it, keep it alive. Until the radar blips behind him, anyway, *blip blip blip blipblipblipblip,* and we break ourselves back in two. His eyes are as bright as I feel, because of the radar and . . . everything else.

"They're back," I say, one part breathless, one part relieved. It can only be Heath and Zesi, and the radar log confirms it. "They're *back*. They made it!"

As far as bad days go, this one could be worse.

41

FROM ENDLESS NIGHT

LEO SQUEEZES MY hand, pulls me in for one more kiss before we head for the hangar. It is quick, much quicker than our first, but with no less power—it is affirmation, it is *this was not a mistake.*

We are business-as-usual as soon as the Control doors open, we are side-by-side-with-purpose. Anyone paying attention would see the newly charged air between us, but at this hour, no one is around to pay attention. We slip into the hangar deck, safe behind its viewing panel windows, just in time to see the runway light up with the electric-purple grav-force glow. Two seconds later, the bee glides smoothly onto the runway, not a scratch on it. I feel a swell of pride for Heath—he did this! He *did* it.

As soon as the pride crests, though, guilt rolls in to replace it: Leo.

While Heath was risking his life for the station—for me—I let myself pretend reality away, if only for a few minutes. And the way I did that, with Leo, even if only for a few minutes, will most certainly hurt Heath if he finds out. Not that I've made any commitment to Heath—but I absolutely do care about him. I hate that what I've done could hurt him, hate that it's too late to change it.

And I hate that if I could go back and do the past hour over again, I'm not entirely sure I'd do it differently.

Heath is first out of the bee after they dock it, and Zesi climbs out right behind him. I wish I could see their faces, see their triumphant smiles through the strong purple glare on their helmets' face shields—they did it, they actually *did* it!

"Mission complete," Heath says, breathless, his words crackling over the viewing room speaker. Rather than triumphant, though, he sounds—defeated? Or maybe it's just exhaustion. That has to be it, seeing as how they were clearly successful at flying there and back, and in retrieving food and fresh filters. Zesi unloads the supply pallets while Heath unfolds a steel pushcart from its hidden storage compartment. The cart looks almost exactly like the gurneys up in Medical, except this one's purpose is to deliver *life* to us, not death.

It takes only a few minutes for them to fill the cart—three SpaceLove pro-pack pallets up top, along with a pair of bulky, awkward items below. A water filter and an extra for backup, I assume. Fingers crossed Zesi can figure out how to switch out our old filter for the new one; he's quick to pick up everything else, so the installation should go smoothly. I hope.

Zesi and Heath maneuver the pushcart through the first air-lock. I find myself holding my breath as the air turns over inside the sealed chamber, remind myself to breathe.

Once they're through the second airlock and back with us in the viewing room, Heath tears his helmet off and barrels straight toward me. He wraps his arms around me, bear-hug-tight, and buries his cheek against the soft bend of my neck—and then he's kissing me, one two three four five, like he's leaving a path of stardust that ends at my lips.

Can he taste Leo on me like I taste starlight on him?

Leo—oh, no. I hear his breath catch behind me, a sound so quiet I easily could have missed it.

I slip out of the kiss, aim for a subtle break so as not to hurt . . . anyone. My cheeks are on fire. "You guys—you—you really did it." It feels like an understatement. Like the words fall completely short at expressing the things I feel but can't bring myself to say:

You didn't crash.

You didn't die.

You've missed a lot.

"Two fresh filters, ready to go," Zesi says, settling his helmet onto its hook. "And everything we could pull that wasn't in contaminated airspace."

My heart dips. "Contaminated airspace?" *Nautilus* is so small the entire chamber could succumb to a contaminant. No room for quarantine on *Nautilus* unless the unaffected spent it outside, in a spacesuit, tethered up with fully loaded ox-tanks.

And even then, that's not the best plan for survival.

I worried so hard over how we could very seriously infect them, I didn't consider the possibility—the reality—

Heath bows his head. "They never answered when Zesi made contact from the bee," he says. "We tried for the entire hour leading up to it . . . but . . ."

"Nothing," Zesi finishes, the look on his face grave.

Fifteen more lives.

Fifteen more deaths.

"We pulled all we could from their hangar deck storage, but the filters weren't in there, so we had to go inside," Heath says. "Got in and out as quickly as possible. It . . . wasn't pretty." His eyes cloud over, like he's staring into death itself.

The four of us stand, silent, for a long minute. I'm trying not to imagine it, the blood and decay and stench of what used to be *life*, brilliant life. I've seen my fair share of death, of course, but we've always cleared it from the station before anyone started to actually decompose. I can't decide what's worse: the idea of being the only one left alive there, or that there *is* no one else left alive.

Heath takes my hand, and what else is there to do when someone has risked his life for the station and seen things that will haunt him for the rest of his days? I don't let go. Things are complicating by the minute with us, but no matter what, he is still one of my very best friends. Right now, this is what he needs.

"That . . . isn't the worst of it," he says. His hand in mine makes all the more sense: this isn't only what *he* needs—it's what he thinks *I* need.

"The crew," Zesi picks up. "Their symptoms looked slightly different than the ones here did."

He goes on to explain the horrific sight on *Nautilus*. No bloodbubbles to speak of—there, they suffered nosebleeds so swift and so devastating, not one crew member had had the chance to clean . . . anything.

Lie low.

Linger.

Explode.

The sickness we know took everyone out quickly, yes, but not all at once.

The sickness we know came with blood—sprinkles of it. Not rivulets.

What if this is not the sickness we know?

I glance at the cartful of SpaceLove supplies, at the suits Heath and Zesi have already shed. What if they've brought back a new strain? An *actual* mutation?

"Lindley. *Linds.*"

I blink, find all three guys staring at me in slack-jawed concern.

"Did it not send up red flags," I say, careful to keep my voice even, without accusation, without coming unhinged, "that you could be bringing a new strain of the virus right back to us? That we might not be immune to this one?" I squeeze my eyes shut, try not to panic.

"It's not like we could just call and ask what you wanted us to do." Zesi's voice teeters on the brink of bitterness, of frustration. "We were already inside when we found them like that, and it was too late to undo it at that point, so we made a judgment call and went forward as planned. Might as well bring back something useful if we were going to come home at all."

If we were going to come home at all. It's easier to forgive when he puts it that way. Because he's right, what else would they have done? Where else could they have gone?

It's a risk, for sure, but Heath has always been the risk taker among us—big risk, big reward, especially when the risks have potential to protect the people he loves. I only hope this risk pays off.

I'm trying to pick out the perfect words—*thank you* feels like too much and too little all at once—when Zesi runs a hand over his dreads, breaking the moment. "I'm taking a shower and then sleeping for a year," he says. Heath could use a shower, too, but I don't want to be the one to say so.

Turns out I don't have to, though. "Come find us at six tonight if we're not around yet," Heath says. "Can the filters wait until then? If you still want us to use them, that is?" His eyelids are heavy now that he doesn't have to be on high alert.

We already have the filters, and I can't see how going forward with the installation will change anything now—if *Lusca* was going to be contaminated with a new strain, it happened the second they entered the airlock. It has an automatic decontam feature built in, but that didn't kill the first virus—why should I expect it to be any different with a new strain?

"We'll do the installation as planned," I say. "Later today." Normally, I'd want to knock it out as soon as possible, but I think we could all use some time to uncoil. "We've waited this long—go get some rest."

And then it's just Leo and me, like we started this day. Alone together.

We meet eyes, and I wonder if we'll pick up where we left off—I want to, but the problems of the day are already creeping in to poke pins in my heart.

"You look like you could use a break, too, Linds." He plants a soft kiss on my forehead, and another on my lips, like he's trying to erase the ones Heath left on me. "Get some rest and meet back at six?"

I nod, caught off guard by the tears filling my eyes. It isn't Leo, it's just . . . everything. Too many emotions, too many extremes.

A break would be nice. A break is necessary.

"Buzz if you need me?" I say.

But Leo shakes his head. "Turn it off, just for today. It's not even a full day—not even a *half* day. I'll knock on your door at a quarter to six, and we'll go from there."

It's an offer too tempting to refuse. It's not *easy*—not easy at all to take this step back, to purposefully put myself in the dark, especially in light of the hard truths I've uncovered today. I press the power button, hold it down until my buzz screen goes dark.

"I'll take care of things," Leo says. "I promise."

I'll take care of you, I hear.

Today is not for leaps of faith, but for the small first steps of it.

42

KNOTS

IT'S LIKE MY left arm has been cut off, not having my buzz screen on—like my mind is constantly searching for this vital part of me, constantly looking for that connection, constantly coming up empty. It isn't restful, not at first. The silence is unnerving: I wonder what I'm missing. At least with the buzz screen on, I'd know for sure no one is trying to get in touch.

After habitually reaching for it three times in a row, I climb up onto the kitchen counter and tuck it deep into the highest cabinet. It might not be out of mind, but at least now it is out of sight.

I drift from kitchen to fireplace to window wall to my bathroom, not quite sure what to do with all these empty hours. I can't remember the last time I had time to decide—usually it's crash on the chair, eat what I can, shower out of necessity. Now that I *have* the time, I wonder if maybe I've been keeping myself busy on purpose without realizing it. When the silence starts to gape, I start thinking about how even another person breathing in the same room, not speaking, can make a place feel alive. When I try to fall asleep—curled up in my bed for once, instead of my mother's chair—my mind turns from nightmare to nightmare, fear to fear.

I turn on the shower to drown out the silence, let the steam fog the mirror so I won't have to face the dark circles that haunt my eyes. I climb in, stand with my back to the deluge of watery needles as they rain down on me. It's good we have a fresh filter ready to go; I haven't had the luxury of a shower like this in weeks.

When I finish, I force myself to crawl back in bed. I stare out my bedroom window and count the stars until they blur, until my eyes are heavy and I lose the number. I must sleep eventually, for a dark and dreamless stretch of hours, because the next thing I hear is Leo at my door, calling my name.

If left to myself, I could possibly have slept forever.

43

INCENDIARY

THIS SPACE IS too tight for the six of us.

Natalin insists she be present for the water filter installation, insists upon seeing it connect with her own eyes—as if, after flinging themselves out into the stars, Zesi and Heath wouldn't do everything in their power to finish things the right way. As if they aren't also in dire need of fresh water like the rest of us. Leo let it slip, on our way down to the water chamber, that Natalin's been buzzing into his ear all day with a too-sharp tongue: *Why not now, why can't they rest later, why is this not a priority for anyone but me?* Leo also mentions that he spent the better part of an hour trying to make contact with Nashville, but still, their silence continues.

I don't regret that I slept through all this.

So now we are crammed onto a catwalk in a tight, dimly lit alcove inside the immense hydro chamber, dwarfed by its massive orbs full of water—one is sparkling and clear, less than half full, while five others are filled with cloudy liquid yet to be purified. A maze of thick pipes connects orbs to filters, with dozens of smaller pipes snaking off to pump clean water through all offshoots of the station. This chamber was clearly built for the water—and a tech or two who know what they're doing—not six people fumbling around in the dark.

"You're blocking the light, Nat," Heath says, holding one of the bulky *Nautilus* filters, as Zesi performs surgery to extract the dying one from its snug compartment. "Could you shift a bit?"

"If I 'shift a bit,' I won't be able to see."

"If you don't move, there won't be anything *to* see," Zesi says. A bead of sweat drips from the tip of his nose to the concrete floor. It's hot in here.

A pinprick beam of white light hits Zesi square between the eyes. "Flashlight?" Natalin says, head cocked. She hasn't budged.

Zesi squints back up at her, one eye hidden behind his dreadlocks. "I just don't get why *all* of us have to be here for this? This is a two-person job at most."

Leo and I had planned to meet Zesi and Heath here, but that was before we discovered just how tight a space it was. Natalin came because she's afraid, I think—afraid of our water running dry, afraid she'll miss an opportunity to step in if something doesn't go as it should. It's like me with my buzz screen, how it's hard to relinquish control even if you aren't actively *doing* anything.

Why Haven is here, I have no idea.

Well, that isn't completely true. She told us flat-out she

didn't want to be the only one out of the loop. I guess what I mean is that I have no idea why she'd choose this over doing *any*thing else—it's pretty miserable down here. I'm going to need another shower.

"We don't all have to hover in this *exact* spot," I say. "I'll be over on the platform if anyone needs me." There's a small balcony that overlooks the orb with clean water; the balcony is lit by a single recessed spotlight and is probably not quite as hot as the filter alcove. Not quite as stuffy, at the very least.

I trail my hand along the catwalk's railing as it curves around the orbs, then climb six small steps to the platform balcony. The catwalk rings the spherical room at about half its height—a high ceiling above, a deep pit equally far beneath—with the orb system suspended in the middle. I sit on the balcony, dangling my feet over its edge, and rest my arms on the lowest rung of the railing.

"Mind if I join you?"

Haven's voice startles me—either her footsteps were unusually quiet as she followed me over, or I was unusually lost in my own head. Probably the latter. Her tank top is dark with sweat, and under the spotlight, every exposed bit of her skin is slick and shimmering.

I inch over as far as I can, gesture to the space beside me. She sits, dangling her legs just like I do. We stare out at the still, clear water.

"You doing okay, Lindley?" she asks after a moment of

silence. "You've been holed up for a couple of days, and I just . . . I'm a little worried, is all."

It isn't that I've been avoiding her, not exactly. It's just that we're both changing lately, for better and not, all at once. She's been extra *You're sure you've got this? You're sure you're okay?* And maybe she means well; maybe she does have faith in me. Maybe she doesn't realize how much it undermines the thin armor of confidence I have to put on every morning. I'm *not* sure I've got this. I'm *not* sure I'm okay.

But that doesn't mean I can't be the leader we need.

I try to hear her question for what it is: a question from my close friend, my close friend who cares enough to ask. Who knows me, and sees me—all of me—even the things I'm ashamed of, the things I'd rather hide. When we were younger, it was so much easier to just come out with the truth of my feelings. I hadn't learned to hide them so well back then. Never felt such a need to.

"Lots on my mind, that's all." It's not quite as much as five-years-ago Lindley would've offered, but it's something. It's honest.

For once, she doesn't jump in immediately with strong opinions on how I should be handling all of this. She sits for so long without saying anything I start to wonder if *she's* okay. And of course she can't be, not completely—none of us can live through what we have and come out without scars.

"What about you?" It shouldn't have taken me this long to

ask; I swallow the guilt down, try to convince myself I'm just an overwhelmed and distracted friend, not a terrible one. "How are you holding up?"

She plasters on a smile, but her eyes fill with tears; an instant later, her smile tightens and the tears recede. Not a single one slips out. "I miss them," she says, watching the water like it can give her clarity. "My parents, I mean. And I miss *us*. All of us, how we used to be. We're all just ghosts now, you know?"

I let her words sink in, tear their layers apart. I hadn't thought of it like this before, but she's right. We'll never be the same people we were before the virus hit. Our flesh and blood might be the same, but we're forever changed.

"Every day is a new day, though, I keep reminding myself," Haven continues. "I can keep fighting, even when I feel like parts of myself have gone missing. People go through hard things all the time and come out much stronger than before, right?" She doesn't give herself the same luxury of silence she afforded me. Tips and tricks and easy fixes, that's how she's making it through.

Maybe I should try her approach instead of letting things weigh on me like I do. Maybe her bright-side attitude actually *is* the secret to how well she seems to be surviving these days.

A loud clang from the filter alcove, followed by a string of curse words, startles us both. Zesi's voice bounces from orb to orb, from ceiling to deep pit.

"Everything okay over there?" I call, jumping to my feet

and hurrying back down to the catwalk. Haven follows me. No one answers, so I pick up the pace. Even once we're back to the alcove, it's dead quiet. I look from Zesi to Heath to Natalin to Leo, each of their faces wearing varying shades of panic.

Panic laced with frustration.

Panic laced with disappointment.

Panic laced with anger.

Panic laced with calm. A failed attempt at calm, anyway, one I can see straight through.

"Someone want to tell me what's going on?" I put edges in my voice, hope they can slice through this silence.

Zesi rises, drenched in sweat. "Filter doesn't fit," he says. "We're screwed." He pushes past Natalin, between Haven and me, his furious footsteps shaking the cool metal catwalk until he exits the chamber.

I've never seen fury and fear like I have on Natalin in this moment. She could spontaneously combust; she could shatter every orb and assail us with a storm of shards.

But she holds herself together. Looks me straight in the eye and says: "Completely. Royally. Screwed."

44

WHEN IN DARKNESS, STRIKE A MATCH

NONE OF US wants to be here.

We don't want to talk about how completely wrecked we are. We don't want to stumble on each other's live, frayed wires, don't want to feel the shock wave of electricity as it radiates through our skin. We would all be better off alone right now.

We don't have that luxury.

I ordered an emergency meeting of our six, again in SSL, with its silent, still forest of glowing pillars. Silent and still is all I crave right now—we have problems upon problems upon problems, and they're not going away unless we find a way to deal with them.

Natalin is the last to arrive. She stalks over to us, paces around the spotlit lab instead of making a place for herself. The rest of us might be steady where we sit and stand, but the tension is palpable. Even Leo's looking cracked and worn down, and Heath—Heath's eyes have never looked so heavy.

I should say something. They're *waiting* for me to say something. I called this meeting, after all. But I'm at a total loss.

How would my mother handle this? How would she deal with this spiral of defeat that grows more hopeless, more bleak, with every hour?

She wouldn't let it crush her, I know that much. But she also wouldn't give false hope just for the sake of lightening the mood.

"We're imploding," I say finally. "I know it, you all know it."

No one says a word. No one moves. Only Leo and Heath meet my eyes, and the others—the others stare at their hands, at the floor.

"Zesi, Heath, thank you again for making the trip to *Nautilus.*" Zesi looks up, his brown eyes hard and cold. It's an unnatural look on him, and for a moment, it steals my breath. Everyone hears what I'm not saying, I'm sure: *thank you for making the trip even though you brought back a useless filter and, possibly, a new strain of sickness.*

"It's particularly devastating," I continue, "to have so much at risk. To think you're making progress, to come so close, only to have it not work out after all. And to have huge consequences on the line, *life* at stake." Now I'm the one who has to look away. "On one hand, it would be easier not to try anymore at all—the higher your hopes, the harder the fall when they don't work out, right? And nothing seems to be working out. At all."

All the emotions I'm trying to swallow are trapped in my throat. I take a moment, close my eyes. Still, no one speaks: we have never had a meeting so silent as this, not once. We are in even worse shape than I thought.

"We may be imploding," I go on, "and we are definitely

frustrated, and tired, and nothing we've tried has *fixed* anything, and we are running out of time to fix it." I don't throw out hard numbers—everyone saw how little clean water was left in that one orb. If we place a station-wide ban on showers, at least we'll have drinking water for another day, maybe two.

"But"—I pause, wait until I have eye contact from each and every one of them, even Natalin—"we aren't dead yet. We can figure this filter thing out, there *has* to be a way."

"And the virus?" Haven cuts in. "Even if we figure the filter out, what's our plan with that?"

"The new strain we might've brought back? Or do you mean the *murders*?" Zesi says, and all heads turn.

"You *told* him?" My words are knives, aimed straight at Leo's heart. How could he? How could he share that, when it took so much faith for me to confide that much in him?

Everyone is talking now, so many voices so many words so much *noise*, so loud loud loud they lace together like a tightly spun spiderweb. I can't pick apart the individual questions, I only know that the faltering hope we had—the tenuous trust we had in each other—just took a major hit. Perhaps a devastating one.

"Yes," I say, my voice like iron as it cuts through all the others. The noise falls away, and I take a deep breath. Like it or not, the terrible secret is out. "The recent deaths—someone killed them on purpose." Someone could be killing again as we speak, and I hate that my time and energy and attention are so desperately fractured right now. There is too much at stake on every front, too little time.

It is also not lost on me that that someone might be in this very room. I don't truly believe that to be the case, because the panic on their faces is *real*. But what kind of scientist would I be to rule an entire group out based purely on my own feelings?

"You weren't going to say anything to us, Lindley?" *To me*, I hear underneath Heath's words. *You weren't going to say anything to* me?

"But *why* would someone do this?" Haven says, her voice rising with every word. "It doesn't make any sense. And how? How did they do it and make it look so . . . so . . . so much like the virus?"

"That's what I've been trying to figure out," I say. "I didn't want anyone to panic, so I've been trying to learn as much as I could on my own before I called for lockdown or told anyone . . . else." I give Leo a pointed look: I still can't believe he told Zesi. I never explicitly told him not to, and I never explicitly mentioned the deeper reasoning behind keeping it a secret—because how do we know, for sure, who *didn't* do it? Leo spilling this secret: not helping my trust issues.

"Figure out the *how* and you'll land on the *who*." Natalin's voice is heavy, sharp. "Maybe you should go get to work on that, Lindley, before anyone else dies? Clearly you don't need our help."

Her eyes are a challenge. I turn mine to steel, straighten my shoulders. She's just anxious, I tell myself. Fearful, and past the point of freaking out. She does this every time, shifts the blame wherever she can—she doesn't want any slight weight of failure to fall on her shoulders. Not *her* fault if I can't figure out how to stop the deaths. Not her fault. *My* fault.

"Yeah, you're right," I say, betraying no emotion. "I should go get to work. I really don't do enough around here."

I don't want to bear the weight of failure, either. I *can't*. A person can only bear so much.

So I won't fail. I promise this to myself, because other people's lives depend on it—and my own life does, too—

I. Will. Not. Fail.

45

SPITFIRE

LEO RUNS OUT after me, calls my name over and over.

I don't stop.

"I'm so sorry, Linds, I'm so sorry"—he is breathless when he catches up to me—"I thought maybe Zesi could help us look through the security feeds, so I told him in private. I thought I was *helping*, Linds, I thought—"

"I told you that in confidence." I pick up the pace, turn left, on autopilot to the lab at Portside. "I almost didn't even tell *you*. Do you not realize it could be anyone? Someone on this station killed them, Leo, and we can't just go making assumptions about who did or did not do it."

"Zesi seemed safe enough—"

"There's your mistake," I say, whirling to face him. "*No one is safe.*"

"I'm safe," he says. "You know I'm safe."

"Are you? Are you really? Okay, I totally believe you because you *told* me you didn't do it." I'm just spitting fire now, and I know he doesn't deserve this, but he's here and I can't stop. "I honestly know you don't have it in you to *murder* people, Leo, but do you see my point? We don't know anything. Not a single thing. Everything I thought I knew flipped on its head the instant I discovered these deaths happened because someone wanted them dead—we can't afford to make assumptions. We make assumptions, we die."

We stand there, staring at each other, for a single moment—and then he nods, conviction taking over: conviction and determination. Something I said must have clicked.

"Okay," he says. "Okay. What can I do? How can I make this up to you, Linds? I'm so sorry. I get it now. I want to help." A beat passes, a breath. "I'm so sorry I messed this up."

"Search the security feeds all the way back through the night when we first found Mila," I say, despite myself. I want to do this alone, but I can't. I physically, emotionally can't do everything on my own. "Buzz me immediately if you flag anything suspicious."

"You got it."

"And tell Haven to call for a station-wide lockdown, effective immediately. Tell her to have them break off into groups of four—make sure no one's alone and everyone's accounted for. Don't tell them why."

"Will do, Linds."

We linger, long enough for me to think *if he were going to kiss me now, he would have already.*

I'm glad he can read me well enough to know not to try.

Lindley, buzz me back.

Lindley, I know you're seeing these.

Lindley.

LINDLEY.

Haven's messages pile up, one on top of another, but I'm in no mood to talk. I have work to do. I already said all I had to say to Leo—she can call him.

Another message buzzes in on the heels of the last: **If you don't buzz me back in the next five minutes, I'm making an announcement about the water situation without your input whenever I call for the lockdown. I know you want input on this, Lindley, so BUZZ ME BACK.**

I close my eyes, breathe in and out deeply, then tap into the screen.

"I *knew* you were just watching my messages roll in," Haven says, not two seconds later.

"I'm trying to focus over here." I keep my voice even, try to stick to business and not feelings. Haven tends to veer toward feelings more often than not. "As far as the announcement goes, I think it'd be best for you to keep it to a bare minimum."

"Bare minimum, like, 'No more showers, only drink what you need, and by the way, we're all going to die'?"

She can't see my face, and that is a good thing.

"Wow, Lindley, *chill*," she says when I say nothing. "That was a joke. Learn to take one."

"This really isn't the time, okay?" She's *wasting* my time.

And how can anyone joke about *we're all going to die* after everything we've been through? After everything we're still going through? I know some people process stress by turning everything into a joke, but come on.

"I can't believe you seriously thought I'd say that." She sighs, a loud and dramatic thing that scrapes at my ears.

I choose to ignore this direction she's trying to take us, shift back to the announcement. "I definitely think it's a good idea to make an announcement about the water, because we're going to run out soon if we aren't careful—we need everyone's help on this so we can buy time while we figure out a new plan." Perhaps it's time to make a leap of faith onto a burning bridge, attempt to reach out directly to Sergeant Vonn since we still haven't been able to make contact with Nashville. Despite the inevitable fallout that would surely follow—I still believe we'd be trading slow-starved death for a miserable future, and everything in me recoils at the thought—we need to figure something out *today*. If our situation doesn't significantly improve within a few hours, I decide, I'm making that call no matter how resistant I feel to it.

"Tell them water access will be restricted to drinking water only, from now until we tell them otherwise," I continue, before she can get a word in. "Twenty ounces per day, per person, max. Toilets are on their own separate system—tell them to proceed as usual, in case there's any question—but showers take a major toll on the supply. No showers for anyone, and please emphasize that."

I already regret this announcement, because ugh. Talk about unpleasant, being stuck in close lockdown quarters without the luxury of keeping clean. Unpleasant is preferable to dead, though. Unpleasant is preferable to displaced.

Haven makes a noise of disgust on the other end, but doesn't argue. "Do you want me to give them any time frame for when things will go back to normal?"

For *when* things will go back to normal. When, not if.

"Let's not make promises we likely can't keep."

She's quiet, and I have no clue what she might be thinking. Finally, she says: "*We* can take showers, though, right? As long as they're quick?"

I knead my temples. "Haven. No. Seriously?" What part of *we're running out of water* does she not understand?

"I just thought, you know, since we're in charge of things, we might have certain privileges—"

"Listen, I really need to get back to work," I say, putting some bite in my voice. That's the only way this conversation is ever going to end. "I'm not going to tell everyone else they're under water restrictions and then go bend the rules for myself, but if that sits well with your conscience, by all means do it."

She hangs up on me.

It's probably for the best.

46

Q

HAVEN'S VOICE COMES through the speakers not a minute later, a shade dimmer than usual. Will the rest of the station pick up on this subtle change in her, or am I simply hyperaware of it in light of the conversation we just had?

The announcement comes to a blunt end, almost as if Haven's intentionally making our situation sound even more bleak than it is—if that's even possible—just to get a rise out of me. I don't regret what I said, though. We shouldn't bend the rules for ourselves; it's our responsibility to do everything in our power to conserve water while we figure this out. Whatever she feels for me right now, maybe my words will make her think twice. Maybe she'll think about the entire station, not just herself.

Not that I don't get the temptation. Didn't I do the exact same thing just this afternoon? I turned off my buzz screen; I tried to sleep. I took a shower, and not a short one. That was before, though—when we were all riding high on the news of Zesi and Heath's successful mission, when I expected we'd have the new filter installed within hours.

I try to push all these distractions from my mind. Focus on the task at hand. I'm back at Portside now, about to run a fresh series of tests on the hair and saliva samples pulled from Jaako and Kerr. This time, I won't be looking for traces of the virus, but for clues as to what actually killed them. Natalin's words replay in my head: *Maybe you should go get to work on that, Lindley, before anyone else dies?* Her caustic tone is like acid to my bones, eating away at me by the minute. Perhaps it was unfair of her to shove all the weight on my shoulders, but it doesn't make what she said any less true. I *should* get to work. I *could* have a breakthrough, stop this madness before someone else dies.

Hopefully lockdown will help; hopefully it won't backfire somehow. It's not my style to make big decisions on the fly, but at least it's something. Hopefully it will be *enough*.

I don't have confirmation through testing yet, obviously, but I have a strong suspicion about the *how* of these deaths: poison. Mila, Jaako, and Kerr were all covered in bloodbubbles—bloodbubbles that were planted on them, as I've already established—but their bodies were absent of flesh wounds. No signs of a struggle, no bruising, nothing at all except quick, silent death. They could have been asphyxiated, of course, but it's far more difficult to run tests on *absence of breath* than it is *presence of toxins*. If my tests come back true-negative, no poison present, it would be a neon sign pointing to asphyxiation as cause of death. I'm almost rooting for poison, though—one killer could not have suffocated both Jaako and Kerr at the same time.

Asphyxiation would mean *two* killers. Two liars. Twice the level of coordination it would take to commit these murders alone.

So. Systematic toxicological analysis it is.

I wish I hadn't been so quick to blame the virus for everything, because otherwise—if I hadn't skipped the autopsies, if I hadn't already had them burned to ash—I'd skip the hair samples and go straight for their livers. Not that I've had anything but textbook experience with livers; hair can simply be a little less reliable, from what I understand. *Now I know for next time,* I think, before I can stop the thought.

No. There will not *be* a next time.

I prepare the preliminary test to see if my toxin theory holds up; it's a two-step process, the first step a simple screening to identify the presence of drugs or other toxicants on the hair. Unlike so many other lab tests, this one won't make me wait even a minute—it will take less than ten seconds for the scanner to give a simple positive or negative analysis. If positive, I'll move on to the next step, which Dr. Safran simply called Q for its ability to run both qualitative and quantitative analysis at the same time. In other words: Q will tell me exactly which toxin—and exactly how much of it—was present in Jaako and Kerr when they died.

The screener blips red even before the full ten seconds have passed. This . . . can't be good. I run a second test on Kerr's hair, just for the sake of being thorough, and it goes red even quicker this time—not even five full seconds, compared to the eight it took for Jaako's.

Well, that's it. Poisoned, both of them. Mila's results would yield the same, I'd bet anything.

I feel a sharp descent coming on—feel my thoughts start to avalanche—but I try my best to hold it off.

Tests first, theories next. Tests will *inform* the theories.

I run Q on both samples, and for both, the results are clear: Jaako and Kerr were killed by belladonna—by off-the-charts, lethal dosages of it.

And there's only one place on the station the killer could have possibly obtained it.

47

TOXIN

OF ALL THE times I've been to SSL, I've never actually used it as a lab.

That changes now.

I enter my access code—my *meaningless* access code, now that Yuki and Grace and stars know who else have it memorized by heart—and head to its central workstation. The countertops are pristine white, but I'm certain there must be substantial equipment in its various underlying doors and drawers. I'm looking for a tablet—a database system, specifically—that will help me make sense of the forest of glowing pillars and their exact contents. There's nowhere else the killer could have found belladonna; the only other place that's even a remote possibility is Medical, but Dr. Safran never kept anything like that lying around. I checked every cabinet there, just to be sure, but—in keeping with my theory—the cabinets were all clear.

I find what I'm looking for in the third drawer, beside a trio of microscopes: a tablet so thin it could be paper, so inflexible it obviously isn't. I handle it carefully, dust it for fingerprints before I do anything else—

It's clean. Because of course it is.

I pinch the lower right corner and its dark screen blooms to light. My limited options are clearly marked: *Storage Index, Compendium of Botanical Specimens, Calculator, Notepad,* and *Settings.* I tap into the compendium, do a search for belladonna. As I suspected, it's in our system. The entry reads:

> Belladonna (Atropa belladonna):
> Plantae > Angiosperms > Eudicots > Asterids > Solanales > Solanaceae > Atropa > A. belladonna
>
> Belladonna has a tortured history; while its value is primarily medicinal, it is most notorious for its toxic qualities. Primary medical benefits: sedative; remedy for bronchial spasms; common ointment for skin, leg, or joint pain; treatment for excessive sweating. Use with caution, use reliable measuring devices for exact dosages, use only if no better alternative is available.
>
> WARNING: When ingested in heedless proportions, belladonna becomes a deadly poison.
>
> Storage Index: F23

I tap F23, which takes me from the compendium directly to belladonna's entry in the storage index app. Now that I know for sure the belladonna originated here in SSL, the index itself isn't as helpful as a map would be. While I can tell enough from this list that Section F is devoted entirely to medicinal plants, it isn't as easy to figure out how the pillars themselves are arranged in this physical room. There are no signs, just row after row after endless row.

In poking around the index, trying to find a map, I stumble on an answer I hadn't even begun to search for yet—by tapping into F23's index entry, I've accidentally pulled up a request form. Its entry fields prompt me to select a quantity, then manually enter an access code. Instead of filling out the form, however, I tap a small, gray link off to the side: *Activity Log.*

There's only one item in the log. Who knew two tiny words, a timestamp, and an access code could be so chilling? *Six leaves,* it says, and is timestamped four hours prior to Mila's death.

The access code is exactly the same as the only one I know, the one that grants entry to this place.

And suddenly, my hopes flip—whereas just a few days ago, I had hoped Yuki and Grace were the only ones who knew the access code outside our core six, now I hope for the opposite. I hope this knowledge is pervasive, a secret everyone knows but no one talks about.

Otherwise, our list of potential killers officially just took a drastic hit.

Otherwise, our list of potential killers now looks like: Yuki, Grace, and the five people I thought I could trust more than anyone in the entire galaxy.

I hope beyond all hope there is something here I'm missing.

Belladonna's pillar is tucked away in the far recesses of the lab. A few more minutes of tapping around pulled up a map, so now I'm leaning against the window full of stars and staring at the bright pillar, as if it will divulge the secrets I want to know.

It could still be anyone. Yuki and Grace had secret intel, and I had no idea, so who's to say there aren't more people wandering around the station with restricted access codes?

This reasoning brings me no comfort, though. No matter how emphatically I try to preach it to myself, my counter-thoughts are louder and more convincing.

Because, by now, we would have found more people in places they shouldn't be: more people trying to access medicinal herbs for their own stress relief or recreation, more activity in the log than two isolated incidents of belladonna and witch hazel retrievals.

Because Akello Regulus would have used the code to access the lab at Portside that early morning. He wouldn't have been yelling at me through the glass door if he could've slipped inside it instead.

There's always the possibility, of course, that someone I'd never suspect has the code and is simply being extremely careful. If they're thinking enough steps ahead to commit murder with such calculation, it makes sense that they'd be smart enough to cover their tracks.

My head hurts.

As much as I'd rather not think about the most likely suspects, it's time.

I know of eight people who have the access code. Leo and Heath and Haven, Zesi and Natalin. Yuki and Grace. Me.

Unless I have deep repressive issues and have somehow blocked out the planning and execution of *three murders*, I'm ruling myself out.

Yuki and Grace are natural suspects, since they have obvious knowledge of how to get into SSL, and more suspiciously, knowledge of how to retrieve botanical matter from the pillars. They were also missing in the hours after Mila's death—but what about the hours leading up to it? When, precisely, did they leave Mikko's party? Was anyone paying close enough attention to know how long they stayed, and when they left? Even if so, I can't think of a way anyone could provide substantial proof of that information. It would also be good to know what time they arrived at the party—if they were there by 9:13 that night, they couldn't have been retrieving belladonna from SSL at the same time.

Next up: Natalin. Natalin has been overly combative with me lately, but that seems to spring from her intense desire to keep people alive. That's not exactly her entire motivation, though—she also has an intense desire to not be at fault, to shove all responsibility on me. It's possible she's so deeply afraid of how the station will look at her if we run out of food that she resorted to creating a diversion: something even more terrible, something even *more* out of our control, than our supply shortage. And cutting down on the number of people who need food while she's at it? Kind of brilliant. Twisted, yes, but this could be killing two birds with one stone at its finest—exactly the sort of calculation needed to pull these murders off.

As for Zesi—he and Leo were the first to find Jaako and Kerr, after the tip-off from Noël. He was the one to bring me their (potentially tampered-with?) samples, and also the one who discovered Mila in the middle of the night. Even if he didn't have a direct hand in their deaths, he's consistently been the first to uncover the news: I can't think of a more brilliant way to position oneself as blameless than to shine a light on the deaths, to be the first swallowed up by grief and shock. On top of all this, he has intimate knowledge of our tech—he could have tampered with our security vid-feeds, or evaded detection altogether.

Haven, Heath, and Leo: it's most difficult for me to wrap my head around any one of them committing these murders. It's difficult to imagine how—like vines grown from the same soil, under the same sun and the same rain—any one of us could have sprouted, not to mention *hidden*, such a homicidal streak.

It's like slicing off a piece of my own heart to set aside my trust in them, even for this single moment. If I'm honest with myself, though, I will reluctantly admit my trust cracked more than a little when Leo shared with Zesi the things I'd confided in him—and when Heath confessed the truth of his bee crash, a secret he'd hidden for well over a year—and it fractures a little more every time Haven pokes and prods at me about how I'm holding up. Those aren't *murder*-level trust issues, though. Right? Those are *we're supposed to be able to share everything with each other* issues. They're *how can I possibly feel supported by you, Haven, when you constantly make me feel like I'm never enough?* issues.

And yet. I *must* consider them.

No matter how small the break, I can't say with absolute certainty that I know every shade—every shadow—of their hearts. We're all changing, each and every one of us. Every minute since the last of our parents died, every minute we've been stranded up here alone. We are as constant as starlight, yet every bit as unreliable: by the time it's obvious a star has died, it's much too late to prepare yourself for the darkness.

48

FEED AND FIRE

THE SUBTLE VIBRATION of my buzz screen pulls me out of a deep sleep. I'm disoriented at first to find myself on SSL's cold, hard floor, in shadows except for the sliver of light where my skin is kissed by the bright white glow of the nearest pillar.

"Hello?" My voice echoes in this cave of a room.

"Zesi figured it out," Leo says. "He figured out some way to adapt the connection, and it's genius, Linds—he fixed it, and it works!" His words fly past, light-years per minute.

"Leo—*Leo*. Slow down." Finally, he falls silent on the other end. "What's *it*?"

"The filter," he says. "He successfully installed it and we won't have to ration like we thought we would! Not as much, anyway."

Now I'm awake. "Wait, seriously?" I'm sitting straight up now. "This is huge."

"Right? He turned the mech room upside down, ended up finding some spare odds and ends in one of the drawers." Leo's energy is palpable, contagious. I'm on my feet in an instant, pacing the length of the panoramic window full of stars.

It's almost unbelievable, to have a crisis just be . . . solved. Nothing else has gone the way it should, so this news is an enormous relief. Not just for the station, what this means for us, but for the state of my own parched hope—we are not terrifyingly low on clean water, and we may not have to reach out for Vonn's help after all! Things have spiraled for so long now it's like I started believing *wrong* was the only way things could go.

"This is . . . this is incredible."

"Yeah, at least that's one thing we don't have to worry about," he says.

"My thoughts, too." And just like that, my joy deflates. One crisis averted, a thousand other things still spinning out of control. "Did you have any luck searching the vid-feeds?"

Leo is dead silent on the other end of the line.

"Leo? You still there?"

"I'm still here," he says, his voice heavy, a complete one-eighty from just two seconds ago. "Trying to figure out how to tell you there's absolutely nothing we can use on the feeds, and in fact, there are a few very significant and suspicious gaps in the footage."

I stop pacing. I am a still shadow against infinite starlight. "I'm sorry, what did you just say?"

He's speaking again now, but all I hear in my head is a blur of panic—he said there's nothing we can use on the feeds, but he's wrong. The fact that there are gaps in the footage *is* something we can use.

But it is the exact opposite of what I wanted to hear.

It is what I've dreaded most, what I didn't want to believe was possible: it's simply too much of a stretch to believe that Yuki or Grace would have been able to sneak into Control without any of us noticing, too much of a stretch that they'd know how to access the vid-feeds in the first place, let alone *alter* them.

The killer was one of us.

The killer
is
one of *us*.

"I, um—I need a minute, okay, Leo? I'll talk to you later." I cut the call short before he can get a single word in.

To his credit, he gives me the space I need. And I do need it—this changes everything. There are only two people who could have altered the feeds in plain sight, and I was just on a call with one of them. Surely Leo wouldn't—*couldn't* have—

Right?

I trusted *him* to go through the feeds, checking for anything suspicious—but what if he spent all this time cutting himself out of the footage so we wouldn't have any incriminating evidence? He was alone up there, too, since Zesi apparently spent the last stretch of time working on fixing our filter.

And speaking of Zesi: this drastically shifts my perspective on his miraculous water filter fix. What if the filter was never a poor fit at all, but he made it *look* like a problem just so he could come in and save the day by "fixing" it? He could have altered the vid-feeds at any time prior to now. I do think he would've been more careful about it, though—he's usually pretty precise at everything he does—but perhaps there's just no elegant way to avoid an obvious splice when removing bits of timestamped footage. Add to that, whoever did it was probably in a hurry.

This isn't to say it could *only* be Zesi or Leo—all of us have had a primer on the vid-feeds, and all of us are decent with the tech in general, thanks to an involved tour of Control Zesi gave us when we first stepped up to lead. Again, though, that points me back to Zesi: Could he have been preparing, even then, to *murder* our people? Could he have been laying groundwork that early to cover his tracks, so it wouldn't be a giant neon arrow over his head when we began to investigate? And—*and*—if he had it in him to poison three of our population, what's to say he wouldn't eventually move on to a much larger scale: we've entrusted him with our water supply, but what if this "fix" was also an excuse to tamper with the water itself? What if our station-wide water supply is laced with belladonna now—what then?

I feel like I'm losing my mind. Like there is no gravity, no sun, no oxygen—like I can't trust my own judgment, or my own memories.

Hope and fear can only coexist as equals for so long before one devours the other.

I only pray the fear will starve when it runs out of crumbs.

49

CATWALK, TIGHTROPE

HOW DO YOU hide, forever, in a place like this?

Where the walls feel like they're closing in—

Where beyond the walls is a suffocating void: from the safe side of the windows, the glittering starlit space is more majesty than instant death—but the safe side of the windows has become every bit as risky.

How do I hide?

If I hide, I'll starve or get trapped in my head, running blind on an endless dark loop. If I hide, I die anyway.

These are my three options: venture beyond *Lusca*'s walls out into the void of space; simply continue on as I always have; never leave my unit again. Two of these hold certain death—are those preferable to the one that comes with betrayal? Secrecy? Manipulation? Death after death after death, all illogical and completely avoidable?

Unfortunately, the option that terrifies me most is the only one that holds a chance at survival.

The water might be perfectly fine, I tell myself.

The water might be perfectly fine.

I can test it in the lab, prove it's safe to drink. But how long do I have before we stumble upon another dead body? Or a *lot* of dead bodies, if the entire supply has been tainted?

I rummage around the drawers in SSL and grab an empty test tube, along with a cork I hope will fit—we've had issues with these tubes in the past, so delicate they crack when corked. Carefully, I fill the tube with water from the lab's tap, then ease the cork into place. The glass holds.

Halfway to Portside, I decide to take a detour down to the hydro chamber. A series of panels near the filter console gives a constant read on the mineral levels in our water supply—they wouldn't necessarily inform me of the presence of belladonna there, but if the levels show any abnormalities, that could be a clue. Aside from that, I simply want to make sure the sample I pulled from the tap is water from the filter Zesi installed, not the little bit left over from before. Each orb self-sanitizes before refilling with water, so it should be fairly easy to tell if my sample came from the dregs of Orb 5 or from full-to-the-brim Orb 1; if there's any water left at all in Orb 5, my lab test will be useless until I can get some that's been through the filter Zesi installed.

I tap in my code, and the door zips open—but I'm stopped dead in my tracks when I hear a pair of hushed voices, sandpaper voices that rub roughly against each other.

The argument cuts off abruptly; their echoes take longer to die. My paranoia crescendos to worst-case scenario in a heartbeat. Anyone outside our core group should be in their cabins on lockdown right now.

"Hello?" I call.

No use pretending I haven't interrupted. They know I'm here—well, they know *someone* is here. I can't see them from where I stand, but that doesn't mean they can't see me. And if they can see me, that's an advantage I'd like to take away. If I've stumbled onto something—if they think I've overheard things I shouldn't—

Now does not seem like the time to place myself in anyone's crosshairs.

"Lindley?"

A wave of relief washes over me. "Heath?"

It's only Heath . . . and . . . who? My relief is quickly chased by a wave of suspicion. What is Heath doing in the hydro chamber? And since when does he get into heated arguments with people?

"Yeah, over here," he says.

I follow the catwalk around toward his voice, find him sitting like Haven and I did earlier, beside . . . Natalin?

My eyes dart back and forth between them. Heath and Natalin? Heath . . . and Natalin. I can't think of a single time I've ever seen them pair off on their own.

Maybe it's because they only pair off in secret. Sort of like now.

I could sit here all day trying to read between the lines, or I could attack the question head-on. What would my mother do?

My mother wouldn't waste her own time or anyone else's.

"Am I interrupting something?"

They exchange a glance, like they're each waiting for the other to start talking. The silence stretches on. Heath rips at his thumbnail with his teeth.

"Seriously, guys." I sharpen my glare, though neither will look at me. "What's going on?"

Every second they don't speak, my suspicion ticks up a notch. Every second they don't speak, I wonder if they—

"It's the food," Heath finally says. "After *all* that, after we risked our effing lives for them, no one will *eat* it because *someone* let it slip that it may be contaminated."

"I did not let anything *slip*," Natalin shoots back before I can get a word in. "It isn't my fault Evi and Elise overheard me talking with Haven—"

"If you're going to let them live with you, you're going to have to figure out how to keep confidential information *confidential*, Natalin." I've never seen Heath so full of pent-up fury. There's a reason he took on the role of peacemaker, peacekeeper: he isn't often moved to anger like this.

I bite down on my temper before it flares. "Evi and Elise know enough to know the food could be contaminated—they don't know why, right? They don't know . . . about *Nautilus*, do they?"

"They know everything," Heath says, eyes trained on Natalin; she dips her head, lets her long, dark hair fall like a curtain between them. Heath shifts his eyes to me. "They. Know. Everything."

Blackness creeps in at the edge of my vision, panic closing in on me. I take a breath. "*Everything*, everything?" That all our recent deaths—that there was no mutation at fault, at least for those—that they were all—

"They overheard me talking to Haven about the food, that's all," Natalin says, as if my thoughts had been tattooed on my face. There's no sting to her words for once; she only sounds tired. "They know we were running out. They know how we got more. They know everyone on *Nautilus* is dead, and they're afraid of dying, too." She kneads her temples. "And they messaged someone about all of these things, probably a lot of someones, and basically . . . now everyone knows."

"And no one will eat," Heath says.

"Yeah." Natalin tucks her hair behind her ear, eyes sparkling in the electric white light of Orb 2. "It's . . . a problem." I've never seen her this close to cracking before, never seen her this raw.

"This . . . ," I begin, but quickly find I'm at a loss for words—there are too many places to start. "This is everything we've been trying to avoid. I mean, exactly how bad is it? *Everyone* knows—*no one* will eat—you've got to be exaggerating, right? There are just a few friends that Evi and Elise told who are being a little pickier than normal—right?" I sound slightly unhinged, even to myself, but can't slow my voice down, can't keep it from rising. "Please tell me it isn't as bad as it sounds."

"I'm *sorry*, Lindley—I—"

"You what?" I snap. "You forgot you had two nine-year-olds living with you? You forgot they could understand every word you say? How could you be so *careless*? What else have they overheard?"

"Linds . . . ," Heath says, like I should stop. Like I should've stopped much earlier.

"No. Don't tell me this isn't a big deal—"

"Linds, I agree with you. I *agree*," Heath says. "It is a *huge* deal, but blaming Nat isn't going to help anything."

"Like you have room to talk? Didn't I just walk in on you arguing about the exact same things?"

Heath recoils. "You have no idea what you overheard."

"Care to enlighten me?"

Heath stands now, makes me feel small by the way he towers a foot taller than me. Natalin sits still as a statue, her cheeks wet with tears. I can't remember ever seeing her cry before. Perhaps I should have swallowed some of those words after all.

"None of us are perfect, Linds." Heath's eyes flicker in the light, searching mine. "Not one of us." There are a million shades in his gray irises, like: Anger. Forgiveness. Frustration. Patience. Panic. Hope. Exhaustion.

None of us are perfect.

You're *not perfect*, I hear.

How does he do it? How does he always *know*?

I'm not perfect. I desperately wish I were.

"We have to do what we can, okay?" He's softer now, but no less intense. "We've gotta move on and work with what we've got."

It's not lost on me that he still hasn't answered my question about what exactly I've just walked in on.

I let it go. For now.

"I shouldn't have gone off on you like that, Natalin." My words echo, echo, die.

"I don't want them to starve." Her voice is a dull knife, twisting. "I would never have compromised that information on purpose."

"I know," I say.

Because I want to believe her. Because I know, more than anything, that I'm giving everything I have to keep as many people alive as possible. Because I want to believe she and I aren't so different at the core—that we clash so often because we both care passionately about the station, and our passion takes an equal-but-opposite approach. I want to believe her. I do.

But the truth is, I *don't* know.

I'm halfway around the catwalk, trying to sneak a secret glance at the water panels before I leave, when Natalin calls out: "What are you doing with the test tube, by the way?"

I think fast, fast. "Running levels on the water, just to make sure the filter's working properly and we're all clear to drink it." True enough. I'm not about to tell her what I'm *specifically* testing for—even if I did trust her fully, it seems unwise to stress her out about the water when people are already refusing the food.

"Didn't Zesi already double-check all of that?" she pushes back. "He tinkered with things for a good ten minutes after he got the filter to work."

I adjust my hairpins, smooth down the nonexistent flyaway wisps. Is she trying to keep me from running another test? Did Zesi really spend ten minutes checking levels, or did he spend some of that time lacing the water with poison? Or—did *Natalin* put something in the water, after Zesi had finished? Did Heath help her?

Surely not, right?

"We can never be too sure," I say, giving her a tight-lipped grin. "Better safe than sick." *Or dead*, I think.

"You're wasting everyone's time," Natalin says, "running the same tests twice instead of trusting that Zesi did it right in the first place."

"You're really going to lecture me about trust right now?" I struggle to tame my voice, to keep it from flaring like it did before. I . . . don't succeed. "You couldn't even keep confidential information to yourself, Natalin, and now it's spread like wildfire through the station. You want me to trust someone did his job the right way, when we've *just* established that none of us are perfect? I don't think so." A buzz comes in, and it's persistent, but I ignore it. "You're right, though, it is a waste of everyone's time. I really should be figuring out how to feed everyone, since you royally screwed up and no one will eat."

She doesn't deny it. She doesn't say anything, and neither does Heath. I take the merciful silence, check the levels on the filter panels like I came down here to do, even though everything is a blur right now and I'm shaking.

Losing control, as it turns out, is a fast track to feeling worse, not better. A lump crawls into my throat, curls up there. I can't even bring myself to apologize, the pride—fear—embarrassment—is so thick. My buzz screen vibrates again, but I just . . . I can't.

I blink back my tears. Try to make sense of the panels. All the numbers, all the charts: they look just as they should. Nothing overtly out of normal range, no blood-red WARNING notifications.

My buzz screen goes off for the third time, and finally, I answer: it's Haven. "Hey," I say. "Everything okay?"

For all her urgency in trying to get through, she's quiet on the other end. "Haven?"

"We—we're all trying not to add more to your plate right now," she says, which is news to me. "But . . . you should know . . . there's been another one." She pauses for a second, for two more. "Another death."

The news knocks the wind out of me. When will this end?

I'm quiet, and for once, Haven doesn't press me. Vaguely, I'm aware of Heath in the background, and of Natalin. *Who?* Heath is saying, and Natalin: *In the mezzanine—and there's already a crowd?* They're not talking to each other. Both are pacing, hands to their ears. On calls of their own, with Leo and Zesi, presumably.

"In the mezzanine?" I ask Haven, and she affirms it. So much for our lockdown—it's not quite as effective if people choose to do their own thing and ignore it. I take a deep breath, squeeze my eyes shut. "I'll be there in five."

50

LIVING IN NIGHTMARES

INDIGO SUTTON: ANOTHER new name on the list. Another new body, undisturbed, when the six of us arrive.

Though the mezzanine is full—practically everyone on the station is here, defying the lockdown order, to a party none of us were invited to—I've never seen it so silent. It's like the life slipped out of everyone all at once, not just the thin frame lying motionless on the floor in the center of some invisible circle no one dares to breach.

It's not hard to piece together what the scene must have looked like just minutes ago. Half-empty liquor bottles— and *empty*-empty liquor bottles—stand in silent judgment all around the room; there are innumerable shot glasses and too-full tumblers and not a piece of food anywhere in sight.

"Have you all had a good night?" I scan the room, meeting as many eyes as possible before they turn down toward the floor. "Did the vodka take the edge off?" More eyes avoid mine.

I'm dangerously close to losing it on the entire station, just like I lost it on Natalin. Deep breaths: one, two, three. Four.

One breath for every one of us who no longer breathes.

I cross the invisible barrier, kneel to examine the body.

A single glance is all it takes to realize: this death is not like the others. I don't even have to run tests to confirm it—I will, of course, but I don't *have* to. There are no bloodbubbles, no *Nautilus*-style nosebleeds, no pretense of virus-related cause. This is what happens when fear turns to escapism turns to too much to drink, in too small a body, with too little food to offset it. It is a poisoning, but not the kind I feared, I'm almost sure of it: this is chaos in motion.

We're all losing it a little. We're all losing it a *lot*.

I open my mouth to speak but can't find the words or the breath or the anything I need to reassure them this is all going to be *okay*, because I'm not sure it is, and I'm not sure it will ever be, and shouldn't I have all the answers? Shouldn't they have someone who can give them the peace they need—the peace they deserve?

I want to.

I want to.

Haven clears her throat. "We're going to get through this." I immediately recognize this as her *good morning* voice, her *let's start the day right!* voice. Fortunately, it is tempered to minimal brightness, the perfect mix of hope and realism that even I need right now.

If I can't give them what they need in this dark moment, perhaps Haven can. Normally, it would irritate me to have her step in like this—to give a statement when I, their acting commander, should be the one doing it.

Right now, all I am is relieved.

"We've been living in nightmares lately, every single one of us," she goes on. One by one, people begin to look up. Look at Haven—like they couldn't look at me. "It's time to *wake up*. Do you want to end up like this?" She gestures to Indigo's lifeless body in front of us. Gives us a minute to see her, really *see* her:

Indigo, with her long black hair and long black lashes and lips that always had a kind word for everyone—with her beautiful voice, often found singing in harmony with Sailor Salvato as he played his guitar in the alcove. I scan the room, find Sailor in the crowd. His face is all numb shock.

"Do you want to end up like this?" Haven repeats. "Like Indigo?" Her words hang in the air. "Do you think we put you on lockdown for no reason? Are you *trying* to die?"

"We're not trying to die." A deep voice speaks up from the far side of the room. Jono Deering: everything about him is exaggerated, from his height to his long black bangs to the kohl he uses to line his piercing green eyes. "We're only trying to forget."

"Try a little more responsibly next time," Leo says, and not gently. His voice catches me off guard; I didn't realize he was so close behind me.

The words are incendiary, flame to a fuse: everyone erupts at once.

Who gave you *all the power?*

Is it true we can't eat the food?

Is it true Mila died from the mutation? What about Jaako? Kerr?

Is it true is it true is it true

Is it true

Is it true

Is it?

Each voice is a hammer to my skull, driving nails down deep to where they stab at my conscience. I want to shout *NO—no, it is NOT true! None of those things are true!*

But then I'd be forced to tell them what is.

They aren't ready.

I'm not ready.

A small voice in my head, pinned to death by the sharp tip of a nail, whispers: *You'll never be ready. You're not meant to be ready for something like this. Serialized murder is not a thing that should happen.*

So what am I waiting for?

If I'm honest, I want to fix it without them ever having to know the truth. Without them ever having to know this *fear.* This heartbreak. Because it *is* heartbreak: whoever is doing this simply would not have done it before. The virus broke us all, when it comes down to it, some more than others. This . . . what's happening now . . . it's like a *heartbreak* virus: when one heart breaks, it wants company, so it breaks another—which in turn breaks more—and more—and on and on from there. We all end up cracked.

"I'll try it," Haven says, her voice cutting through the noise in my head and outside it. "Someone bring me a couple of pouches of *Nautilus* food, and I'll try it, right here in front of you all. This paranoia needs to end, or else you're all going to starve."

Natalin throws a grateful look her way. I wish I'd thought of the idea, but at least one of us did. This is good—this is a start.

I volunteer to retrieve a sampling for her just so I can get out of the mezzanine for a few minutes, walk off my nerves that are so on edge. What I don't count on is how they insist I take someone with me—anyone who is not in our core six—as witness, to prove I've actually pulled the food in question from the *Nautilus* supplies and not from a high corner of our own pantry. A petite girl named Story Lutheborough, with delicate dark skin and bouncy curls and bright-eyed wonder despite all that has happened—*how?*—steps up to join me.

We set off together, quick steps through empty corridors, to retrieve a meal from the storage pantry where the *Nautilus* crates are stowed, as informed by Natalin. I can tell Story wants to take advantage of our alone time—prod me with questions, pry the truth out with sheer persistence—but, to her credit, she reads me well enough not to. To *my* credit, I'm in full commander mode right now: shoulders back, eyes trained on the path ahead, unsmiling. I make myself a wall, and it works. No use throwing pebbles at iron and expecting it to collapse.

I let her choose Haven's meal. All the options look the same, really, in their SpaceLove packaging, each stamped with *NAUTILUS SHIPMENT 1032C-2B* in gray-purple ink. She plucks a crowd favorite from the shelf, mashed sweet potato, along with a notoriously disgusting smoothie made of beet, parsley, spirulina, wheatgrass, carrot, celery, and spinach.

"Let's get this over with," Haven says as soon as we return, and I couldn't agree more. I need to get to toxicology as soon as possible, need to take care of Indigo's body before too much time passes.

Everyone watches eagerly as Haven eats the potatoes straight from the pouch, ingesting half the contents in a single squeeze. Story massages the smoothie pouch—as if that will help its texture or flavor at all—before handing it over.

I'm sure not even Haven likes this particular combination, but it's obvious she's determined to take it in and keep it down. "See?" she says, after a forced swallow. "Not terrible." A couple of fourteen-year-olds nearby stifle drunken giggles; Natalin cuts her eyes at them and the giggles come to an abrupt stop.

Haven gulps down the rest of the smoothie before she can think twice about it. When she's finished, she hands the empty pouches back to Story. "Show them," Haven tells her.

"*Nautilus* shipment," Story reads. Her voice is loud and clear, unexpectedly authoritative for such a young person, and for such a small frame. And *lucid*—no way she could've been drinking as much as the others tonight. Nice to know we're not all spiraling in self-destructive ways. "And"—she squeezes both pouches, holds them up on display—"she downed all the food."

This seems to satisfy the crowd, so I step in for an announcement before they start to disperse. "We're going to need you all to keep clear of the mezzanine for the rest of the night so we can . . . take care of things," I say. "If any of you would like dinner, you know where to find it—find Natalin if you have any issues with the dispensers in your cabins. And I know we're having a rough season right now, but please, everyone—please take care of yoursel—"

A loud *thwack* cuts me off: Haven.

She's passed out cold, and she's hit the floor hard. The barest rivulet of blood seeps out from where her temple connected, starts to pool, dyes her golden-blonde waves dark red.

"Everyone out," I say, tears springing to my eyes despite my increasingly complicated relationship with Haven. "Everyone *out!*"

But no one moves.

Everyone is slack-jawed and gaping for one single second as we all realize, collectively: we're screwed.

"NOW!" I yell, putting some grit into my voice. Heath and Zesi and Leo herd them out the various exits; Natalin kneels down beside me, beside Haven. She's not dead—not *yet*, anyway—and the bleeding doesn't look as bad as it did with the initial shock, once I take a closer look.

But.

This.

Is.

The.

Last.

Thing.

We.

Need.

"Do you know how to fix this?" Natalin asks, her face drained of all color. "Is it . . . fixable?"

Nothing else seems to be, I want to say.

"Get a gurney, get her to Medical. Get the guys to help." It's as much of an answer as I can give. I sift through the litany of first-aid procedures I memorized years ago, at Dr. Safran's insistence. "Find a clean cloth—rip a shirt apart if you have to—and press it to the wound for the next fifteen minutes at least. And don't use your bare hands, there are latex gloves in Portside, have Leo run for them while Zesi and Heath get the gurney." I rattle off instructions, while at the same time running scenarios in my head on how to treat the injury. She passed out *before* she hit her head, so her lack of consciousness isn't necessarily a sign of a concussion—and the wound does look relatively small, even though it is in a sensitive place. I think a bit of antiseptic and a few stitches with a sterilized needle will go a long way. As for what made her pass out in the first place . . . I wish I had an easy answer.

"Okay," Natalin says, hands shaking. She looks around for help, some sort of reassurance, but the guys are still herding away the last of the gawking onlookers. "Okay, we can do this. I can do this."

I leave her, alone with the dead and the bleeding, trusting that she and Leo and Heath and Zesi will get the job done.

I'm halfway up to Medical when I come out of crisis-mode fog and I realize: I've just put a world's worth of trust in my short list of murder suspects.

51

A SEA OF THORNS AND GLASS

I DO MY best to block out how little time I have to prepare, how very many urgent things I'll need to take care of once I finish stitching Haven's wound. I set my buzz notifications to *do not disturb*, just for now, so I can focus while I work on her. Seconds blur to minutes, chaos blurs to blackness. By the time Zesi and Heath deliver Haven to me on that wretched squeaky-wheeled gurney, my focus is as narrow and sharp as the needle in my hand.

"Do . . . you need any help, Linds?" Heath looks as shell-shocked as I feel, eyes tired from taking in blast after merciless blast.

"Not a two-person job," I say. "But thanks."

He wants to say something else, I can tell—he hesitates, lips slightly parted like there are words on the tip of his tongue—but then his mouth falls shut. He dips his head. "Need anything, just let us know, okay?"

I give him a tight-lipped smile, the best I can muster. I'm not in the mood for small talk, or a pep talk, or any kind of talk—I just want to get this over with already. Heath and Zesi take the hint, leave without another word.

"Okay, Haven," I whisper, when it's just me and her unconscious body, which looks too much like death. "I'm going to get you through this." I slip a tiny tablet into her mouth, under her tongue, count to ten while it dissolves; this way, she won't wake when my needle pierces her skin.

I clean the wound, dab at the blood, which has already started to dry. The antiseptic has a strong chemical smell that brings me straight back to the day Dr. Safran first taught me how to stitch a person up. It seems like a lifetime ago that he was here with me, right in this very room, guiding my every move. My hands trembled viciously that night I first learned—we'd just sterilized the wound and were about to stitch up a six-foot-six tech who'd had a bad run-in with a low steel beam. *Count to five, and slowly,* Dr. Safran told me. I did as he said, and it worked, my hands steadying with each passing second.

Today I pass five—and ten—and fifteen—before the shaking stops.

I make careful stitches with the curved needle, a perfect row of *x*'s sewn in dark navy thread. It isn't a deep wound, and it isn't a terribly long one, either—a few minutes later, the job is done. Haven breathes lightly, looking more like a sleeping princess now that I've cleaned her up. She'll wake when the meds I gave her wear off.

If only I could solve all our problems so neatly: focus, plan, fix.

While she's out, I take the opportunity to swab inside her mouth. If what happened to her is at all related to the strain that took *Nautilus* out, it should show up in test results. She didn't get a nosebleed, though—and even though it looks like the deaths over there happened more immediately than the ones here, her collapse seems like it was a little *too* immediate. I prepare the test using Dr. Safran's equipment, right here in Medical. Sit. Wait.

I lean my elbows on the cool metal of the gurney, rest my head in my palms. What are we going to do? No way our people will eat the *Nautilus* food now, not after what happened with Haven—even if the test comes back clean, I doubt I'll be able to convince them it's fine. We'll have to stretch what little food we have left from our own shipment. And I still haven't had a chance to run labs on the *water* sample yet—what if it's tainted? The panels looked promising back in the hydro chamber, but if there's anything today taught me, appearances aren't reliable. Story picked those pouches out from the shelf right before my eyes, and they looked fine to both of us, unexpired with an unbroken seal. *Something* happened with the food, no question there. Maybe she just got a bad batch, and took it all in too quickly? Can a person pass out from simply being so disgusted that their body overcompensates to block all memories of it happening?

Maybe it really is time to swallow my pride. It seemed like such a risk before to reach out to Vonn—but at this point, what *isn't*? He could bring another shipment. Our people would eat it, I'm certain of it, because if the station on Radix is all alive and well, their food can't possibly be contaminated. I was afraid of looking weak before, of looking like we can't run the station every bit as well as our parents did—

But, well.

We're doing our best. It isn't enough.

I'm doing my best and there's still a *serial killer* within our walls. I've dreamed, for so long, of running the station every bit as well as my mother did—I've dreamed of earning my place.

I never dreamed of this.

There's a light knock on the glass behind me. I look over my shoulder, see that Heath has returned. He makes a motion, like *Mind if I join you?*

I'm too tired to tell him no.

Heath slips through the doors after I wave him in, and retrieves Medical's second silver stool. Dr. Safran preferred that one, even though they're practically identical—the only difference is that the wheels on his are worn down to the quick from years of use. I haven't touched it since he passed.

"How're you holding up?" Heath asks, pulling the stool close to mine. Not *too* close. Just close.

"I . . ." I look around the sterile room, look for answers on the walls. The walls are blank.

All I want is to know I can trust Heath, to know I can trust *everyone* again. That, and I want the memory of him and Natalin, there in the hydro chamber, gone from my mind. *You have no idea what you overheard*, Heath snapped at me, just before we rushed off to the mezzanine.

"Linds?"

His eyes are like fire turned to ashes. I've never seen him look this . . . defeated.

"I'm sorry," he begins. A second passes where he can't meet my eyes; when he looks back at me again, they're sparkling and sad. "In the hydro chamber—what you heard—Natalin was trying to convince me you could handle the truth, all of it." His gaze drops again, and this time, it stays there. "I didn't think it was a good idea. I'm sorry, Linds. I know you're stronger than that. I just—I didn't want you to break, is all, and I thought maybe it'd be best if we just tried to handle things ourselves." His fingers tap a slow, nervous rhythm on the gurney near a wave of his sister's silky blonde hair.

"*That's* what you were arguing about?" Haven's odd comment makes much more sense—*We're all trying not to add more to your plate right now*, she'd said. "Does *everyone* think they need to walk on eggshells around me?" I struggle to keep my voice from shaking, from rising. It's hard enough to admit to myself that I might not be strong enough or smart enough or *enough* enough to save my people.

It's another thing entirely to hear it from Heath: that he thinks I'm breaking, break*able*. So much so that they need to hide the truth.

"I'm sorry, Lindley. You've just been through so much lately, and putting so much pressure on yourself—" He cuts himself off with a rough exhale. "We thought we could fix things without you having to stress about it."

And just like that, the sharp blade of my own logic cuts clean through my heart: Have I not been doing the exact same thing?

I didn't want the station to panic, so I hid the truth. I thought I could fix everything before they ever had to know there was even a problem.

But people have died under my watch—and not from the virus. *Four* people have died.

I've been operating under the assumption that I'd only make things worse if I told them the truth, but perhaps that isn't the case at all. Perhaps they'd be alert, not more reckless. Perhaps the deaths would stop entirely if the murderer knew so many eyes were trained toward suspicious behavior.

"I committed myself to this sort of stress when I stepped up as commander," I say. "I *asked* for it."

Heath nods, presses his lips into a thin line.

"What?"

His buzz screen vibrates, but he silences it at once. For another brief second, he hesitates, then says, "It's just—none of us knew what we were getting into, Linds. It's *okay* to feel out of your depth, you know?"

"Is it? Is it *really*?" I close my eyes, but all I see is Indigo's face, her body still and unmoving on the mezzanine's cold, hard floor. Nothing left but her empty, blank stare. "I can't solve a problem if I don't know it exists," I say. "And I appreciate the sentiment, but from now on, please pass it on that *I* decide when I'm out of my depth." He suddenly feels far too close, even though he hasn't budged a centimeter since sitting down beside me. I stand, pace to the far side of the room, busy myself with Haven's test results. They're as clean as my lab on a stressful day, which should be good—*great!*—except that I still have no idea what could've made her pass out. Added to that, clean lab work doesn't necessarily rule out the possibility of a new strain being present on our station; it only means Haven's collapse was not the result of one.

I just want answers. I want *easy*. I close my eyes, grip the counter's ledge until I feel my fingertips go numb.

"*We* can't solve problems *we* don't know exist, either, you know." His voice is like shattered glass—broken, and with the sharpest edges. "You tell Leo your secrets, but you can't tell me? You can trust me, you *know* you can. Let me help, Linds."

I *am* out of my depth. Far, far out of my depth. Drowning, nearly.

But I can't afford to trust anyone but myself. If I ask for help—in solving the murders, particularly—how do I know I'm not asking *the killer* for help? I don't. Confiding my suspicions would only give the killer inside knowledge, an advantage in how to further avoid being found out.

Part of me wants to sit back on my stool, let him see every fear and every worry, talk his ear off for hours in strategy.

When this is all over, I'll ask his forgiveness. He'll understand why I can't tell him, he will. He'll *have* to. I hope.

I can't meet his eyes. "I shouldn't have even told Leo," I say, keeping my voice even. This is a prime example of how I can't assume anyone is a safe place for my trust, not even my closest friends: Leo spilled the most sensitive secret I ever told him, and now Heath—good intentions notwithstanding—has wrapped a thorny layer of guilt around the burdens I'm carrying.

He starts to speak, but I change the subject abruptly before he can begin. "I'm going to put a call in to Vonn tonight. I think it's time we take them up on those supplies from Radix."

"But aren't you worried—"

"Stay here with Haven until she wakes up," I say, speaking right over him. "Send me a buzz when she's up, or else I'll worry. Shouldn't be more than half an hour."

"Linds—"

"Thanks for checking on me, Heath. We'll talk more later, I promise."

I slip out of Medical without a backward glance. I'm headed to Control, about to do the thing I swore I'd never do: ask that the man who showed less than zero respect to my mother please send help.

We may be indebted to him forever, and I may sacrifice my dignity, but at least we'll be *alive*.

52

HALF-GLOW

THE SMELL OF days-old coffee hits me full force as the doors to Control slide open. Leo must've left the auxiliary lights on when he was here last; they bathe everything in a dim half-glow that makes the room feel like it's on its dying breaths.

Something about the half-light, and the stale smell, and the stillness of this silence, digs under my skin like splintered glass. All at once, I realize: *there is no going back.* There is no *like before.*

No amount of effort to save the station—if I can even manage *that* at this point—can bring Lieutenants Brady and Black back to their places at the Control deck. No amount of effort can rewind time, send us hurtling down a path far away from the nightmare we've been living in.

Nothing can bring back my mother.

I close my eyes, try for just a few seconds to remember what it felt like to have her here, to not have death shadowing my every move. Time ticks by as I grasp at ghosts: Hers. Mine.

When all of this settles, will I ever feel truly alive again?

Not *when,* I correct myself. *If.*

What would my mother think of my decision to reach out for help from Vonn? It feels like a betrayal, in a way. Like all of her sleepless nights, and all of her stubborn resolve, were for nothing: like in one swift call, I'd be saying *You were right all along, Vonn. We'd be nothing without you.* I can't help but think about how he may help us live but would never let us live it down.

In desperation, though, I think my mother would arrive at the same conclusion I have: saving lives is more important than saving pride.

I slide onto a metal stool, identical to the ones we have in Medical, and roll over to the panel deck's message screen. I mentally prepare myself for the call as I pull up the directory, hope the systems on Radix have better connectivity than the ones down in Nashville. But as I swipe past our call history, I notice three new calls in the log—three new calls from Shapiro! I take a closer look: they're all dated today, just this past half hour, two of them flagged as *missed*. The third is timestamped at three minutes long.

He's alive—Shapiro is *alive*!

And this is *not* the way I should be finding out about it. My blood goes from relief to simmer to boil in an instant. I buzz Leo immediately, without hesitation. As far as I know, he's the only one who's been around Control today, to look over the vid-feeds.

"Why didn't you tell me you'd spoken with Shapiro?" My words are a swarm of wasps before he even says hello. "I shouldn't be finding this out from a blasted communications log, Leo. You know how anxious I've been to get in touch with him!"

"He'd called twice before—twice in a row—"

"That's when you call *me*. Not him."

Leo's exhale crackles loudly in my ear. "You were stitching Haven up when he called, Linds, and I panicked, okay? I tried buzzing Heath to see if he could let you know, but he didn't answer, so eventually I just picked up."

"You could have at least sent me a message."

"I *did*."

I don't believe him—but when I check, sure enough, there it is: **Shapiro calling. Should I answer or wait for you?** Looks like I completely forgot to switch off *do not disturb*. Fortunately, it doesn't look like I missed anything else.

"He was only calling to check in on us, that's *it*. But he asked to speak with . . . with your mother?"

The bottom drops out of my stomach. "And what did you tell him?" I say carefully.

Leo's not the only one who's been less than honest. I should have told him the truth about the conversation I had with Shapiro. I should have told *Shapiro* the truth. I would have, if I'd gotten the chance.

"I told him she was unavailable. That's it, I swear, Linds." He waits a beat, then adds, "What did *you* tell him?"

I bite my lip. "I told him I was her."

He's quiet on the other end. He doesn't heap burning coals on my head, like: *How could you?* or *How could you keep that from me?* He doesn't drag me through fire.

He must know he has no room to talk. He really could have tried harder than just sending me a single text half an hour ago.

"So that's it, then?" I ask when he doesn't offer any more. "Did he ask you to pass her a message?" It doesn't sit quite right, that he'd call three times in a row after such an ominous stretch of silence, ask for my mother, and say nothing else. I told him we were holding up well, last we spoke—and would he not trust my mother's word implicitly?

Of course, he's probably been every bit as worried about us as I've been about them—and he'd be right to be worried. He doesn't even know the half of it.

My heart twists at the thought of Shapiro finding out my mother is dead. Not just because there will surely be consequences for my lies, but because I know how it feels to be wrung out by grief. Of blood and sweat and tears running dry—like life is being drained, leaving nothing behind but dust—because how can you go on like today is just any other day when she *can't*? When she never will again?

"He didn't leave a message, no," Leo says. I hear a noise in the background, steel scraping steel, and then a resounding thud.

"What was that?"

"That was Zesi attempting to move Indigo Sutton without my help." He cuts himself off abruptly, then says, "Wait—you *did* want us to take care of the body like usual, right?"

I resist the urge to tear my hair out. Indigo was almost certainly not a *murder victim*, judging by the details that don't add up—but, I mean, performing an autopsy would have been good to do, just to make sure. What kind of detective am I—or *scientist*, for that matter—if I operate purely based on empirical assumptions?

"And if I didn't?" I ask, knowing the answer before it leaves his mouth.

"Too late, as of . . . ten seconds ago." He sighs on the other end. "Sorry, Linds. I totally screwed up, thought I was being helpful by just taking initiative."

I close my eyes, count to five. Try to keep the full weight of my ever-increasing suspicion from exploding. "It's okay," I say, more to myself than to Leo. "It isn't like I have extra time for an autopsy right now anyway."

He's dead silent on the other end of the call. I wait, knowing him well enough to be sure it isn't for lack of things he'd *like* to say—sometimes it simply takes him a minute to put his thoughts into words.

"I'm sorry, Linds," he says finally. "I don't know what to tell you. I wish I could fix it, but—"

"I get it," I say. Because what else *is* there to say? Another long silence stretches between us. Unlike before, though—unlike *ever* before—it just feels like empty space.

"Do . . . you want me up there with you?" he asks, and, oh—

Suddenly it feels like we're talking about something else entirely.

I pause for a split second too long, processing it all, but just as I'm about to answer, he says, "You know, never mind—I actually need to take care of a few things for River back at our cabin."

"Okay," I say automatically. "Good luck with that."

I had just been about to tell him not to come, anyway. So why are these tears springing up in my eyes?

Nothing is predictable these days, not even me.

"Leo . . . we'll talk again in a bit, okay?"

"Yeah," he says. "Sure."

I close my eyes, not entirely certain how to gracefully end the call. Soon, though, his silence turns flat, and I know: he's cut it off first.

53

WHITE-HOT BLACK HOLE

AIMLESSLY, I SWIPE my finger across the panel deck's message screen several times in a row, a repetitive motion that's calming for my nerves. I'm not looking for anything in particular—yet to my surprise, the image on-screen shifts to another inbox, one I've never seen before. What is this?

I take a deep breath, shake things off. Focus on the screen, not on how I left things with Leo.

An indicator proclaims *New Messages: 2*—but there's a closed padlock icon beside it. I tap the padlock and six empty rectangles appear on the screen, along with a keypad. It looks just like every entry panel where we have to input our codes for access.

I try the universal code I already know, but it's rejected immediately. Whose inbox is this? All other communication has come through the main channel, so it's logical that Lieutenants Brady and Black used that one on a regular basis. Shapiro even called for my mother on that line—so what is this one?

Padlock icon, hidden behind the main screen, no flashing indicator light to call attention to it: the only thing I can come up with is that it is for top-secret private messages, an inbox meant for a very select set of eyes and ears.

The person of highest rank was my mother.

What if Shapiro didn't leave a message with Leo because it was so sensitive he had to do it in private? What if these two new messages are from him—what if they change *everything*? That would add up to five urgent calls in a row this morning. It would probably be smart to be informed before reaching out for help.

If this inbox was my mother's, surely I can crack the code . . . eventually. I don't have eventually, though. All I have is this moment.

Six boxes. Her first name—Linsey—is six letters long, but that would be so easy to crack it is not even worth considering. Still, I try it, because watch it be so simple it's impossible.

Rejected.

Okay, then. I run through as many iterations of birthdays and initials as I can think of—hers, mine. I don't know very much about my father, except that my mother would never talk about him and that it had something to do with flight school.

But, ahhh—what if—

My mother took the same day off, every single year, and devoted it entirely to *us* time. We'd play cards by the fire, drink hot cocoa with huge marshmallows Shapiro sent up for us—at her insistence, I'm sure—and connect the stars for each other, each trying to come up with the most creative constellation for every letter of the alphabet. *A for Armchair, B for Bicycle, C for*

Crown, D for Dragonfly, and on and on. We took turns, but she always won—my scope of knowledge was rather limited, especially when I was younger, to what I'd grown up with on the station. She taught me about so many Earth things, though. With my head in her lap, her gentle hand smoothing my hair until it was soft as silk, I'd search the stars and try to imagine how a *real* dragonfly might move. We'd often end up forgetting the game altogether as she told me story after story, until I fell asleep.

She never told me why we celebrated that particular day, and I never asked. All I know is that I always looked forward to it, the one day each year when I had my mother's full attention. June 6 was the date—I try several combinations with our mutual initials, LH0606 and 0606LH and L0606H, and then I flip them all backward.

Finally, *finally,* one combination works: 060654.

Our special day plus my birth year.

As I suspected, one of the messages is from Shapiro, time-stamped immediately after the call Leo answered. The other is from a garble of letters and numbers that is confusing and slightly alarming.

I tap Shapiro's first.

Linsey, he says, his voice clear in the speaker, *a young male answered when I called Control just now—a breach of protocol, as you are aware. I'm contacting you here so said breach will remain off the main record, encrypted, for the protection and security of your position. But Lins, I—I'm so sorry we went completely dark for so long. We've finally resumed control over our own systems after suffering a cyberattack coordinated by the Antarcticans.*

I blink, surprised. Of all the scenarios I'd considered, that was not on my radar at all.

When you didn't answer, he goes on, *I feared the worst. I know you well enough to know you'd never breach protocol unless you were far in over your head.*

To say the least, I think.

Nautilus *has been similarly unresponsive, though the body heat sensors aboard their station unfortunately confirm our greatest fears—there've been no survivors.* He pauses, takes a deep breath. *Oddly, their sensors picked up an aberration in body heat just yesterday—it's suspect, to say the least. And as far as* Lusca *goes, your heat readings don't line up with what you told me on our most recent call.*

My stomach twists. This . . . is not good. How can I possibly come clean without burning the final splinters of my dreams to ash? I'm going to have to, of course. It's just not going to be pleasant.

I was actually calling with good news, he goes on, *but I fear I may be too late. I wanted to reassure you that we were still able to launch a fresh batch of supplies for you as planned—and we've managed to push the birds to about 1.6 times their usual speed. You can expect them to make contact in just under four days.*

I do the math—four days—four days! It's so close we might not have to ask for Vonn's intervention after all! We can stretch our supplies just long enough, if all of us eat only the bare essentials. If the station will eat at all, anyway—but as long as Haven makes a full recovery, that shouldn't be as much of a problem. Hopefully.

There are a number of deeply concerning issues here, to say the least, he says, *but I trust there must be a logical explanation for it all. We'll talk head counts and refresher teams when this is over, Lins, since you've obviously got the world on your shoulders—and—and I hope this shipment will help. I hope* . . . His voice cracks, breaks. *I hope you're holding up okay.* He clears his throat. *All my love, Lins. Call when you can, but take care of your people first.*

Tears sting my eyes. *All my love.*

For once, I don't try to stop them. I've held it together long enough, and no one is here to see me fall apart, and I just. Can't. Help it. I'm not even entirely sure what this flood of emotion is made of—grief? Relief? Relief for the shipment, for sure, and relief that the topic of relocation is tabled for now. Also, though, because it's an enormous weight off to realize I'm not the only one left who loves her so fiercely. While there are billions of stars still in the sky, I can't help but wish for one more, the one so bright it burned out too fast.

When Shapiro finds out the truth, he'll feel the exact same way, I *know* he will. I hate it for him just like I hate it for me. For the first time in weeks, though, I don't feel utterly alone.

I take a moment, two, three—time I don't have, but time I *need*. I let myself remember her, even though it makes me feel broken. So much of *me* was tied up in *her*. She'd be proud of me, I think. All I want is to hear her voice, feel her soft hands in my hair as she tells me about fireflies and zebras and what snow is like as it melts on your tongue, as she tells me I've done *enough*—that I *am* enough.

I'm not sure I'd ever actually believe it. It would still be nice to hear.

Minutes pass, I don't know how many. After a little while, when my eyes are far past dry, I lift my head. Take a deep breath. Pull myself together.

I tap on the second message, the one from the garbled username. My blood runs cold as soon as I hear the voice, a bass so low and gravelly it feels like fire to my ears.

Vonn here, the voice says, as if his two words aren't nuclear bombs to the relief I'd just started to feel. *Heard from Shapiro there's been a breach of protocol under your watch,* he goes on. *You and I have never seen eye to eye, but if there's one thing I know, it's that you're too stubborn to risk a breach.*

Shapiro instructed me to wait it out, but he'll be sorry to hear I'm going over his head on this one—his judgment is beyond clouded by the feelings we all know he has for you, Hamilton, and the board is with me on this.

Before you hang up on me, hear me out.

We have confirmation that the Antarcticans infected our Earth-based systems units with a virus, in an attempt to seize control over all intergalactic operations; the board and I are concerned that the man Shapiro spoke with on your Control deck might actually be one of them. If they've sent someone to strip our off-planet systems, it would also explain the body heat abnormality detected on

Nautilus. *Call me paranoid or call me brilliant—I don't care what you call me, as you are well aware—but we're already on our way, an entire speed fleet, and are prepared to take out any unfriendly presence before it has a chance to strike first.*

Reach out if you're still there, Hamilton, using the handle attached to this call in the log—but be aware, we may not answer if we're in dark space.

Vonn, over and out.

I sit, stunned, do the math in my head. *Speed fleet* is code for max velocity, which means they won't be loaded down with supplies—supply shipments take two to three times longer, if I'm remembering right. Heath would know this off the top of his head.

Two days. Two days, and an entire fleet will be here, ready to attack. I have no idea how much of that is dark space, but I'm guessing quite a lot—especially on the first half of their trip, since they're so far out. They'd be close enough to Radix to borrow its satellites for a little while, but by now, at the speed they'd need to travel to get here so quickly . . . they'd be well out of range already, I'd estimate.

I call the garbled handle, ten—twenty—thirty—unsuccessful attempts in a row. Not even a message system picks up.

Over and over, I jam my finger at the screen, as if pressing harder will make any difference at all. I keep going, don't even notice the door slide open behind me or Haven's presence at my back before she speaks:

"What are you doing?"

"I . . ." I spin around, slowly, to face her. "We need . . . I need to call an emergency meeting."

"Yeah," she says. "We do." She takes in my face, bites her lip in concern. "This is the last thing you want to hear right now, I know, but—there've been three more. Three more deaths, like . . . like Mila. Like Jaako and Kerr."

In the vast, arid place where so many of my conflicting feelings have strangled each other's roots, one last tough weed sprouts up like a vine: I thought I was far past numb, maxed out on feeling *anything* after feeling so many things, so strongly, tonight. I was wrong.

"Call the meeting," I say, through my teeth. "We'll have it here, right now."

I'm shaking, livid. This has to *stop*.

It should have stopped a long time ago. I could have warned them, and I didn't.

I didn't.

Three. More.

I can't stop shaking.

Our secrecy ends tonight.

54

SEVEN AND COUNTING

"SEVEN," I SAY, once the others have joined Haven and me in Control. "We've lost *seven*."

All six of us are here; I look from face to face. Despite our various shades of skin, despite our height or lack of it, despite our each and every difference, in this moment we are all the same: Exhausted. Defeated. Sparks of fire simmer in our eyes, even so.

"This. Must. End." I can't meet their eyes for long. There are too many faces I want to trust, too many faces I've trusted forever. Maybe I'm wrong, maybe the killer isn't one of us after all, maybe whoever did it set everything up as one giant distraction so we'd focus our investigation inward. Maybe I've been looking in the wrong place all along. I hope I'm wrong. I *want* to be wrong.

But just in case I'm not, I can't show my hand.

If I'm right, and if I'm the only person close to finding out the truth, what would a killer naturally do to protect themselves?

Take out the one person who could shine a spotlight on all of their shadows.

I can't give my suspicions away.

"Seven is too many," I say. "*One* was too many."

"Let us *help* you, then," Haven says. "You've been taking everything on alone, and you don't *have* to, Lindley. That's what we're here for, right? You don't have to do this alone. Your mother didn't."

Your mother didn't. It stings like salt on raw skin. "This isn't about *me*. And it certainly isn't about my mother."

"I'm just saying, maybe we'd be more effective as a team. Y'know, like we initially decided when we took over? As a *group?*"

The thing is, I agree with her. And I *want* help, more than anything.

I only wish I knew for sure that I could trust them.

I take a deep breath. "I'm going to tell the station the truth," I say. "All of it. Everything. They need to know there's no threat of viral mutation at this point—they need to know there's a *killer* within our walls. No one else needs to die." I think of our latest victims: two girls, Nieva Taylor and Emme Davenport, found dead in an alcove with Sailor Salvato, who was slumped over his guitar. "Maybe if they know to be on guard, they'll be alert and aware. Maybe someone will even catch the killer in the act of trying." And maybe, I think, the killer won't try at all if they know so many eyes will be watching out for suspicious behavior.

"You don't think they'll panic when they find out?" Zesi says, shaking his dreads away so both eyes are clearly visible.

"They . . . might?" I say. "But it can't be any worse than the party earlier, right?" Let's hope, anyway. "I think that particular risk is worth it."

"I think we should've told them a long time ago," Heath says. It's not lost on me how he says *we*. Like the blame doesn't clearly fall just on my shoulders. Like we've been acting as a team, even though I really have been going lone ranger for so much of this, like Haven said.

I glance at him, send him a silent *thank you* with my eyes. "Any objections?" I ask, more as a formality than anything. The least I can give, basically, to make it seem like a team effort instead of just a *me* effort.

For a long moment, no one says a word. Finally, Leo claps his hands together. "Well," he says, "that's settled. We'll tell them first thing in the morning?"

"I was thinking we'd tell them tonight, right after we're done here?" It's already past eleven. We'll have to wake some people up, but many of them stay up much later than that anyway.

Natalin glances at the clock. "Tonight? Sure you don't want to wait until morning, when they've slept off everything they had to drink?"

I *don't* want to wait, but she makes a good point. It's important that they're lucid enough for the warnings to make a deep impression. "What if something happens in the meantime, though? I feel like we should call for lockdown again." Even as I say the words, they feel empty. Lockdown didn't work before—why should it work tonight?

"You heard them out there, Linds," Leo says. "It's obvious they're going to do whatever they want no matter what we say. If we call for lockdown again tonight, it could be the last straw. They might not show up to hear what we have to say in the morning, you know?"

"Gut feeling?" Haven chimes in. "We've got to give them a little space if we want them to keep listening to us. It's not like we're their parents—we'll lose them if we push too hard."

She's right, and I know it, but still. Just because we're not their parents, it doesn't mean they don't need people looking out for their best interests. Can't they see we're only trying to protect them? At the same time, I get it—I would not take kindly to someone close to my own age telling *me* what I'm not allowed to do.

"Okay," I say, still a bit reluctant about the whole thing. "Tomorrow at ten-thirty sharp, we'll meet in the mezzanine. Haven, get the word out when you do your morning announcement, okay? Make sure to mention it's extremely important that they show up." I hesitate to say *mandatory* after what happened with lockdown—*mandatory* seems to have lost all meaning.

"Great, so can we go to bed now?" Natalin says. She's been two seconds from sleep this entire time, and after the week we've had, who can blame her?

The main reason I even wanted to call this meeting, before

Haven came in and heaped more terrible news on, was to tell them about Shapiro, about Vonn—ugh. I'm tempted to dismiss them all, stay here all night until I make successful contact with Vonn's fleet. But have I not learned my lesson? In this, at least, I can try to rely on more than just myself. Not even a murderer will want to suffer an attack at the hands of Vonn—I *hope*—or be relocated when they discover we're merely unattached youth and not a hostile team of Antarctican agents—so I take a leap of faith and rely heavily on one fundamental assumption: that everyone in this room has a strong sense of self-preservation, at preserving their own freedom.

Not that freedom awaits the guilty, if I have any say in the matter.

"Sorry," I say. "One last thing, before we go." I fill them in on the good news first—that relief is on its way, even as we speak!—that we just need to stretch our food supply a little longer, and we'll be in the clear. Natalin, especially, perks up a bit at this.

And then I drop the bad news.

"So . . . what do we do?" Zesi says, when I've finished telling them about the attack fleet headed our way.

"At this point, there's not much we *can* do." I survey the vast expanse of buttons on the control deck. "Are we equipped for defense, Zesi, do you know? And if so, are you capable of deploying it?"

He stares, unblinking, at the control deck. "No scientist or engineer worth anything would strand us up here without a way to protect ourselves," he says. "I'll figure it out." If anyone could do it, Zesi could. He's been connecting invisible dots since most of us were still learning the alphabet. He's frighteningly brilliant.

I make a two-second snap decision: it would be smart to not leave him alone in here. "I can reach out to Shapiro, attempt to explain before it's too late—and I plan to continue my attempts at direct contact with Vonn's team. Anyone want to take shifts with me tonight?" I want to delegate this completely, but what if someone answers and we can't manage to convince them we're *not* war-prone Antarcticans? Maybe they'll hear traces of my mother in my voice, like Shapiro did before. I can't stay up all night, though. I need help, much as I hate to admit it.

"Nat and I will take shifts with you," Haven says, obviously pleased I'm taking her advice to make this more of a team effort. "Want to sleep while I take the first one?"

I glance at Natalin, who looks the furthest thing from alert right now. "I'll take the first," I say. "You can relieve me at four, and I'll take over again when it's time for you to make morning announcements at eight. Good?"

And then we break again: Natalin floats off to her bed to sleep off the day, as does Haven, so she can rest up for her shift. Leo and Heath head out to deal with the latest bodies—it's beyond pointless to bother with autopsies at this point, when our time is being stretched in so many different directions. Just in case, I have them put them on ice instead of fire. Zesi and

I settle in at Control; he's already pulled up two sets of *Lusca* blueprints on his pair of display screens.

I make mindless work of clearing the old coffee mugs away, something easy and well within my control, something to do while mentally preparing for tonight; for tomorrow. I pour the dregs down the sinks in the nearest facility, and rinse off the days-old grime until the mugs are far past the point of being clean. I use a white cotton cloth to scrub them until they sparkle.

When I finally take a seat on my stool, on the opposite end of the control deck as Zesi, I'm ready to begin.

I log back into my mother's private message inbox, jam my finger at Vonn's garbled contact handle.

No answer, again. Even the most advanced tech can't connect in deep, dark space. Fine by me—I need time to think of how to navigate my call with Shapiro, what I could possibly say to convince him I'm a competent leader after all of this, what I could possibly say to convince the board to let us keep our home. And I need time to think about tomorrow morning, how I'll lay out the stark, bleak truth to the entire station about six of the seven we've lost. So very many delicate, dreadful conversations.

This is going to be a long night.

55

MESSAGE FROM THE DEAD AND DYING

SOMETIME AROUND TWO-MORNING, I give it a rest. Not a permanent rest—just a much-needed one. My body needs to move.

I haven't yet worked up the nerve to have my difficult conversation with Shapiro, and my attempts at getting through to Vonn have proven fruitless. I've been circling an idea, though. Earlier, Haven broke the news about the recent deaths right here in Control—there's no way the vid-feeds could've been tampered with since then. I've been here the entire time, and Zesi's been completely wrapped up in file after file of complicated blueprints and diagrams.

I want to go through the footage, but how do I do that with him sitting four feet away? What if he is our murderer and I see him poison Sailor and Emme and Nieva *right there* on the screen? What if he *sees* me see it? We're alone together in the dead of night.

This is what I've been thinking about for two hours.

I keep thinking maybe he'll doze off, or use the facilities for more than just half a minute. Hasn't happened yet.

"Lindley?" Zesi says, breaking our silence.

"Hmm?"

"Maybe it's time you try Nashville?"

I'm surprised it took him this long to bring it up, honestly. I had hoped that if I just waited, I'd feel ready, but each passing hour has only served to heighten my nerves.

I glance at the clock, do quick math. "Isn't it, like, four-morning there?"

If anyone can get through to Vonn's fleet once it's out of dark space, surely it would be Shapiro. I wouldn't put it past Vonn to ignore even him, though—especially given what Vonn said in his last message, that he and Shapiro disagree about what's going on here on the station. That Vonn's taken it upon himself to go over his head to the rest of the board.

Even so, it makes sense to try.

I'm going to have to come clean about my lies at some point . . . I just hope I don't accidentally flip things to Vonn's favor in the process. What if my attempt to tell the truth backfires and makes Shapiro inclined to believe the enemy really *has* invaded our station? How am I supposed to prove I'm the actual daughter of Commander Linsey Hamilton, and not just an Antarctican looking for a way to hide her true identity?

Still. These are flimsy excuses and I know it.

"Okay, fine," I say, tapping back into the private message

inbox, ignoring the piercing look Zesi's giving me. It's like his eyes are burning holes through my conscience. "You're right. I'll try that first."

Even if it *is* four-morning, Shapiro won't want us to destroy each other. I put the call through before I can talk myself out of it. It rings, rings, rings—longer than usual, for sure. On the fifth ring, finally, someone picks up.

"Hello?" I say. "This is Commander Lin—"

"Julian Shapiro's department," interrupts the voice of what can only be an intern slapped with a string of graveyard shifts. She can't be much older than I am, from the sound of it. Her voice is full of sleep. "Please state your clearance code?"

"This is Lindley Hamilton, daughter of—"

"Your clearance code, please?"

My heart beats in my throat. My only guess—the same code my mother used for the passcode to this private inbox—is definitely the wrong one. Clearance codes are an entirely different level of complicated, company-issued garbles of letters, numbers, and symbols meant to be unguessable and unbreakable; I know this because Dr. Safran made an offhand comment about it during our final day together, how he'd memorized the entire periodic table as an eleven-year-old and could teach me nearly anything I'd need to keep the station running. *Just don't ask what my clearance code is*, he said. *They change every year—started losing track after the first four. Never needed mine anyway, though, not once. Ask your mother for hers if you want to cover all your bases.*

I wish I'd had the chance. His mind was slipping even then, because my mother was already long gone.

"I'm aboard the space station *Lusca*, and this is an emergency," I say, my voice rising. "Could you please connect me with—"

"I'm sorry," she says, not sounding the least bit sorry to keep cutting me off. "Due to a recent breach of security protocol, I cannot speak further or connect you unless you provide the correct clearance—"

I end the call.

Zesi lets out a long, loud exhale. "Well."

It's the beginning and the end of his commentary on the matter.

I should do something. I should do anything besides sitting here, staring at the message log like it could, at any minute, produce magic answers to all our problems. If only. I slip into the facilities, close myself inside its claustrophobic walls. Take my time. Put my head in my hands, wait for it to stop spinning.

We are alone up here, we are going to die, my best is not enough—and it never will be.

I've made a thousand mistakes.

The station deserves better.

Surely there is a way to salvage this. Surely we can make it four more days, until our shipment comes, without getting destroyed—or without destroying each other.

Surely.

When I finally come out again, Zesi's standing right outside the door. He holds his buzz screen in my face, so close the words blur. "What the hell?" he says.

"What? What is that?" I pluck the buzz screen from his hand before he can protest, take a closer look for myself.

Do not tell them the truth, the message on the screen reads, **or one of you will be the next to die. The virus has mutated, and it's getting worse: that's the official word.**

"Zesi . . ." A chill races up my spine, splintering like ice between the bones. "What *is* this?"

My eyes shift on instinct up to the name at the top: *Mila Harper.*

"What were you doing in the bathroom?" he asks, a vaguely accusing tone to his voice that's completely unlike him. "Do you have your buzz with you?"

For a split second I'm speechless. "Are you implying that *I* sent this?" I shoot back. "How do I know *you* didn't send it?"

"That's not an answer."

The clothes I'm wearing right now have only three pockets, total, and I turn all of them out. "I left my buzz on the control board, where I've been sitting all night. Check the facilities if you want, but you're not going to find anything."

I don't ask him to turn his pockets out—he's not stupid. Far from it, actually. If he's somehow the one behind this message, not to mention everything else, the evidence will be long gone by now.

He beats me to the control board, holds my buzz up so I can see it. "Looks like you got it, too."

A second message flashes onto the screen while he's holding it—from Haven this time. **What the eff is this message? Tell me I'm not the only one who got this?** A screenshot pops up right on its heels, identical to the one Zesi and I received.

I take my buzz screen from Zesi, type out: **I got it, and Zesi did, too. Same exact thing.** I hit enter, then add, **Try to sleep a little more before your shift, k? No luck here yet.**

She writes back immediately: **How am I supposed to sleep when Mila is haunting us from beyond the dead????? x.X**

Srsly, you need to try, I type out but delete it immediately; it's likely to rub her the wrong way, especially at this hour. I decide to go with **If you figure it out, let me know when you get here** instead.

I sit down on my stool, bury my face in my hands. *Do not tell them the truth, or one of you will be the next to die.* I could spin out another theory: Did someone plant a bug here in Control? Did someone plant a bug on one of *us*? Could someone have figured out how to eavesdrop through . . . the pipes? But at this point, it only seems like a way to put off the truth I'm so reluctant to accept.

Only the six of us were in this room tonight.

Only the six of us know about our plans to come clean with the station.

One of the six of us sent this message. One of the six of us is willing to kill a close friend in order to keep their secret safe.

This . . . I . . . I can't.

I didn't think it could get worse. This is *beyond* worse.

"What, so we're just . . . not going to talk about this?" Zesi says. His blueprints and diagrams have gone dark, and he's pacing pacing pacing pacing. He's frantic, and I wish I could go back to trusting what's right in front of my eyes instead of assuming everything is a vicious lie. *Someone* is a vicious liar, that's the only thing I know for sure.

I have to get out of here.

"No." My reply is sharp and short.

I zip my zipper all the way up to my neck, tug my hood up over my head so there's nothing in my peripheral vision. I want to disappear.

"What are you going to do?" he asks. "What are you going to tell everyone?"

The doors slide closed, eating his words.

56

FEAR IS A PILE OF FEATHERS

UNSURPRISING: THE REC center's jogging track is deserted when I arrive. It's nearly half past two-morning. Not only is the track deserted, I have yet to see another soul on this entire deck. Good. I may only be able to run in circles—not *away*, like I'd prefer—but at least I'm able to *run*. And run alone.

I pound a fast rhythm, until the neon art installations on the wall are nothing but a blur of bright streaks. I run and run and run, like I'm flying on wings made of fear and adrenaline, shedding dead weight as I go:

First, the paranoia—for this moment, at least, I can breathe.

Then, the numbness that's turned me to stone.

Next, the sting of betrayal.

I leave these behind, knowing they'll chase me down and climb back on the very second I stop, but for now, it feels good to forget.

It's harder to shed the anger. Anger fuels my every step, my every thought, my every breath. I just can't get past why someone would do this—or *how*. Not *how* as in *death by bella-donna cocktail*, but *how* as in *I cannot comprehend the mind of this killer*. I imagine the mind of a murderer to be a twisted, tangled thing, the good parts suffocating while the terrible ones thrive the only way they know how: take, take, take. No remorse, no regret. Survival, and misery-loves-company, and *if I'm dying inside, you get to, too*.

That, I get. What I cannot wrap my thoughts around is how that twisted and tangled mess could possibly exist inside a person I've known my entire life. Haven, Heath. Leo, Zesi. Natalin. We've grown up together, here, inside the same walls, forever. We've experienced *everything* together. We lost our parents together.

More than anything, that is the thorn that digs. I want nothing more than to be able to erase everyone's pain: to stitch up the places where the things we love have been torn away. To heal. I want to make it *better*—I know what it feels like to wake up in the dead of night, sweating cold from nightmares. I would give anything to take all the nightmares away.

I do not understand the instinct to *create* them.

Why, why, why, why: my feet beat the word into the track. And this latest message—does whoever sent it really expect me to blatantly lie after we've resolved to tell the truth? Lying would do nothing but hand over even more power. It's not like it would prevent the deaths altogether—it would only prevent certain *specific* deaths.

I've already lost too many people I love, but I am the leader of this station. I cannot, *will* not, prioritize my own comfort above everyone else's.

That's the heart of a killer, not a leader.

I run until everything burns, legs and lungs, and then I run more. I don't stop until I feel peace with my decision. It's a tough spot I'm in, and whoever's pushed me here knows it— something terrible is going to happen no matter what I do. The deaths will keep coming, I'm sure of it.

There's very little left I can control, very little I can do to ease my conscience. As I work through my options, I realize there's really only one I can live with: turn the target on myself. If I continue on with our original plan—tell the station the truth—perhaps the killer will come for me, and not another of our core six. It's a risk, for sure. They may not take the bait at all . . . or if they do, I may not recognize what's happening until it's too late.

I'll just have to see them coming. End it before it begins.

I've been fumbling in a dark and chaotic world since the moment my mother left it. Nothing is like it was before, nothing is *sure*—not anymore.

But if there's one thing I know, it's this: I've been ruled by fear for far too long now.

I refuse to bow down any longer.

57

SHADE UPON SHADOW

"WHERE WERE YOU this morning?" Haven greets me just outside the doors to the mezzanine balcony. "Not like you to no-show."

I haven't even peeked inside and the noise is already earsplitting. It's a relief: I've been dreading the possibility of silence. "Needed some space," I reply. I adjust my hoodie, try to make it look fresh after being worn for so many hours in a row.

"You could've *told* me before I dragged myself out of bed in the dead of night," she says. "You could've left the passcode or Vonn's contact info behind, at the very least. You should've—"

"I know," I cut her off. "I should have."

I woke, on a patch of barren rec center floor, to the sound of Haven's voice echoing from the speakers. She gave the morning announcement as planned, put out the call for our station-wide meeting.

It was only *after* the announcement that I noticed all the missed messages on my buzz screen. Tons from Haven—**Where**

are you??? and **How do I call Vonn?? Instructions, plz?** and **Are we still going forward with our announcement, in light of that certain disturbing message we received last night???** Mixed in with those were a slew of missed calls and other texts from Leo, Heath, and Natalin when they woke up to the mysterious threat from "Mila"—all equally freaked out, all with their questions questions questions—and a set of messages from Zesi, wondering where I'd disappeared to, if I would be coming back, **Sorry Lindley I can't stay awake any longer, headed to bed now,** and on and on.

I ignored everything.

I did stop by Control, hoping Vonn had finally made it out of dark space—but when I logged in to the private inbox and resumed my futile attempts at contact, I was met with more of the same: utter silence. We've got little more than a day before they storm our station, maybe less if our estimated calculations are off—there's still time to stop the attack, but not much. I'll have to go back in a few hours, try again.

"So . . . um . . . ," she says, snapping me back to this present moment. "What are you going to do?" She dips her head toward the balcony doors.

I press my lips into a straight line. *Undecided*, I want to say—but I can't even lie to Haven, who I've known forever, who would absolutely forgive me once all of this ends. How does anyone expect me to lie to our entire station, if I can't breathe this one small dishonest word?

When she meets my eyes again, the look on her face is sheer terror.

"Whoa, Haven—are you okay?"

Her irises are unearthly green in this light, shade upon shadow. "I don't want to die, Linds. I don't—" Her voice catches, and she shakes her head. "I want to *live*. I want to do great things, *be* great. Don't you want that, too? Don't you think our *parents* would want that—wouldn't they want us to continue their legacy?" She presses her lips into a tight line, blinks up at the recessed spotlights in the ceiling to clear the shine in her eyes. "Don't do this to us."

If we burn out there'll really be nothing left of them, she doesn't have to say. *No one who remembers them. No legacy left behind.*

It's enough to shake me. Enough to make my almost-lie—*undecided*—true. Because she's right, none of our parents would wish us dead. They'd be heartbroken to see what's happened here, what's happen*ing*. The thought of letting my mother down, of *what if the truth is just another mistake*, is crushing.

But I'm resolved to tell the truth, not just to the station, but to myself.

No one who remembers them, no legacy left behind: those are lies, if I really break them down. Even if I die for this choice—possible self-sacrifice, me for my people—a legacy of integrity is the greatest thing I could offer. It's certainly preferable to a life propped up by fear and lies. Sooner or later, that life would collapse.

I smooth my hair down, adjust the pins. "No one wants to die, Haven."

She opens her mouth to speak, but it's 10:01 and I have nothing left to say that she'll want to hear. I open the balcony doors, step out to face the room.

The noise dies down as soon as they see me: a half-here-half-not ghost with dark circles under her eyes, who ran her heart out in the middle of the night, who trusts no one but herself—and even then, only barely. Lindley Hamilton, a girl who's closer to falling apart than they might've guessed before this moment.

I look from face to face, take in the souls behind their eyes: Akello Regulus. Story Lutheborough, who helped me just yesterday before Haven collapsed. Yuki and Grace, Mikko and Dash, Siena Lawson. Eight-year-old River, standing arms crossed next to Leo. Evi and Elise. Natalin. Heath and Zesi, at the back of the room. So many, many others. There are seventy-eight of us in total, down from our original number of eighty-five station-born. The crowd looks thinner for it.

Someone in this room poisoned at least six of the seven who are gone.

Someone in this room is about to witness, firsthand, my refusal to bow to their threats.

I hold my head high. If I'm going to do this, I'm going to do it all the way, with as much confidence as my mother would have shown.

"I've called you here today," I begin, my clear voice echoing from even the farthest wall, "because you deserve to know the truth. I wanted to"—I cut myself off before the word *apologize* slips out, not because I don't mean it, but because it could undermine their impression of my leadership—"let you all know that the recent deaths on our station are not, in fact, due to viral mutation."

I take a deep breath, resist the urge to glance at Haven, who's beside me on the balcony. If I were to look, I'd see a silent struggle, no doubt: public support masking private panic.

"The deaths were . . . intentional. To be clear, someone has gone out of their way to make them look as if the virus is spreading, when in fact, that is not the case."

For one brief second, my words hang in the air—and then there's an explosion of whispers as they go from zero to full-volume *fast*.

"Are you trying to tell us someone *killed* them?" Akello's deep, resonant voice cuts through the noise from the far end of the front row.

"That is exactly—" I begin, but cut myself off. My voice alone isn't enough to overpower them. I wait it out for half a minute before trying once more, and again: I'm not enough.

And then, from the back of the crowd: "EVERYONE STOP TALKING!"

Heath.

I meet eyes with him as their voices die down, hope he hears my silent *thank you* loud and clear. A pinprick beam of hope pierces right through me: maybe I can trust him. If he's trying to help me get the truth out, even though it means it puts him at risk, too—

Maybe.

"Yes," I say, shifting my attention to Akello. "That is exactly what I'm trying to tell you." The noise starts to swell again, but I quell it at once: "I'm telling you this so you'll know how to protect yourselves. What to watch for, and—and what *isn't* a factor." I take a deep breath. Screw it: an apology can't possibly undermine my own leadership more than my mistakes have. If anything, maybe it can *save* it.

"I'm deeply sorry I've kept this information from you," I go on. "It's reached a tipping point now where it is no longer in anyone's best interests to keep the truth private." *Except for those of us who are now explicit targets thanks to this confession,* my conscience fires back. I shove it down. "There is currently no need for quarantine, no obvious resurgence of viral threat to your health—full disclosure, though, we are keeping a close eye out for a possible strain brought over from *Nautilus,* but haven't seen any actual worrisome symptoms at this point. What I ask of you is this: be wary of your beverages. Don't take your eyes off your drinks, not for one second. Don't allow anyone to get a drink *for* you, or food, for that matter." Probably good to add that in. With everyone aware of the threat, a smart killer would look for a less obvious approach. Telling people to keep a close eye on their drinks *and* food drastically reduces the likelihood of anyone ingesting belladonna—to pretty much zero, I'd guess.

"Mostly," I say as I scan the room, taking in as many faces as I can, "keep your eyes open. If you see anything suspicious, you're under strict orders to report it to me at once. And if you *do* see something suspicious, take immediate action by yelling '*Fire!*'—you'll draw more attention that way." It's a trick my mother taught me when I was young. I've never had to use it, never *seen* anyone have to use it. There's a first for everything, I guess.

"I'd open the floor up for questions, but I'm sorry to say I don't have the answers you want just yet. Stay on guard, be vigilant. Don't panic. I'll report more when I can." As soon as the words are out, I give a deep nod and retreat through the balcony doors, out into the quiet corridor.

Haven follows.

"We're dead," she says with bite. "I hope you know that."

I wish I knew for certain that I've done the right thing.

I wish I could tell her she's wrong.

Truth is—right or wrong—it's too late to go back.

All we can do now is try to stay alive.

58

FUSION

HAVEN WALKS AWAY without a second glance, and I'm alone.

No one's made it up to this deck yet. From the sound of the noise—which hasn't let up since the doors closed at my back—everyone's still in the mezzanine, like an audience waiting for an encore. Like if they're loud enough, I'll come back out: put on a good show, dance gracefully through their questions, trick their eyes with a blinding spotlight that twists darkness into nothing more than an afterthought. Like if I say just the right thing, tell them exactly what they want to hear, they'll feel better.

I'm not here for that show, not anymore.

I lean my back on the cool steel of the wall and sink down until I'm sitting on the floor. There are probably a thousand things I should be doing instead, but I hold myself still. Curl my knees into my chest. Rest my head. Listen to my own heartbeat.

It's a strange feeling, the urge I already have to check in on the others of our six, to make sure they're not dead. I care so deeply for each of them—and yet.

Love is complicated right now.

What will it feel like when I figure out who our killer is? Will my love blink out, like it never happened at all—or is it possible I'll experience an emotional paradox, where love and fury coexist? When a heart breaks, do the pieces just . . . crumble? Or do they fuse back together, all gnarled and deformed?

"Mind if I sit?"

I don't have to look up to know it's Heath who's found me. "Go ahead," I mumble into my knees.

He sinks down beside me, so close my entire left side warms at his presence. I don't shift away from him, not even slightly, not even with the small voice in my head saying *trust no one*. Minutes tick by, both of us silent and still in the small space of this alcove. Soon, the voice in my head quiets down. He is such a force of *calm*.

"You're brave, Linds," he says. "You are so unbelievably brave."

Finally, I lift my head. Look up at him. "You really think so?"

He nods, slowly. "I like to hope I would've done the same thing," he says with a sad smile. "Don't think I could've gone through with it, though."

"I get it," I say. "We're all afraid of dying, I think."

"I'm too afraid of *you* dying."

He looks deep into my eyes, and I take him in—how could I have ever questioned him, for even a single second? Heath never would've put me in this position. Heath is like me: he wants to bind people up, not break them.

Before I know it, I'm closing the space between us, kissing him full on the mouth. I can't help it—it's overwhelming—it is almost certainly a mistake—

But in this moment, it is *everything* to me to know I'm not alone.

To know he sought me out to tell me this, to comfort me—even though I chose to put us all in the crosshairs—

He kisses me back, with the same soft hunger. We fit perfectly, and it is perfectly thrilling, perfectly warm. He understands the risk I've taken. He forgives me for it. He *admires* me for it. If I can trust no one else, at least I know this: Heath is safe. And I am safe with him.

We stay in the alcove, and we don't watch the time. Today could be our last day alive, and everything is falling apart all around us, but this—*this* is good. At the very least, there is one good and true thing left. I plan to hold on to it for as long as I can.

And I do—until Heath's buzz screen starts vibrating like there's no tomorrow. He pulls away, cheeks flushed. "Sorry," he says, glancing at the display screen. "So sorry, but I'd better take it." He holds it up for me to see: Leo's calling.

"Hey," he says. "Yeah, no. Yeah." He pauses, listens. Then, abruptly, he stands and starts pacing small circles in this tiny alcove. "Are you badly hurt?"

At that, I sit straight up. "Wait, what? What happened?"

"Yeah, she's okay," Heath says to Leo. "She's right here." There's another brief pause; I try to eavesdrop, but it's hard to make anything out. "Can you get to Medical? We'll meet you there in five unless you need help."

Medical—that doesn't sound good, not at all. On the upside, at least he doesn't obviously need to be rolled there on our gurney. Or worse.

"Okay, see you there—yeah, I'll tell her. Be there in a few."

I'm on my feet and peppering him with questions before he's even fully off the call. "What happened? Did someone—did someone try—"

To murder him. Those are the words that won't come out.

We walk briskly together toward Medical. "No, not that," Heath says. "I don't think so, at least. A fight broke out near him, he said, and when he tried to stop it someone sliced at him with a razor blade."

Again with the razor blades. "Cameron and Mikko, like before?"

Perhaps I've been too quick to rule out the possibility that our murderer could be someone outside our six. I don't know *how* they would've secured top-secret intel from our private meeting last night, but is it outside the realm of possibility that someone *could* have? I have to admit it isn't.

Heath nods. "Yeah, both of them. Leo's got the razor now, at least—managed to confiscate it after he got cut," he says. "Well, technically, he said *Akello* confiscated it when he helped Leo break up the fight."

Bless Akello and his large, intimidating frame. Not that Leo's small, by any means—he can handle himself. But when it comes to blade versus body, quick blood versus slow-blooming bruises, it's not a fair fight.

Heath and I arrive at Medical before Leo does. The room is spotless, just like I left it, all sparkle and shine. I pull out an array of surgical tools and my favorite silver tray, spread everything out in perfect order. The tray holds everything I could possibly need, from simple antibiotic cream to my stitches kit, with extra cloth on hand in case he won't stop bleeding.

Two minutes pass—then three—then six, and ten. Leo still hasn't arrived.

"He'll be here," Heath says behind me, closer than I realized. "He's on his way, Linds."

He puts both hands on my shoulders, stilling my nerves. Gently, he turns me around to face him.

"We should try buzzing him," I say. "Have you tried—"

"Linds. He'll *be* here." His eyes say it all: he did try buzzing him, yet here we are. He lets out a long exhale, pulls me in close. "I'll try again if he's not here in five, okay?"

Five minutes. It's nothing, compared to the millions of minutes that make up an entire lifetime—yet entire lifetimes can end in less time than that. One blink, one breath. One step too far.

I rest my head on Heath's chest, let him hold me together. For how close we were in the alcove, this is a different sort of closeness: the alcove was spark and flame and fire, but this? This is water. Cool and still, as close to peace as I can hope for on a day like today.

"Thank you," I say, so quietly my words get lost in the fabric of his shirt. My eyes flutter shut as he runs his hand over my hair, the rhythm soft and slow. "This . . . today . . . I needed it."

He breathes deeply, his chest rising underneath me. I hear his heartbeat pick up, feel him press a kiss lightly to the top of my head. "You're not the only one," he says. "I've missed you, Linds." He waits a beat, then adds, "It's been hard watching you push everyone away."

I press my lips shut. I can't possibly tell him the real reason I've been keeping him—*everyone*—at arm's length. He doesn't seem to hold it against me that I explicitly, knowingly, purposefully defied that threat and, therefore, put our core six at risk . . . but even if he's forgiven me that, would he ever be able to forget the depths of my suspicion? *I pushed you away because I didn't know if I could trust you—because you could've been the killer.* It's a betrayal of a different kind to believe someone capable of the horrendous things that have happened between our walls. It's the sort of betrayal that cracks the foundation of a relationship forever.

He can never know. He might understand—he *would* understand, I think, because he assumes the best in me even though

I've been terrible at returning those feelings. But still. Understanding doesn't make a person immune to pain.

The doors slide open, and we break apart. Not quickly enough, I can tell—Leo saw enough to raise eyebrows—but he doesn't comment. He holds up his left forearm, the back of which is covered in a sickening amount of partially dried blood. "You can fix this, yeah?"

I take a hard swallow, nod. "Yes," I say, then clear my throat. "Sit on the table, okay? Okay."

Heath helps me clean Leo's arm, and passes me everything I ask for. It's a long slice, about five inches stretching from near his elbow most of the way down to his wrist. Fortunately, only the top inch or so is deep; the rest should close up quickly. Still, it's going to be painful while it heals, not to mention debilitating—Leo's left-handed.

My work is quick: a few stitches to close the deepest part, antibiotic cream on the rest, white surgical tape wrapped protectively around most of his arm, making his light bronze skin look even darker in contrast.

"There," I say as Leo examines my work, twisting his arm to see it from all angles. It's neat, precise. I'm proud to have managed such clean work on a day like today. "You'll feel it for a couple of days, but it should heal pretty quickly."

He meets my eyes, finally, for the first time since walking in on us here, Heath and me, so close together. Leo's eyes are deep brown, half-moons turned down at their corners, at once beautiful and hopeful and sad: it's the same look he had when he came to my place to deliver the news about Jaako and Kerr— when he discovered Heath and me, together, our lips still pink from that first real kiss.

I'm sorry, I want to say. But for what? Am I sorry for being so close with Heath—or am I only sorry Leo had to see it happen?

I'm honestly not sure. Every kiss I've shared—with Heath *and* with Leo—felt real in the moment. Felt like *everything*.

I should know by now that feelings are unreliable.

My world tips on its axis: *I* am unreliable.

"Thank you, Lindley." Leo gives me a tight-lipped grin, eyes still every bit as bright. He looks away, slides down from the table, and my heart cracks:

I cannot remember the last time he used my full name.

Fix one thing, break another.

59

LIKE WISHES ON THE
VERGE OF BURNING OUT

I HAVE TO leave—I can't be in this room with them anymore, with Heath and Leo and the *feelings*.

"Anyone needs me, I'll be up in Control in about an hour," I say, settling my metal tray on the countertop with more of a clatter than I intended.

"Anything you need us to do?" Heath asks as I breeze past him.

"Just . . . stay alive, okay?"

I resist the urge to look over my shoulder as I walk out.

Not that I know where I'm going, exactly—all I know is I need to sort myself out. I'm a mess, and everything I touch is a mess, and I'm sick and tired of doing my best to save us all only to end up hurting people in the process.

I thought I could do this.

I thought I could do it half as well as she did, just because we share blood.

She made leading look easy. It's anything but.

Almost every place I can think to go is likely to amplify the anxiety I feel, not calm it: the labs, the hydro chamber, Control. Even in the rec center, I'll feel pressured to run, do anything but sit still and take some time to *think*. And besides, the track is just another reminder of my futile desire to run *away* when I can only run in circles.

Before I've really decided where I'm headed, I end up at my own front door. Inside, it's every bit as empty as I left it. Will I ever get over it? Will it ever feel normal that our place is now mine and mine alone—that she'll never be waiting for me again?

I turn the fire up as high as it will go, settle into the leather chair. It's familiar against my skin, cool from lack of use. I curl up into a tight ball and stare so long at the flames I start to see myself in them: ravenous and relentless, never satisfied, blooming and bursting like wishes on the verge of burning out.

I could save this place or burn it down, I think, and I'd never have what I truly want.

What I've lost can never be recovered. What I've lost can never be replaced.

What happens when what I've lost . . . when part of it is *myself*?

She died and took part of me with her.

She died and I've been looking for her ever since: in Leo. In Heath. In my ability to pick up the work she left behind, save the station she loved. In anyone who'll look at me like I'm not just a shadow of who I was before the brightest parts of me burned out. In anyone who'll look at me like I'm *enough*.

I hate this, and I didn't ask for any of it. But there is work to be done, and I am still my mother's daughter, and there are still lives at stake—mine included. Not just what could be taken away by one swift swallow of poison, either; a person can eat and sleep and breathe, but still be ash inside. I'm not quite to ashes yet, and I don't want to be.

All I can do is my best, I tell myself. *And my best will be enough. It has to be.*

I repeat it, over and over again in my head, until I start to believe it.

It's only embers, but it's something.

60

SKELETON SPHERE

THREE QUARTERS OF an hour pass, and I spend their entirety still as stone in my chair.

Before finally heading to Control, I strip my layers of exhaustion away: my tired, rumpled clothes. The sheen of sweat on my skin. The pins in my hair that haven't done a thing to keep the flyaways from slipping out.

All I can do is my best. My best will be enough.

No one else has died, not yet, or else I would've heard about it. It's only a matter of time, I'm sure—not if, but when.

Zesi's already at the panel deck when I arrive at Control. Not trying to murder anyone, I note, which seems promising. Gone are the blueprints, the diagrams—his display screens are mostly black now, save for the overlay of a faint white three-dimensional grid: our radar. It's like the skeleton of a sphere, bones sprouting out like a starburst from its center. He has a thin headset frame wrapped around the back of his head, and he's practically shouting into its microphone. I can't hear what's in his ears.

He's oblivious to my presence until I rip the headphones from his head. I press my thumb to the on/off sensor, and immediately, a voice I don't recognize starts blaring through the main speakers.

It doesn't take long to realize it's a recording. A woman's serene voice, at odds with her words: YOU HAVE NOT BEEN GRANTED ACCESS TO THIS LINE OF COMMUNICATION.

"Zesi . . . what . . . ?"

"You left it unlocked," he says, dipping his head toward the message system. "Thought I'd try to pick up where you left off."

"I . . . I could've sworn I logged out this morning." But sure enough, the display screen is open to the secret inbox, my mother's private one. Perhaps I was more out of it than I realized after so little sleep, under so much pressure. The passcode was difficult enough for even me to crack, so this must have been my own mistake. I scroll through the call log, see ten new attempts at contact since the last time I stopped trying. "And you've gotten that message every time?"

"I'm starting to hate her voice," he replies.

It doesn't make any sense. Vonn explicitly directed me—well, my mother—to contact him with that handle. At least they're out of dark space now. In theory, they're close enough to receive our calls, but in reality . . . we should probably focus our attention on stopping them. If they've blocked us, there will be no getting through unless they are the ones to initiate.

"Any sign of them on the radar?" He's been swiping at the

spherical grid ever since I arrived, spinning and examining it from all angles. I haven't seen anything unusual on the display, but then again, I am not our resident expert.

He pinches the screen, zooming out to reveal a wider view of the space around us; the skeleton grid from before is so small now it's just a white circle at the center of an even bigger sphere. He spins the image 180 degrees and a tiny blip flashes against the black.

"There," he says. "They'll be here earlier than we thought—I've been searching the field for any sign of smaller bees or firebirds they might've launched from their main ship. If they're trying to catch us off guard, that'd be the way to do it."

I take in the screen, think. "Did you ever figure out if we're equipped to, uh . . . defend?"

"Oh, we're definitely equipped," he says. He swipes the screen with three fingers, and there are the blueprints again, this time highlighted in yellow in a number of places. Each yellow place has a tag attached to it, like A10 and F3. They're scattered all over our various decks, with the heaviest concentrations on each of the station's main faces. "Take your pick."

"What . . . do the tags mean?"

"We have tons of A tags—those are the smallest. They do minimal damage, but with maximum output that we can coordinate for large effect," he says. "H is full blast. There's only one of those, but it's on an internal magnetic track between the outermost layers of *Lusca*'s shell; I can shift it to one of thirty-two positions, easy, in less than fifteen seconds flat."

"And all of the others?"

"Varying degrees of destruction."

As relieved as I am that we'll be able to protect ourselves, if it comes down to it, I don't want to *destroy*. I cannot stand Vonn, but these are our own people—they're on our team. They just don't know it yet.

A wave of dread hits me. Same team, same strategy: our defense mechanisms are only reassuring until I think of the exact same weapons being turned *against* us.

"Are they—will they be equally equipped?"

"Depends on the craft, depends on their approach," Zesi says. "Their main ship will be loaded, for sure. But if they're sending firebirds out first, the only advantage they'll have is the advantage of surprise."

I exhale, pace the room until I'm looking out the huge window where we take our coffee breaks, resting my elbows on the metal ledge. I prefer this view—endless constellations of stars instead of a finite smattering of control panel buttons. What to do? Assuming we are unable to get in touch, since that seems like a lost cause at this point, it would be wise to plan for their attack.

"How devastating would *full blast* be, exactly?" I ask, as if Zesi has any way of knowing for certain.

"Could breach an entire segment, if I had to guess. If anything cracks the outermost shell, it'll trigger automatic airlocks all over the station"—he pauses, and I hear his fingers tapping away at the display—"they're these giant metal panel sheets, from what I can tell in the prints. Emergency barriers that'll snap together from the floors and ceiling . . . probably best not to get caught on the wrong side of them."

His words trigger a memory long buried: all those years ago, when we were taking precautions against the solar flare, my mother told me something similar. Usually, when I think of that day, I think of sitting with Leo in that gray box of a safe room at the station's core, our backs together, and Haven talking nonstop. I think of my mother telling me *I'm the heart* when I asked why she couldn't come with us.

What I haven't thought about since then is *why* I was so afraid of her staying on duty. *They snap together like teeth*, I remember her saying. *I need to make sure they don't eat you.* I couldn't find the words to tell her how very much I needed her to stay alive, too.

An idea sprouts: we could pile everyone into the safe room—it was built for twice as many people as we have left, at least. "Any idea how much time we have until Vonn closes in on us?"

"An hour?" he says. "*Maybe* two? Could be even less if they've launched the birds. A firebird could zip here in as little as half an hour, depending on how far out it was before takeoff."

I want to wait as long as possible before asking people to camp out in such a dim, depressing room, but it sounds like we're working with a very narrow window of time. You'd think the designers could've made it more hopeful-looking, since it would only be used during times of extreme duress—but no. It's a plain gray cube, cement except for the requisite air vents.

No windows, no neon, no cushions; even the benches are made of steel and cement. Fire hazards and all that, I can only guess. People are unpredictable, especially under stress.

Which . . . makes me reconsider locking everyone down in the safe room altogether, given our circumstances.

Would it be worse to take our chances on Vonn's attack—stop it before it starts, somehow?—or to put our increasingly volatile population together in a dark room where they can't escape? What sort of safe room does it become when you're locked inside it with a mystery murderer who hasn't hesitated to kill six people just like you?

Still. We could lose *many* of our people if things go worst-case scenario with Vonn.

There is no surefire win here.

I close my eyes, make the call.

"Haven?" I say as soon as she picks up. "I'm going to need you to make an emergency announcement."

61

PANDORA

WE HAVEN'T HAD need for the safe room in so many years that half our people aren't old enough to remember how to get there. Fifteen minutes pass in a blur as Heath, Haven, Leo, and I position ourselves in the most heavily trafficked areas around the station, guiding people in the right direction and making sure they actually do what we've asked them to this time. Zesi stays behind to monitor the radar, while Natalin gathers up as many SpaceLove packs as she can pile on the cart—hopefully our people won't have to stay in the safe room for too long, but we can't be careful enough.

When no one passes through my corridor for two minutes straight, I run and find Haven, who's nearest to me on the opposite end of this deck.

"Hey," I say, cutting her off as soon as she's given directions to a trio of sisters. "I'm going back up to Control now. I need you and the guys to check all the residential wings, and also the rec center—make sure no one's unaccounted for, okay?"

She gives me an easy grin. "Go. We've *got* this."

"And after that, could you send Leo up to Control? And the rest of you could stay behind with—"

"*Seriously*, Lindley. Go," she says with a little shove. "And yes, I'll pass all that on."

"And—"

She tilts her head, gives me a look.

"Okay. Okay, thank you, Haven—buzz if you need me."

"We'll be *fiiiine*."

I head back up to Control as quickly as I can, less sure of myself than I look. Ever since I made the call to direct everyone to the safe room, I've been turning the decision over in my head. Eventually, I landed on splitting our core six into two groups: two of us with Heath, the other two with me. Heath will be able to handle anything that gets out of hand in the safe room, and my gut says I can trust him. As for the decision to bring Leo up to Control—mostly, I just want someone else in the room with me besides Zesi. Even though Zesi's beyond preoccupied at the moment, it doesn't mean he's not our killer . . . it only means his sense of self-preservation is as strong as the rest of ours. And just in case, I'd rather not get on the wrong side of said self-preservation.

Besides, having more eyes and ears and hands around should prove helpful, especially since Leo's good under pressure. Zesi hasn't buzzed, so we're not under immediate threat just yet— but that could change at any second.

"Anything new?" I ask as soon as I'm back. Zesi is exactly where I left him, only now he's standing over the display screen instead of sitting on his stool. It's a subtle change, and it carries with it a new sense of authority.

He shakes his head. "They've stalled out here"—he swipes to rotate the radar's sphere, doesn't even have to zoom out this time—"and I'm not quite sure what to make of it."

"Still no word from them?"

"Nothing." He sighs. "On the plus side, I haven't picked up any firebirds just yet."

"And on the down side?"

"They could be stalled out for any number of reasons—to fake us out, or to prepare their shields in case we go on the offensive as soon as they're within shooting range. Or they could be planning to launch a coordinated advance of firebirds," he says. "Easier to send more than two if the ship's not moving."

None of this is good.

"And we don't have any way of moving closer to them on our own, right? Or away?" I ask, just to be sure. We're a station, not a ship—by definition, we are a *stopping* place.

"Not unless we send Heath out in one of our firebirds."

I bite my lip. It isn't the worst idea, and actually, I'm surprised I haven't thought of it before. Maybe Heath could get a call through from one of the crafts instead—maybe *those* lines won't be blocked. For that matter, maybe our regular channels would work. Hope blossoms inside me as I make fast work of our message system, tapping and dragging Vonn's handle from the private inbox over to the main one. I put in the call, and it's working, it's really working—

"Hello?" I say breathlessly as the call connects. "Hello, this is Acting Commander Lindley Hamilton speaking?"

"IT IS WITH REGRET THAT I MUST INFORM YOU," the recorded voice says, speaking right over me. "YOU HAVE NOT BEEN GRANTED ACCESS TO THIS LINE—"

I jam my finger into the screen, end the call. "No, no, *no*."

"She's the worst," Zesi mutters. "The absolute worst."

"Could Heath call from one of the birds?" I ask. "Would that get through, you think?"

"At this point, I think about the only thing that would get through to them is if Heath flew all the way out and raised a white flag."

I'm quiet, weighing pros and cons. It's a total risk—I mean, what if they fire an array of shots at him before he has the chance to prove his approach is a peaceful one? Vonn is the type to assume the worst, obviously. What if they hit him—what if—

"You're not actually considering that terrible idea, are you?" Zesi asks, straightening.

Heath could die. But . . . he could also succeed.

If nothing else, he could try to make contact using one of the birds' communication systems down on the hangar deck—he might not have to fly anywhere at all. The only potential drawback is that it'd leave Haven and Natalin to fend for themselves with everyone down in the safe room. Haven's constantly offering to step in, insisting she can help me handle things. Maybe it's time I let her.

"Lindley?"

"Look, it isn't the *worst* of ideas—I'm all ears if you have a better one." I cross my arms, challenge him with my eyes.

A brief blip sounds from the radar, and Zesi mutters a curse.

"What?" The blurred world snaps clearly back into focus, and I'm at his side in less than two seconds.

There's movement on the grid. Six tiny white specks break off from the larger white dot at the edge of the sphere: Vonn's ship. They move toward us in synchrony.

"How . . . how long do we have?" The words taste like dying stars.

Zesi's deep brown eyes meet mine, dark with steely resolve. "Long enough for Heath to have a chance at holding them off, if you get him in the bird *now*." He glances at the grid, his mouth a grim line. "Maybe less."

There's no time for *what now*, no time for *what if*.

"See you on the other side of this," I say, already halfway out the door. "Do your best here, and I'll do mine."

I only hope our best is enough.

62

MADE OF SPLINTERS

MY STEPS ARE full of fire, my heart is full of ash.

I fly from Control and buzz Heath on the way.

"Linds?" he says, not two seconds after I initiate the call. I hear the din of chaos in the background, everyone crammed into the safe room. "What's happened?"

"No deaths, nothing like that," I say, even as the word *yet* sprouts up in my head. I fill him in quickly on Vonn, on the firebirds. On the rickety splinters I'm calling Our Plan. "Meet me on the hangar deck as soon as you can, okay?" I'm so fast and focused I nearly bump into Leo as I turn the corner, clearly on his way up to Control. *Change of plans*, I mouth at him, and immediately, he does a 180 and falls into step beside me. "I'm talking five minutes, not fifteen," I add to Heath.

"Got it," Heath says. "I'll be there in three."

We end the call, and Leo says, "Hangar deck?"

"Last resort," I reply.

By the time we reach the hangar deck's viewing room, Leo's all caught up and I'm ready to stop talking, ready to actually *fix* this. We've set aside the awkwardness of our last interaction for now, both of us more than eager to focus on the black-and-white task at hand. Heath arrives just a moment after we do, and begins suiting up immediately. I flip a switch on the motherboard, watch the electric-purple grav-force glow bloom out on the runway. In this precise moment, I have déjà vu—step for step, we are a living memory, floating on autopilot through the exact same routine we took before Heath and Zesi set off for *Nautilus*.

So much has shifted since then, and it's only been, what—days?

I've lost all sense of time.

All I know is that every minute brings something heavier than the last, and that I long for the days when our most pressing problem was a possible viral mutation.

Heath settles his helmet into place, the final piece of protection. Leo watches him, and I watch Leo: I watch as his eyes shift to study the second suit, the one Zesi wore out to *Nautilus*.

"Think that would fit me?" Leo asks. Zesi's a medium at most; Leo's thick arms alone would likely make that suit a tight fit.

His words hang in the air. I hear what he *isn't* saying: he wants to go out.

With Heath.

With zero experience.

"No way," I say at the exact same time Heath says, "More suits in the closet."

I shoot Heath a look.

"What?" he says, his voice electronic and thin through the helmet's vocalization processing unit.

"No way is he going out with you, is what I meant."

"It's not a three-person job in here," Leo says. "I can run comms like Zesi did when they went out, let Heath focus on the flying."

I hate that he always has a point. Still, though. I'm not risking *both* of them. There's very little time left to attempt putting a call through to Vonn, or one of his firebirds; *six* are headed our way, and just one of them firing shots could cause damage. Flying out in peaceful surrender—having Heath settle in one spot, unmoving, with the bird's tail side in their face so it's obvious our weapons won't be deployed at them—that's the most powerful symbol I can think of to keep them from launching an all-out attack.

Whether they feel the same way is another question. This strategy is not without its risks.

I refuse to lose them both.

"You've never been in a bird, Leo. You don't have that much experience with the comm systems, not like Zesi. You've got stitches in your dominant arm." I tick my arguments off on my fingers. "And . . . the . . . other suits might be too tight?"

My case isn't strong enough and we all know it.

"Suit up," says Heath. "I'll go prep the bird."

The next minutes pass in slow motion.

Heath strides confidently across the glowing runway to

where our firebirds are docked. Where the runway cuts off at each of its faraway ends, there are no walls, no windows—it's nothing but wide-open space, yawning like a mouth full of glitter. I can't even begin to count the stars.

In the closet at my back, Leo has found a suit, a perfect fit. Once he locks the helmet in place, it's easy to forget he's never worn one before; he looks like a natural. He looks like Heath.

"You're sure about this?" I ask. "You're *sure?*"

I've never known life without Leo in it. As much as I'm growing to crave Heath's presence, Leo's is like gravity itself.

"We'll be back, Linds," he says with a sad smile that isn't reassuring in the least. "Have a little hope."

A half laugh falls out of me. *Hope.*

I glance out the viewing panels, see Heath standing beside the bird. He's positioned it in the precise center of the runway, and is motioning for Leo to join him. "Guess that's your cue."

He takes one last, long look at me.

"Don't lose yourself out there," I say, recalling our conversation back in the lab. *If you ever lose yourself, I'll come find you,* I told him. What a broken promise. At least I intended to keep it when I made it. Back then, I thought I could save everything. Everyone.

"Deal works both ways, remember?" he says. "If it takes losing myself to save you . . . then . . . that's what it takes."

That's not how it works, I want to say.

Losing him would kill me a thousand times, not save me.

A loud buzzing noise crescendos outside the viewing panels,

and we both snap our heads to look just as it reaches full volume—then cuts off to silence—and the electric-purple glow blinks out to pitch blackness.

"What the—what was *that*?" I depress the button that will put my voice directly into Heath's helmet. "Are you okay?"

The lights flicker back on just as he starts to respond—just in time for Leo and me to see both Heath and the bird slam down onto the runway.

"Did the *grav force* just go out on you?! Are you hurt?" My voice spirals toward panic, but then Heath stands, slowly, shaking out his left arm. He moves to inspect the bird's tail, on the side I can't see, and is limping almost imperceptibly. Hopefully neither of them are badly damaged.

I'm getting an incoming buzz, so I motion for Leo to take over with Heath. A piercing alarm sounds, drowning out the voice in my ears as it says my name.

"Zesi?" I say, glancing down at the name on the incoming call. "What the hell is going on? Are they here already? Did we get hit? What is that alarm?" My questions burst like tiny bombs.

I hear him trying to respond, but the alarm is so loud I only get bits and pieces, fragments of curses. Another call tries to cut in—Haven or Natalin, to be sure—but I ignore it. I have so many questions for Zesi; I need to know if we're under attack. Leo's out on the open deck now, working with Heath to inspect the bird. Do I call them back in? Send them out as planned?

The piercing wail dies out a few seconds later.

"That was all my fault, sorry, all of it—it was—" Zesi's breathless, more panicked than I've ever heard him. He pauses, takes a breath so loud it crackles in my ear. "I was just testing our defense shields, trying to see how fast I could get them up. Required more energy than I realized to shift 'em at top speed—glitched out the power in some sectors of the station."

"And set off an alarm, apparently."

"Apparently. Yes."

I pinch the bridge of my nose. "So no one's shooting at us?"

"They will be, if Heath doesn't get out there, like, *now*."

"Got it," I say. "Thanks for working on the shields—don't go with top speed again unless it's absolutely necessary."

As soon as we end the call, my buzz screen goes off again—Natalin, like I guessed—but as much as I need to take it, I let it go. Whatever's going on down in the safe room . . . it can't be good, but it can't be *our station is about to get decimated* levels of urgent. I'll call her back as soon as I can, but I have to get Heath and Leo out of here *now*.

"Are you good?" I ask, putting my voice directly into Heath's and Leo's helmets. "Is the bird good?"

They've moved on from the tail, each with one hand firmly on the bird's body—like they're trying to hold everything in place to minimize the damage if the glitch happens again. I look down, find myself gripping the edges of the motherboard; I wasn't even out there when the grav force went out, yet my knuckles are turning white.

Gravity: one more thing that's proven unreliable as of late.

We all trust in the world we know until it proves it shouldn't be trusted, I guess.

"Good enough," Heath says.

I don't want to say goodbye, but it doesn't matter. There isn't time for that anyway.

"Go *fast*, okay?" I grit my teeth until I feel pain in my jaw, will my eyes to keep dry.

They climb in, pull their straps tight. The protective shield lowers over them. Seals them inside.

I blink and they're gone, a tiny blip of a vessel out in the endless, glittering sky.

I take in this moment.

This silence.

This could be it. I could be this alone forever.

I didn't think there could be anything emptier than being on my own, forever, without the people I love. But when I think about losing Leo—and Heath—and my mother, of course—it's like bits of my soul are being chipped away with a sharp knife. There's something worse than being alone, and it is this: my soul, scraped into a fine pile of shadow. A fading star eclipsed by dust, not quite dead and not quite living.

Natalin buzzes again, and the sound of the vibration is too loud in this empty room, now that everything is still. I don't want to take the call, don't want to hear anyone tell me how I *should* be handling this mess. I never wanted any of it. I want it to be over—all of it, with all of us at peace, all of us together. All of us alive.

None of us murderers.

I close my eyes. Answer.

"Hey." My voice splinters.

"It's getting pretty overwhelming in here—everyone's freaking out about that alarm," she says. "And it's about a thousand degrees, and it smells horrible, and—"

There's a commotion in the background, and she yells something that does nothing to calm it. If anything, the volume gets worse. "Sorry if that was loud in your ear," she goes on. "Anyway, can you please send Leo and Haven back here to help me?"

My stomach flips. "Leo's out with Heath in a bird, won't be back for . . . a while. I thought Haven was with you, though?"

"She said Grace came to her panicked about Yuki having a nosebleed or something? That was twelve minutes ago—she should've been back with the witch hazel by . . . now . . . well, wait, that's weird." She pauses. I imagine her thick eyebrows knitting together like they always do when she's perplexed about a problem. "Yuki's asleep—Grace, too. And yes, because I know you're about to ask, I can see them breathing from here. I don't see any sign of nosebleed, though?"

"I *was* about to ask. And you're right, that's weird. Can you wake Grace up and ask her about it?"

"Already on it." I hear all sorts of noise in the background, but less than a minute later, Grace's small voice cuts through it. *Haven? I haven't seen her today, why?*

"Grace says she hasn't—"

"I heard her."

Natalin and I are both silent on either end of the call.

If she's like me, she's trying to stop thinking the worst.

If she's like me, she's unsuccessful.

Zesi's busy with our defenses—the gravity glitch confirmed it, as did the blaring alarm. Heath and Leo aren't even on the station right now, and Natalin? Natalin sounds too genuinely panicked to be lying. That leaves only me, only Haven.

"Lindley?"

I make a small noise, something sad and unintelligible, just to let her know I'm still listening.

"You . . . should probably go look for her, yeah?"

This: this is the thing that pulls my tears out of hiding.

This is the hopeless part.

I don't know how I didn't see it before, but now that I've put things together, they are blinding. Such a blatant lie told straight to Natalin's face, so deliberately—if not for that, I'd be fearing for Haven's life right now, that her lingering absence meant she'd become our next victim.

I am not fearing for Haven's life. Instead, I fear the stranger she's become.

Haven.

Haven.

63

THE LIES THAT BLIND

HAVEN AND I are six months apart down to the minute. Heath is just a few minutes younger; Haven likes to remind us. I'm older than them both.

We've known each other since our mothers spoon-fed us SpaceLove puree packs.

We've traced so many circles in these endless station corridors, it's hard to know which one of us is following the other's footsteps. Sometimes it feels like I'm following her, even though I set off on the path first—between us, she's the vibrant one, the magnetic one, the one everyone loves despite her strong stubborn streak. I'm the one with my nose in a book, with needles and scalpels and surgical tools in my hands. I've been told my tendency to be unfailingly direct makes people uncomfortable.

My chest is caving in.

I never saw her break. Maybe I never truly saw her at all.

64

HEART, PETRIFIED

HAVEN COULD BE anywhere.

The station is sprawling, deck upon deck of residential wings and common areas and labs, not to mention the hydro chamber and an entire host of energy banks tucked deeply out of sight. With everyone down in the safe room, every turn leads to yet another unsettlingly empty corridor. I've never seen a place so dead in my entire life.

Would she have gone to SSL, true to the excuse she gave Natalin? Or was that just a reason to leave? I keep quiet, step carefully. She could be around the next corner. She could be looking for *me*—or lying in wait. It seems unlikely that she'd go after Zesi; keeping him alive means keeping herself alive, given that he's actively running defense against Vonn up in Control. Last Haven knew, though, I was in Control, too, not down on the hangar deck sending Leo and Heath out into the stars.

I need to warn Zesi. As soon as I find a place where I'm sure she won't hear me, where there's no chance my voice will carry, I'll call. The second she knows *I* know she's our killer—our *killer*—I still cannot even begin to reconcile it—I lose my advantage.

Every private place I can think of to make the call could put me at risk. Assuming she's actively targeting me, no place of my own is safe. I imagine all the places she could be:

In Portside, tucked in between lifeless appliances at one of its many unused lab stations.

In Medical, guessing code after code in an attempt to unlock my stash of surgical tools.

In my home.

She has clearance to enter every single room because I trusted her. I *trusted* her.

There is no perfect spot without risk: that place does not exist. An alcove lies just ahead—it's a dead end, nowhere to hide if she discovers me. Nowhere to run. I doubt she'd use something so subtle as belladonna this time, not when confronted with someone who knows the truth. Also, a belladonna-laced beverage would be too easy for me to refuse.

When I reach the alcove, I dart inside and crouch down, cramming myself into a tight spot between a sofa and the window. I'm partially hidden this way, at least, and maybe the plush cushions of the sofa will deaden my voice. These steel walls are unforgiving.

I buzz Zesi, my hands more than a little unsteady. He answers immediately.

"You haven't seen Haven, have you?" My voice is a low rasp,

as quiet as I can make it without him having to guess at my words.

"Haven? No, why?" I hear blips and beeps in the background. Heath and Leo should meet Vonn's firebirds soon, if they haven't already. I try to suppress the anxiety I feel over . . . well, everything. Zesi would have buzzed me already if an attack had flared up. Right?

I shake my head, try to clear it. Focus on what you can *control*, Lindley.

"*Do not* let Haven into Control under any circumstances, okay? Change the passcode if you have to, do whatever it takes—I'm pretty sure she's our killer, Zesi."

He mutters a curse. Leaves it at that.

"My thoughts exactly." It's a relief to have told someone, and it's also terrible: saying it out loud makes it feel real. I wish it weren't real. "If you have a second"—I'm pushing it, but I've gone undiscovered this long, might as well see if he can help—"let me know if you see anything off on the vid-feeds from SSL?"

He doesn't say a word, but I hear him shifting and clicking buttons. "I don't see *her* . . . only thing I see is a tablet out on the main countertop, and a drawer left half open. Helpful?"

I nod, my throat constricting. It's confirmation enough that she's been to SSL tonight, that she's likely *still* there. "Yeah," I force out. Scraaaape goes the knife against my increasingly stony heart.

A faint string of beeps goes off; I wish I knew the radar well enough to decode their meaning. "I—I've gotta go," he says, an urgency to his voice that wasn't there before.

"Everything okay?" On instinct, I glance out the window beside me. I can't see a thing from here. "What's happening?"

"The guys are within radio space of Vonn's team," he says. "Let *me* worry about this, okay, Lindley? Try not to think about it. I'll handle it."

I have every reason in the galaxy to crave control.

Every reason to want to handle it myself.

But I am not enough.

I am not enough for everyone, at every time, in every crisis— Haven was right, at least about this. I do need help. And I need to learn how to accept it.

"Okay." My voice is small but clear. "Okay," I repeat, with a little more conviction. "I'll try not to think about it."

"*Good*." I hear him tapping rapid-fire on the keyboard, multitasking at its finest. "And Lindley?" There's a break in his typing, just for a moment. "Go get her."

I'm shaking as I end the call, my muscles starting to cramp from being held in such a tight, awkward position. *Go get her.*

The knife carves a more substantial piece from my heart: a block of petrified, tangled roots. Memories. Questions.

I kill this part of myself, because it's the only way to deaden the nerves, raw and stinging. It's the only way I can face the truth without crumbling entirely. And I do need to face the truth—

For Sailor, Emme, Nieva.

For Jaako and Kerr.

For Mila.

For those who will be next, if I don't put a stop to it.

This. Ends. Now.

65

ECLIPSE

STARBOARD-SIDE LAB: EVEN from outside its glass doors, clear and sparkling, row after row of illuminated pillars cast an eerie glow on the otherwise pitch-black room. Not a hint of shadow mars the perfect white light; wherever Haven is, she must be deep in the forest.

I press my back to the cool steel wall just outside the door, collect my breath. Now that this moment is here, all I want is to never have to face it. What do you say when someone you've known forever reveals herself to be skin and bones and cobwebs? Did she ever truly have a soul, and if not, how did she hide it? If so, where did it go? When she looks in the mirror, does she feel remorse for the terrible choices she's made?

Or does she only feel alive?

My lashes flutter closed, and I will my eyes dry. *Be strong for the station*, I tell myself. *Be brave.*

I'm not so much afraid of dying—it's looking in her eyes that's hard to think about. Looking inside, searching for any sign of the friend I thought I knew. Finding her already dead.

I take a deep breath and tap in my entrance code. A blast of cold air escapes as the doors part, like it can't leave the room fast enough. I slip into the shadows, let the doors seal me inside. I'm here, and I'm not leaving until this is over. Even if she does show a hint of compassion, humanity, remorse—what then? How am I to know it's real, and not just another false act of desperate self-preservation?

And what will I do with her when I find her? I've focused so thoroughly on discovering the truth that I didn't stop to think about how to ensure justice. This is unprecedented on the station, really. I don't remember anyone ever having to face serious consequences for anything. Perhaps I can send her down to Nashville, let the board figure out how to deal with her. Or, worse: perhaps I could send her with Vonn.

If I can just make it to the lab station, I can check the tablet to confirm my suspicions—that she's at pillar F23, *Atropa belladonna*. Because why else would she be here? Not for witch hazel, certainly. I can't remember ever telling Haven about Yuki's nosebleeds, now that I think about it. A shiver raises the hair on my arms. Maybe Heath told her?

The spotlit lab station isn't far from SSL's entrance, but it's not terribly close, either. Nothing will hide me except darkness until I'm there, and then—if Haven happens to look that way at just the right moment—I'll be bathed in bright light.

On second thought, maybe I should head straight for F23: in the forest of pillars, at least, I can hide. I can slip out of sight, disappear in the darkness.

If only I remembered, for sure, how to find the pillar I need.

It is utterly silent in this room, and I make myself a ghost: I match her, silence for silence, as I edge toward the first row. The pillars are arranged in a large grid, more than a hundred in each row, planted evenly from this end of the room all the way to the far side.

I take careful steps, seeking out the deep-black shadows between pillars where their glow doesn't reach. My reflection is distorted in every curved bit of glass, and my eyes are too bright, like I'm starry-eyed with hope, when what I truly feel is the precise opposite. I'm almost afraid to breathe, for fear of giving myself away; I get light-headed quickly from all the shallow breaths, dizzy from all the paranoia.

What could she be doing here, for so long, so quietly, in such secrecy?

I'm deep into the forest when the lights flicker—every pillar, dark, for a split second, before they hold, steady and bright.

I hear a gasp.

She isn't far. She could be as close as a few pillars away.

My heartbeat picks up, trying to run straight out the back of me instead of continuing on in the direction we're moving. It's so strong, and so fierce, I eventually give in: I crouch, in a spot of pitch-blackness, try to calm down. I'm shaking.

The lights flicker again, and this time it's followed by the blaring alarm, same as before. What's happened? What's happen*ing*? Did Zesi activate the defense shields like before—did he activate them for *real*? Are we under attack? I want to call him. Desperately, I want to, and it takes everything in me to keep from buzzing him.

Instead, I stay where I am.

I hug my knees. Feel my heart pound against them.

The alarm cuts off abruptly, mid-blare, but my ears keep ringing. Steady, steady: I breathe. Wait. Wish for my mother. Try to trust everyone else to handle what I can't—try to trust I can handle what I must.

Haven isn't buzzing anyone, I can't help but notice. All those offers to help, all those professions of loyalty to the station, and to me—yet when the alarm sounds she is silent. I'm only silent because it would give me away.

Dread falls over me: Does she know she isn't alone?

Slowly, I stand. The backs of my knees tingle as I straighten. SSL's sliding doors are pretty quiet against the hum of all the pillars, but if she was listening for them, it's not impossible that she could've heard me come in. Perhaps we've even been circling each other, she on her way out, me venturing ever deeper. If I don't act quickly, she could disappear, slip into any single room of the station, hide there indefinitely. It would take forever to find her.

I take careful steps toward the sound of the gasp I heard, do my best to stay in the darkest spots. It's impossible to avoid *all* of the light. Still, I'm pretty successful at keeping myself hidden.

And then.

I see her, sitting on the floor, her back to me. Unlike me, she isn't shrouded in darkness: she's sitting close to the pillar, practically drowning in its light. She's bent over, working on something, a curtain of her shiny blonde hair hanging down on the right side like always.

She looks so achingly familiar—so much like she's looked on countless late nights when we sat, cross-legged, eating midnight chocolate from my mother's stash and playing chess. The sight knocks the wind out of me. I can't move.

I stand, staring, not sure what to say or do—

And then I'm getting a call, the vibration loud enough to rip steel, and that's it, it's over.

Haven turns, on her feet in an instant. On the floor is a tray of leaves, shredded.

My eyes travel up, up: to the razor blade in her hand. Traces of belladonna cling to its sharp edges.

I find my voice before she finds hers. "That . . . isn't witch hazel, Haven."

We meet eyes, and she knows, I can tell—she knows I've figured out the truth. I've caught her in her lies. I watch the full spectrum of fight or flight cross her face, her beautiful face that so perfectly covers such a horrific mind.

She doesn't run.

She doesn't move.

The second one of us so much as flinches, it'll be the beginning of the end. For now, it is checkmate.

My throat constricts. "Why?"

It's broken, nothing more than a whisper.

She shakes her head, slowly at first, eyebrows knitting

together, and the expression deepens and twists until it's pain upon pain, painful to look at. Her careful mask is gone. I'll never be able to unsee this.

And then she smiles, like she has nothing left to lose. "Why *not*?" The smile falters as she falls apart. "All my life, forever, *always*, I just . . . I wanted . . . I didn't want *this*, but I never get what I want, so it doesn't really matter, does it?" There's a look in her eye like she's surrounded by a thousand fun-house mirrors, all of them bending reality, all of them covered in distorted versions of herself. It's almost as if she isn't speaking to me at all. "But you don't know how that feels, do you? Commander's daughter—Commander *Lindley*. You don't know what it's like to live in your shadow, or your perfect brother's shadow, or to never get *credit* for the things you do, because no one sees them at all, right? I only wanted to do something that matters, I swear!" She swerves from pain to laughter and back again. "I was trying to help! They were dead weight and you know it—I was doing my part to save everyone else, Linds, can't you see?"

My eyes are full of tears that won't spill. "You wanted to do something that *matters*? You wanted to *help*?" My voice is like rough rock, like a snarl through sharp teeth. "You wanted to be *remembered*." I shake my head, and the tears fall. "You offered to help me when you knew *exactly* what was going on." Even as the words are still coming out, her disjointed logic suddenly makes sick sense: I get it now, and it's unbelievable. "You offered to help because you knew the answers all along—you created problems only you could fix, a crisis so huge it could only be outshined by the person who ended it. You wanted to be *praised* for solving murders you committed—that is seriously disturbing, Haven."

She waves a hand in the air. "Sounds kind of horrible when you say it like that, honestly." Bright white light winks from the razor blade as she tightens her grip on it. "But the best part is—I still will be praised for it all."

Her mouth quirks up at one corner.

I *run*.

She's fast but so am I, and I have the advantage of slightly longer legs—I run past pillar after pillar, brilliant white and pitch darkness alternating like a strobe light. If she catches me, if she *murders* me, she can create the truth: I won't be alive to tell anyone otherwise. She can be the hero, she can be the one who saved the station from *me*. And of course the deaths will end, because she'll assume the role of commander. She'll deftly erase any traces of herself on the vid-feeds, and all Zesi will know is that there was a tablet left out on the station counter—for all he knows, I could've been the one who put it there. Haven could plant seeds in his mind to undermine what I told him earlier, when I accused her of being our murderer; she could tell Natalin *I* asked her to get the witch hazel. She'll lie, and she'll pull it off.

I cannot let that happen.

She's gaining on me; I turn a sharp corner, weave into darkness, try to lose her so I can get behind her somehow and knock the blade from her hand. She'll be nothing without it—we'll be evenly matched, at best. A belladonna-laced blade will be my certain death, though, if I let her get close enough. I have no doubt now that she'll go through with it. She's delusional, clearly. If the praise she craves is finally within reach, she'll shred me like a paper snowflake and call it self-defense.

I dart around another pillar, catch a glimpse of the spotlit station. If Zesi happens to look at the vid-feeds at just the right moment—if we're not *under attack*, which we could be, for all I know, though it's at least slightly reassuring there haven't been any more alarms—if Zesi sees us on the screen, he'll have to know I'm the one being hunted, and not the other way around.

I head that way, and she completely takes the bait, follows me. She's losing ground with every step, out of practice and unable to keep matching my pace. It gives me a split second longer to figure out a plan—I eye the open drawer, look for anything I can use. There are no blades, only microscopes and empty petri dishes and a handful of zip ties.

It isn't much. But zip ties worked on Akello, when he was yelling outside my door that morning. If I can bind her wrists without getting cut by the razor—

I grab several zip ties, and a microscope for good measure. It's relatively large, with decent heft, and it's blunt; I've lost my lead, and she's closing in on me now, and I swear I don't see anything behind her eyes as she lunges, blade-first.

I ram the base of the microscope out on instinct, feel it connect with her knuckles as she cries out in pain. The blade clatters to the floor, glints under the spotlight—there is blood, only a drop or two—was she cut by the blade, or by the blunt edges of the base? She dives for the blade, so whatever happened didn't faze her. I kick it away, far out of her reach.

Instead of scrambling after it like I expect, she springs back up, wrenches the microscope away from me, and the next thing I know it's coming toward my head. I barely dodge a direct hit. If Zesi is seeing any of this go down, he's not buzzing me, and he's certainly not here in time to help. Haven swings at me again, and this time, manages to graze my temple. It sends a stinging shock through my head, but the room isn't swaying or sliding or spinning. Not yet.

We meet eyes, only briefly—finally, *finally*, there is a hint at recognition there, that I do not deserve this, that *no one* deserves this. I let out a breath, one I've been saving in case it happens to be my last. But just as I start to relax, her eyes eclipse again: rings of hazel gold around pupils so dark and dreadful I can't bear to look.

I hate this. So much, I hate it—

But there is no time to think, because she tries to take full advantage of my hesitation, flinches like she's going to strike again—and harder this time. Before she gets the chance, I seize her wrist so tightly the microscope falls to the tile; I wrench her arm behind her, not gently, pin her to the lab counter as firmly as I can. I make fast work of the zip ties, twisting her other arm around to meet the first, securing both wrists tightly to each other—

And then it is done.

She could run, yes. But without a blade—or the ability to put in a passcode at any door, with her hands bound behind her, and the fact that I'm already buzzing Zesi before either of us has even caught a full breath—she has nowhere to go. She is no hero, will never be, and we both know it.

I pick up the razor. Toss it into the sink, deep into the drain, where it's physically impossible for her to dig it out—where it's physically impossible for *me* to dig it out and do something I'd forever regret.

Zesi answers on the first try. "*Told* you I'd take care of us!" His voice is light, almost jubilant on the other end. "We're good. We're *good*, Lindley! Boys are on their way back as we speak!" He's clearly riding a victory high and has no idea what I've just been through.

"That's—that's incredible, Zesi." Relief tears spring up, blurring my vision. "Really incredible."

I can't take my eyes off Haven, and she won't take hers off me.

It's hardly a moment of celebration.

It takes Zesi a few seconds to register my silence. "You okay?" he finally asks. "Need anything?"

What *don't* I need?

"Help," I reply. For once, I'm eager to ask for it. "Also, a long break."

Haven lowers her eyes.

I don't know what's going on behind them.

I don't know her at all.

All I know is that it's over.

66

BEGINNINGS

I KNOW A lot of things about a lot of things.

I know about supernovas, black holes.

I know there are stars that radiate green light but appear white, true colors hidden until untangled by a prism.

I know people are the same way.

It's been four days since I bound Haven Winters's wrists with zip ties.

Three days since I confessed the full truth to Shapiro. *You've done remarkably well, considering all you've been through,* he said. It's Vonn he's angry with, not me—though I did get a strong reprimand for not coming clean immediately. There will be some immediate restructuring, including a number of fresh faces on our own station to help us transition, but we don't have to leave—and they won't be staying forever. Not here, anyway. For once, the board sided with Shapiro on something: Radix will have a permanent change in leadership, and we get to keep our *home.*

Two days ago, the supply shipment arrived. People are eating again, and no one is dying. Haven eventually admitted to faking the food incident, her dramatic collapse, everything—what a disturbing level of commitment, to go so far as to slice her head open, so far as to need stitches.

It isn't lost on me that I stitched up the very person who later tried to kill me.

We've still seen no sign of *Nautilus*-like symptoms; Shapiro told me to rest easy about that, that they likely suffered from the same strain as our parents did—that it wouldn't be out of the question for it to present itself more aggressively in such a relatively tiny station. They'll have a team up to do full autopsies soon, just to be sure, but we appear to be in the clear.

It's been two hours since Heath told Haven goodbye. He was the only one allowed, being her twin. The rest of us passed the time in speculation, wondering if she'll like it on Earth. Probably not, I'd guess—of all the places there are to see down on the planet, she'll be taken to somewhere smaller than our station's safe room, somewhere every bit as bleak. My heart cracks a little more every time I think about it.

Only five minutes have passed since I last wished for my mother.

Five minutes is progress.

Heath and Leo are here, at least, with me in my home. It's a quiet night. It's been a quiet several days. Shapiro had tucked away a fresh stash of coffee and chocolate in the shipment before he found out the truth about my mother; Leo's brewing a French press now. It's a bit late for coffee, but it won't matter. None of us has managed a good night of sleep yet.

The thing that keeps me awake at night, the thing I dream of that eventually pulls me swiftly out of sleep: there is no going back to how things were, not for any of us. I thought you could only change the future, not the past. But the past is constantly shifting when I think about it. Memories that fall apart when I think of Haven. Memories I see in a new light when I think of all that's happened since the first time Heath—and Leo— kissed me. The shifting past makes it hard to know what to do with the future. None of us are sure we even know ourselves right now, honestly. We're trying to help each other remember.

I've tucked a new memory away, too, another thing Shapiro said at the very end of our call. *You sound so much like her*, he told me.

The words got stuck in his throat.

After we'd both sat in mutual silence for several minutes— the only two people left in the world who knew her, and knew her well—he told me this: *You are so much like her. She'd be proud.*

Only a few words, yet they were *everything.*

We'll help each other remember, too.

Leo brings the French press over to where I'm sitting at the window; Heath brings the mugs. We sit in a row, Leo and Heath on either side of me. We take long, slow sips of our coffee. We watch the stars. All we have is this moment—not the future, not the past. For once, I'm trying to embrace it.

Right now, we are alive.

Right now, we have each other.

We've lost so much—but we've survived even more. I search the sky, lose myself in its silent, splintered starlight. *You are so much like her. She'd be proud.* The stars flicker, a thousand thousand fireflies frozen in flight. A deep calm settles over me, settles into a place I feared would be empty forever.

I've never been so happy to be wrong.

ACKNOWLEDGMENTS

To the world's most wonderful literary agents, Holly Root and Taylor Haggerty: thank you for believing in my work, and for the way you work so hard on behalf of all your clients. I am forever grateful for you and think the world of you both. To Mary Pender and Heather Baror-Shapiro, thank you for always championing my work in the film and foreign rights spheres, respectively—you are both brilliant at what you do, and I can't thank you enough for all you've done on my behalf over the years.

To my editors—Emilia Rhodes, who brought this book into the world, and Elizabeth Lynch, who saw it through—I feel so lucky to have worked with both of you on this project! And to everyone else at HarperTeen who had a hand in making this book happen and getting it in front of readers—Jessie Gang (design), Jon Howard (production editor), Bess Braswell and Michael D'Angelo (marketing), Vanessa Nuttry (production manager), Jessica White (copy editor), Dan Janeck (proof-reader), and Gina Rizzo (publicist extraordinaire!)—I'm so grateful for all the time, heart, and energy you put into this project. Thank you!

This book would not be what it is without the wonderful,

talented author friends whose insight and encouragement helped shape this book:

Tracey Neithercott, who read this book in a single day—on her birthday!—and offered brilliant suggestions when I needed them most;

Emily Bain Murphy, whose unfailing support and encouragement kept me going on the most difficult of days;

Carlie Sorosiak, who traded drafts with me when I couldn't wait for *Wild Blue Wonder*, and who sent the most excellent string of messages upon finishing mine;

Anna Priemaza, who did endless productivity sprints with me when we were both on tight deadlines;

Alison Cherry, whose invaluable beta-reading skills are always so thoughtful and thorough;

Karen M. McManus, whose blurb for this book means so much to me—I adored *One of Us Is Lying*, and I hope the fact that I've written a mystery means we'll get to do more events together in the future!

When I was in the earliest stages of drafting this book, I flung small snippets of it out to various friends—their enthusiasm for this project was so motivating! Thank you to all of you who expressed excitement along the way: Alex Higgins, China DeSpain, Mark O'Brien, Amanda Olivieri, Lola Sharp, Nadine Jolie Courtney, Gwen Cole, Heather Kaczynski, and Kristen Orlando.

Lodge of Death friends (you know who you are): reading these pages at our various retreats helped fuel the project immensely, as did the innumerable hours I spent working on it at my favorite window, surrounded by all of you.

To #TheSandwolves—especially Stephanie, Carole, Charlotte, and Belle—thank you all for the light you shine into my life! I'm grateful for each of you, and can't wait to share this book with you. Thank you, too, to my bookstagram friends who helped out with the cover reveal (Melissa at @thereaderandthechef, Heather at @read.write.coffee, and Bridget at @darkfaerietales_)—you do such beautiful work, and I'm grateful you took the time to support mine!

Finally, to my family: Mama and Daddy and Lori, thank you so much for your wonderful support and for believing I could do anything I set my mind to. To my vast network of grandparents, aunts and uncles, cousins, and in-laws—thank you for being at my various events, despite long hours on the highways, and for being so excited with me about all of this.

Andrew, I cannot put into words how much I love you. You are my very best friend, and I'm grateful for every single minute we've spent together. Thank you for being the sweetest, most wonderful husband a girl could dream of—your love and support mean everything to me. James, you are brilliant and kind and thoughtful and creative, and I cannot wait to see what you do in this world. Thank you for being you: you inspire me every day to be more thoughtful, giving, and kind to the world around me. I love you both so, so much.

In memory of Theo Freeman Malone, Darryl "Cujo" Malone, and Ross Clayton Lehmberg. When I started writing this book,

I had not tasted grief like I would over the years to come. By the time this book comes out, I might have tasted more. To Jesus, my savior, who sustains me through every season: When I am overwhelmed, I cast my anxiety on you. Whether heartbroken or bursting with joy, my hope is in you. Where I am not enough, you are. | Philippians 4:6–7

TURN THE PAGE FOR A PEEK AT ANOTHER
HIGH-STAKES ADVENTURE BY KAYLA OLSON

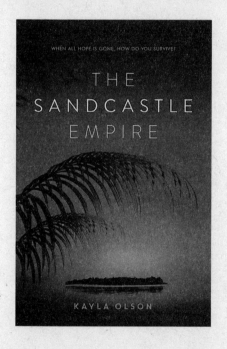

ONE

I WON'T MISS these mornings.

I won't miss the sand, the sea, the salt air. The splintered wood of the old, worn boardwalk, burrowing beneath my skin. I won't miss the sun, bright and blinding, a spotlight on me as I watch and wait. I won't miss the silence.

No, I won't miss these mornings at all.

Day after day, I slip down to the boardwalk when it's still dark. I've worked hard to make it look like I'm simply a girl who loves sunrises, a girl who'd never shove back. One of those is true, at least. The Wolves who guard this beach hardly blink at me anymore, a rare show of indifference bought by my consistency, my patience. Two *years* of consistency and patience, every single morning since they plucked us from lives we loved and shoved us into gulags. I sit where the guards can see me—where *I* can see *them*—where I can see everything. I watch the water, I watch the waves. I watch more than water, more than waves. I look for cracks.

There've been no cracks. The guards' routine has forever been solid, impenetrable, the only reason I haven't yet made a break for it. I will, though. I am a bird, determined to fly despite clipped wings and splintered feet. This cage of an island won't hold me forever.

One day, when the war ends, I will eat ice cream again. I will run barefoot on the beach without fear of stepping on a mine. I will go into a bookstore, or a coffee shop, or any of the hundreds of places currently occupied by Wolves, and I will sit there for hours just because I can. I will do all of these things, and more. If I survive.

I am always ready for a way out, always looking to leave. I carry my past wherever it fits: tucked in at my back, hanging from my neck, buried deep in my pocket. A tattered yellow book. A heavy ring on its heavy chain. A vial of blood and teeth. My empty hands are my advantage—with nothing but my own skin to dig my nails into, with no one left to cling to, I'm free to take back this war-stained world. If everything goes as planned, that is.

It may not be obvious to anyone else, but things are changing. I see subtle signs of it everywhere, for better and worse all at once. Where there used to be only two guards at this beachfront station, now there are four. Where the guards once stepped casually around certain patches of sand—they've been loud and clear in warning us of the land mines buried there— they now step carefully, single file, if they even leave their station at all. Until last week, their post was equipped with a blood-red speedboat. Now they've traded sleek for simple, a no-frills green sailboat in its place meant to disadvantage anyone who tries to use it to escape. As if any of us could make it that far without being blown to pieces.

This quiet shifting of routine assures me the rumors are true.

Someone escaped last week, people say. Someone else plans to try. Today, tomorrow, next week, next month, I've heard it all. The rumors aren't about me—I'd never be allowed to sit here now, watching as always, if they were. This worked out exactly the way I hoped, that my being close to the beach triggers the assumption that I am up to nothing, nothing at all out of the ordinary. To change my routine would be suspicious.

Now I wait only for the guards to turn their backs on me, as they sometimes do, when they go for coffee refills inside their bare-bones old beach tower. They are far too comfortable with me looking comfortable. Too confident I'll stay put. They keep their eyes trained on the seawall, on those who've taken a sudden interest in the sunrise.

The boardwalk has been lonely for the better part of two years, but not now. Not yesterday, either, or the day before. Whether the others are plotting an escape or just hoping to glimpse one, who knows? This is undoubtedly the best spot for either, I figured that out my first week. From every other side of this island, the water leads straight back to mainland Texas. Better open ocean than that.

These fresh faces that peek out over the seawall and divert attention away from me—it's good, and it's not. Anyone could make a run for it at any time. The Wolves will redouble their security measures when that happens, no doubt, rain bullets and bombs over the entire camp. I can't be around when that happens. I need to make a run for the boat today, this morning, *now*, or I might never get the chance.

I have to be first.

Dawn breaks, a hundred thousand shades of it, so brilliant the sky can hardly contain it.

Two guards go inside their post, and the third turns—this is it this is it this is it—but then the air shifts. It starts with a seagull, warning on its wings as it flies straight for the ocean, like it wants to get far, far away. The two remaining guards meet eyes. I hear the rumble of footsteps, not from the beach but from beyond the seawall at my back, toward barracks and breakfast and the silk lab I've left behind.

A distant explosion shakes the entire island. Two more follow on its heels, five more after that. Gunfire, like a storm—so many blasted bullets I lose count—screaming, chaos. It's louder with every second. Louder and *closer*.

I freeze, every muscle in my body stiff. I'm too late, a split second too late—someone must have attempted escape from the wrong side of the island.

Looks like I'm not the only one who wanted to be first.

All four officers are out of the post now, running their tight zigzag pattern through the sand, toward the noise, careful not to blow themselves to pieces. They don't look my way as they pass.

I should have gone for it in the dead of night, shouldn't have waited for perfect timing—there is no perfect. These bullets and bombs are the consequences, I'm sure of it, security measures on steroids. I've missed my chance.

Or maybe not.

The green sailboat bobs idly at the end of their dock. No one has stayed behind to guard it.

I shift, about to make a break for it—but then that miserable seagull settles itself on the sand in the wrong place and sets off a mine. The earsplitting explosion is close enough to scare me still. Smoke and feathers obscure the guards' sandy footsteps, obliterating my only clue as to where the safe path is. Before last week, when they planted hundreds of fresh mines, I could have run it in my sleep. Not now.

People come spilling over the seawall, five and ten and fifteen, more with every second. If they're desperate enough to run this way, straight toward the sand and the mines, I don't want to know what they're running *from*. I scramble to the edge of the boardwalk. There's an opening below it, where wind has blown the sand away from the posts and planks. I will wait this out and try again, or I will die. It's a tight squeeze, just enough room for me but hardly enough room to breathe. My breaths are shallow anyway, shallow and quick. Sand sticks to the slick sweat on my neck and cheek, coating the entire right side of me. The grit is everywhere: inside my nose, between my teeth, behind my eyelids. But I breathe, never having felt so alive as I do in this moment, so close to death.

The noise is inescapable now, the sound of the desperate as

they run from death to destruction. Footsteps pound the board-walk, shaking it. If it gives out, I will be splintered and crushed beneath it.

Sand scatters under the first pair of brave feet, not terribly far away from me. Two more pairs follow, and ten more after that. Then twenty.

The mines spray sand and skin high into the air. All over the beach, explosions burst like fireworks. Yet the feet keep coming, winding through pillars of smoke until—*pop!*—they are forced to stop.

It isn't pretty. It is a sickening, revolting mess.

Something heavy slams into the boardwalk, directly above me. The boards creak, sagging so low they press into my shoul-der blades. Quickly, the pressure recedes—but then there are fingers, long and tan and delicate, curling over the plank's edge two inches from my face. A noise almost slips out of me; I bite it back.

Shots ring out, cracking wood, deafening and close. I don't feel anything—but would a bullet burn like fire, or would it be a blast of numb shock? The fingers grip tighter, knuckles white even in these shadows, and then they are gone. I shift, as much as I can in this tight space, and see three perfect circles of sun-light streaming through the wood just past my head.

Another shot rings out, and then, just like that, darkness overtakes the light—there is a *thud* above me, even heavier than the first, and a limp arm hanging over the boardwalk's edge. A limp arm clothed in crisp, tan fabric that would blend into the sand if not for the blood.

An officer. An officer is down, and they will find him, and if I stay where I am I will be covered in his blood as it drips through the cracks.

I could run now. I could follow the footsteps of the dead, step only in places where the sand has been tested. I could make it to the sailboat, if I am smart. If I am smart and quick. I could finally, finally sail to Sanctuary.

I inch out of my hiding place, careful to stay low. An enemy of an officer is a friend of mine, but that doesn't mean I'm safe—I still need to be as careful as possible, and quiet. A blast of salt-water breeze hits me, cool against damp sweat.

"Wait."

I freeze, though I've obviously already been seen.

"The guards are making rounds," the voice says. Soft, urgent. "They're not close, but they'll see me if you run."

I turn my head, just slightly, enough to look at her. She's petite, Asian—I don't recognize her. Her long, tan fingers ravage the fallen officer's pockets. Could this girl really have killed him, David against Goliath?

"Here," she says, tossing me a lanyard heavy with keys. Clever, an attempt to share the blame if someone sees, because why else would she hand over this freedom? Not that I'm complaining—I don't plan to be around long enough for blame. She stuffs his ID tags into her pockets and tucks his pistol into the back of her shorts. "I'm coming with you."

The pistol makes me nervous, but at least it isn't aimed at

me. "You don't even know where I'm going."

She tilts her head to the beach, to the sickening display of blood and bone before us. "I know you're not staying here," she says. "That's all I need to know."

"Is it clear yet?" Still crouched on the low side of the board-walk, all I can see is the girl, and the officer at her feet. Even this much blood turns my stomach, but I keep it together. I have to.

"Clear enough that we'll have a head start. People are avoiding this beach now. . . ." Her eyes drift to the mess of death in the sand. The tide doesn't reach far enough to lick any of the blood away, and neither of us can look for more than a few seconds. "It's only a matter of time until they're all killed. The guards won't be distracted for long."

"Okay," I say. "Okay. We can do this."

"We *have* to do this. What else is there?"

She's right. And it isn't like I have anyone to go back for, not anymore. I take a deep breath. "Follow—"

"Crap, they're on the seawall—they see us. They see us! Go!"

I spring to standing and take off. The smoke has cleared, not completely, but enough. I don't look behind me to see if she's there. I don't look at what remains of all the people I might have eaten breakfast with later this morning. I only look ahead, at the ravaged sand, darting left and right like the officers did when they first noticed the air shifting.

Bullets burrow into the sand, into bodies already dead, into a wake of people who trail behind us. So many bullets from only—I risk a glance—two guards. I dodge their shots, keep running until the sand is smooth ahead of me, untested. I stop short, not sure exactly how to proceed, and the girl from the boardwalk barrels into me. It's everything I can do to keep from losing my balance, from taking one wrong step that could end everything.

But of those who've fallen in with us, only two stop. The others push past us, sights set on the sailboat. Between their footsteps and the spray of bullets that follows them, the sand is broken—and they are dead—in a matter of seconds.

I suck in a breath, choke on sand and smoke, but force myself to keep going. The boardwalk girl follows, along with the two girls who stopped with us. I recognize both their faces from the seawall, peeking over, today and yesterday and the day before.

I lead the way, fast as I can. The guards' boat isn't far now. If we press on we might actually make it. More shots ring out, but this time they're fired by the boardwalk girl, directed at the officer who usually guards the boat—bullet and blood, he collapses before he can make it back to the dock—then at the other guards who chase us, their pistols dead. This girl is an impressive shot, unsettlingly so. She keeps pulling the trigger long after she runs out of bullets.

No one shoots at us anymore.

No one follows us at all.

But I keep running. I can't stop. We're past the minefield now, into guards' quarters—where the guards would be if they weren't dead or hunting—and down the endless dock where their boat is tied up.

I climb up and over the boat's side, collapse just long enough to catch my breath. I'm vaguely aware of the three other girls as they join me, one of them a blonde who works to untie the knotted rope, our only anchor to the dock. The sky starts to sway as the tide pulls us out to sea. It hurts to breathe, it hurts to think. Everything hurts.

It is worth it.

Don't miss these action-packed survival stories from KAYLA OLSON!

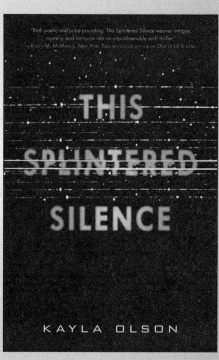

JOIN THE

Epic Reads

COMMUNITY

THE ULTIMATE YA DESTINATION

◀ **DISCOVER** ▶

your next favorite read

◀ **MEET** ▶

new authors to love

◀ **WIN** ▶

free books

◀ **SHARE** ▶

infographics, playlists, quizzes, and more

◀ **WATCH** ▶

the latest videos